MAN OF STEELE

A Daggers & Steele Mystery

ALEX P. BERG

BATDOG PRESS

KNOXVILLE, TN

Batdog Press
www.batdogpress.com

Publisher's Note: This is a work of fiction. Names, characters, places, and incidents portrayed in this novel are a product of the author's imagination.

Cover Art: Damon Za
Book Layout: ©2013 BookDesignTemplates.com

Man of Steele/ Alex P. Berg — 1st ed.
ISBN 978-1-942274-29-2

1

believe in all sorts of wild notions. I believe in elemental magic and mind control and necromancy. I believe in the existence of griffins and unicorns and dragons, and that vampires, werewolves, and other superhuman creatures walk among us. I have good reason to. I've seen them all firsthand.

I also believe in things that run contrary to observation, like in fate or the existence of almighty gods or the usefulness of differential calculus. I believe in both the inherent good nature of man and in our species' ever-present duplicity, as contradictory as those things might seem. So I shouldn't have been surprised to find out I'd been lied to—but I was.

Our rickshaw pulled up under an awning of red and gold brocaded cloth. A red rug stretched from the foot of the sidewalk to a pair of heavy golden doors, one flanked by two young men in matching black uniforms trimmed with red and gold satin.

I glanced at the sign over the doors. "Hold on... The *Empress of Welwic?* You said Quinto invited us to *dinner.*"

"He did," said Shay. "A fancy dinner, here at the *Empress*. Why do you think I forced you to dress up?"

I glanced at my suit, cool gray in color with prominent black stitching and a black silk border along the lapel. It was one of the ones I'd kept following our gambling sting aboard the luxury cruise liner, the *Prodigious*. I wouldn't be caught dead in it normally, certainly not in the waning days of summer, but Shay had insisted.

"A fancy dinner, sure," I said. "This is beyond that. More like voluntary extortion."

Shay batted her eyes at me. "You know I love you, Daggers, cynical attitude and all, but don't ruin this. By all accounts, the *Empress* is one of the three best restaurants in New Welwic, and as much as I enjoy the dives we normally dine at, it's not as if I'd turn down an invitation like this. Besides, Quinto must've been planning it for months. Do you have any idea how hard it is to get reservations here?"

Shay gave me one of those sly smiles she and I both knew I couldn't resist. Her chocolate brown hair, ever so slightly curled, draped lazily over her shoulders, ending at the top of her strapless yellow gown. Her azure eyes shone more brightly than usual, brought to life by a touch of mascara and eye shadow. I should've known something was afoot as soon as I saw her donning makeup.

"I won't be too much of a sourpuss, I promise," I said. "I'm more surprised is all. Quinto's never been much of a gourmand."

"He may not be," said Shay. "But who's to say Cairny isn't?"

One of the doormen approached the rickshaw. He tipped his cap and held out a hand. "Miss?"

Shay lifted her skirt off her feet with one hand and took the man's assistance with her other. The remaining doorman opened the golden gates for us and stood to the side as we walked in.

I locked my jaw into place to avoid looking like a yokel. The ceiling stretched three stories above us, a curved golden dome inlaid with gemstones that looked suspiciously like rubies from my vantage point. A frieze depicting scenes from popular mythology wrapped around the base, hand-carved in painstaking detail despite the fact that no one would ever get close enough to it for it to be worth the bother. Red velvet sofas lined the walls, interspersed with ten foot paintings in golden frames. As I took it all in, my wallet hurled a curse and punched me in the thigh.

A maître d' nodded to us as we approached his station. "Sir. Miss. Your names?"

Shay saved me the ignominy of fumbling for the right words as I gawked at the surroundings. "Shay Steele and Jake Daggers. We're with the Quinto party."

The maître d' made a note on a sheet hidden by the lip of his kiosk and smiled. "Wonderful. Welcome to the Empress. If you'd be so kind as to follow me."

He beckoned and turned, leading us down a hallway whose arched ceilings were as golden and brilliant as those in the foyer but only two stories high instead of three. I spotted dining halls past doorways adorned with red velvet drapes, but rather than usher us into one of them, the maître d' stopped in front of a glass-paneled door.

He opened it and extended a hand. "Enjoy your evenings, sir. Miss."

I was through the door before it occurred to me that I didn't know where I should sit, but as my eyes adjusted to the darkened room, I managed to figure things out. To my right I found a table with place settings for twelve, each of them arranged with a tumbler and a wine glass, a trio of plates, and more pieces of silverware than there were ways to consume food. A few tall, round tables also populated the room. At the nearest one, I saw a familiar couple.

"Daggers. Steele. You made it."

Detective Gordon Rodgers set his drink upon the tall table and extended a hand. I shook it and clapped my longtime pal on the back.

"Rodgers. Good to see you. And Allison. How long has it been? Three months?" I gave Rodgers' wife a friendly hug.

"Try six or seven," she said. "Last time we got together was in the middle of winter. Remember that awful grapefruit sorbet? Hi, Shay. It's been too long."

My partner hugged Allison as I pulled away. "Daggers probably blocked it out, but I remember. It was grainy and bitter. *Yech.* Anyway, how are you? You look fantastic."

It was true. I'd always considered Allison a bit of a Plain Jane, with her collarbone-length brown hair, soft-featured face, and slight figure, but the scarlet dress she'd picked out masterfully used layers of bunched fabric to give her curves that weren't really there.

"This?" said Allison offhandedly. "Oh, I just picked it out."

Women... "No need for modesty. Shay's right. You look great. You make Rodgers look like he rolled out of bed."

"Hey, now," said Rodgers. "I dressed up, same as you. The only difference is I make my suit look *good*." He adjusted the lapels of his charcoal blazer for emphasis, flashing me one of his trademark white smiles.

"As if that's something to be proud of," I said. "With your blonde hair and baby blue eyes, you could make a potato sack look good. The fact that *I* look good is a miracle."

"Oh, it's not a miracle," said Shay. "Hard work on the part of *one* of us, more like."

Allison smiled. "It always is. You think Gordon looks this good without my help?"

I gasped, covering my mouth. "You pick out his clothes for him? He's had us thinking for years that his sense of style was innate."

Rodgers held up a hand. "I get pointers on color co-ordination, that's it."

"Sure you do," I said with a wink. "So where are Quinto and Cairny?"

"They disappeared in back," said Allison. "Said they needed to check on some things."

"Isn't that what the wait staff is for?"

Allison shrugged. "Beats me."

Shay gestured toward the table. "Who else is coming?"

"No idea," said Rodgers. "I was under the impression it was the big guy, Cairny, and the four of us."

A waiter wearing black pleated pants and a matching jacket emerged from a door at the room's side. He offered a platter, a quartet of champagne flutes bubbling merrily atop it. "Ladies. Gentlemen. A drink?"

Rodgers and his wife waved the man off, pointing to their half-finished beverages on the table, but Shay accepted one. "Don't mind if I do. Thank you."

The waiter gave me a nod. "Sir?"

I lifted a hand. "No thanks. A cocktail, though? An apricot whiskey sour, if you could."

"Certainly, sir. We use Glendale whiskey unless otherwise requested."

I nodded my approval, my wallet leg continuing to ache as the man left. *Glendale?* What did he think I did for a living, embezzle money from the working class?

Shay snickered and shook her head. "You're losing your touch, Daggers. You had champagne right in front of you, not to mention a captive audience, and you didn't make a single crack about spoiled grapes."

"This place is too fancy for thinly veiled sarcasm," I said. "Trust me, if I were smoking an imported cigar, I would've blown the smoke into all of your faces while disparaging the champagne's insufficient vintage. All in a drawling, condescending tone of voice, to be sure."

"You may have lost weight since the last time I saw you, Daggers," said Allison, "but it's good to see your sense of humor hasn't gone anywhere."

"Some things never change," said Shay. "It's alright. I love him all the same."

She smiled, melting my heart in the process.

I smiled back. "I would, you know. Change. If you wanted me to."

"You already have," she said. "But I'd hate to lose your running commentary on life, the universe, and everything in between. I can't imagine how boring my days would grow without it."

"Oh, it wouldn't be so bad. Trust me. I know."

I turned, not having heard the door open behind me. I couldn't believe who stood there. "Captain Armstrong. What the hell are you doing here?"

"Hopefully about to enjoy a fine dinner, same as the rest of you," said the old bulldog, his hair a little thinner and grayer than the last time I'd seen him. Much of the latent tension in his jaw and brow had melted away. Even his trademark jowls seemed less prominent, mostly because he wasn't actively frowning.

He gestured to the woman beside him. "Daggers. Rodgers. You remember my wife, Lizbeth. Steele, I don't think you've had the pleasure."

The short, gentle-faced woman beside him seemed the antithesis of everything I remembered about our old Captain—mild, calm, and on the rounder side—and though I was sure I'd met her at some point over the past decade, I couldn't for the life of me recall when. Maybe at a police ball.

"Pleasure to meet you, Mrs. Armstrong," said Steele, taking her hand. "I have to imagine you've been loving having your husband around these past few months."

"For the most part," she said with a smile. "He can get underfoot as often as he helps, so it's a mixed bag. But he seems to be enjoying himself, which is all I could've hoped for."

"Turns out forced early retirement was the best piece of ill luck that could've befallen me," said the Captain. "Not that I realized it at the time, but since leaving the precinct, I feel like a twenty ton weight's been lifted from my back. My doctor jokes I might've regained some of the ten years stress and lack of sleep cut from my lifespan. And all it took was freeing myself from your overflowing font of aggravation, Daggers."

"That's me," I said. "I'm like a fountain of youth in reverse. The less of me you experience the longer you live. But as great as that is to hear, that doesn't explain—*Captain Knox?*"

I was about to ask what Captain Armstrong was doing here, but the arrival of Captain Knox left me even more befuddled. Our diminutive current captain, wearing a forest green dress that accentuated her faded copper hair, joined the party, arm in arm with a handsome silver fox who was about my height and looked far more comfortable than me in a suit.

"Evening, Detectives," said Knox with a tip of her head. "Abe, nice to see you here as well. Everyone, this is my husband, Richard."

Introductions and handshakes abounded, but I was a little behind the eight ball. I glanced between my former and current captains. "The two of you are friends? And there are no...hard feelings?"

Captain Armstrong frowned at me. "Come on, Daggers. The police chief pushed me out, but it wasn't without my input. You don't think Beverly and I failed to meet before she took over the department, do you?"

I gave them a blank look.

Captain Knox chortled and shot Abe a sly smile. "Often, a lack of an answer is as good as the real thing. To be fair, he never asked. Not that I provided an opportunity. I've kept him busy."

"Or the city has, at least," said Rodgers. "No shortage of murders since you left, that's for sure, Captain."

While I struggled to grasp the congeniality shared between my two captains, a new pair arrived. Together they about outweighed the entire party assembled to date: Quinto's brother, Felix, as tall and broad as his older brother but a few pounds trimmer, wearing a snazzy purple suit and striped tie, and next to him, Quinto's mother, a full-blooded troll with tusk-like fangs, roughly seven feet tall and tipping the scales at a good four or five hundred pounds. Her long black hair had been curled into a neat updo, and though she looked awkward and self-aware in the flowing indigo gown she wore, she smiled and nodded nonetheless.

"Norma," said Shay, gathering her wits quicker than the rest of us. "And Felix. What a surprise to see the two of you here."

The big troll woman joined the group. "Yes, well, I'm surprised to be here, to be honest. It's been a while since I've travelled to the city. I've forgotten how crowded it gets. After so many years in Aragosto, it feels suffocating. Hard to believe I used to barely notice it."

"I don't think we've met. Captain Beverly Knox." She extended a hand. "You're Detective Quinto's mother, I take it?"

I tugged on Steele's elbow as the rest of the assembled parties shared introductions. "Shay?" I tilted my head toward a corner.

She followed my lead, bringing her champagne with her. "What is it?"

I spoke quietly. "Did you know about any of this?"

She shook her head. "No. I thought it was going to be us, Quinto, Cairny, Rodgers, and Allison."

"Right. So Captain Armstrong? Captain Knox? *Quinto's mom?* You see where I'm going with this, right?"

"I know. It's exciting."

I blinked. "*Exciting?* How could you be cavalier about this?"

Shay blinked and stared at me.

"Quinto's getting promoted," I said. "We're the senior detectives at the 5th. That means he's getting transferred to a new precinct. I can't believe Captain Knox didn't say anything!"

Shay lifted a brow. "Daggers... I don't think that's what's happening."

"No? Well then how—"

A deep-throated "Ahem!" cut me off. I turned to find Quinto standing in front of the table, dressed in a rich dark suit that draped his considerable frame. His left arm wrapped around Cairny, who was dressed in a spectacular gown—black, of course—that flowed down her body in a waterfall of satin. For once, she'd done more with her hair than let if fall over her shoulders, pinning it up and adorning it with pink and purple flowers. A smile stretched her painted lips, as did one for Quinto, whose mismatched buckteeth were on full display.

"Welcome, everyone," said Quinto. "Gosh, it's good to see you all here. It warms my heart to know we have such a great group of friends and family. I only wish Cairny's folks could've been here, but they had out of town matters that kept them away."

"I'm sure I could've persuaded them if I'd known," said Cairny with a grin.

"You could've, but that would've defeated the purpose of all of this, wouldn't it?"

Rodgers held his hand out as he shot his partner a perfect smile. "Well, go on. It's pretty clear we're not here for a run of the mill friend's dinner. Lay it on us."

Quinto took a deep breath. "No point in dallying, I suppose. As you all know, Cairny and I have been dating for a while now. We're best of friends. Partners, intellectually and physically. I've never met anyone as amazing and inspiring and insightful as her, and as crazy as it would've seemed to me even a year ago, I can't imagine spending a day of my life without her." He glanced lovingly at Cairny. "Thankfully, it turns out she feels the same way."

Cairny extended her left hand. It sparkled more than I'd remembered. "Quinto proposed. I said yes."

Shay squeaked and leapt forward to give her friend a hug. "Oh, Cairny! Quinto! I'm so happy for the two of you. This is fantastic!"

Everyone surged forward, inundating Quinto and Cairny in a flood of congratulations, hugs, and friendly pats on the shoulders. I stood there, bewildered, letting everyone take their cracks at the newly-engaged pair while I fought off my embarrassment.

Engaged... Of course they'd gotten engaged! Only a dolt like me could've failed to see it coming. Even with Shay's continued guidance, I couldn't shake my blind spot when it came to interpersonal relationships.

Waiters came in with more champagne, including the one who'd previously taken my order. He handed me a whiskey sour as Quinto and Cairny ushered people toward the place settings.

Quinto came over to check on me. "Daggers. You doing okay?"

"*Okay?*" I clapped him on the back. "Why wouldn't I be?"

"You seem out of it. Shay isn't the only one who can read you, you know."

"It's nothing. I'm a dolt. Don't worry about me. This night's about you. And I couldn't be happier for you. You and Cairny are going to make the rest of us jealous, I know it. Couldn't have happened to a better guy."

Quinto smiled. "Thanks, Daggers. It means a lot coming from you."

I nodded toward the table. "Quite a feat you pulled off, though. Cairny didn't know until this evening? You didn't even tell Rodgers?"

Quinto shook his head. "I didn't tell a soul. Well, that's not true. I sent a message to Cairny's folks. They gave me their blessing, even though they couldn't make it."

A swell of chatter rose from the table as everyone settled into their spots. The waiters who'd distributed champagne exited as another crew laden with appetizers, bottles of wine, and pitchers of water followed in their wake. I wasn't sure what exactly lay under the waiters' trays, but it smelled earthy, savory, and *delicious*.

Quinto held out a hand. "Should we join the others?"

My stomach rumbled, and for the time being, its concerns drowned out those of my wallet. "Are you kidding? Let's feast."

2

I groaned and leaned back in my chair, my stomach stretched to capacity after finishing the last of a dark chocolate pomegranate mousse. After the first five courses, I'd promised myself I'd only sample the dessert, a promise I immediately broke. I'd wolfed down half of it before regaining my self control. Then the waiters swept by with another round of drinks and left the mousse lingering before me, tempting me with its decadent flavor.

I'd tried to resist, but a man can only hold chocolate at arms length for so long.

Captain Armstrong and his wife had just left, and the rest of the party had splintered into smaller groups. Many of them chose to stand and stretch their legs, possibly as a means to help their meals settle.

Shay twittered with Allison across the table, who'd been abandoned after Rodgers left to chat with Quinto and Captain Knox. I glanced at the clock in the corner. It read quarter after nine.

I placed a hand on Steele's shoulder. "Shay?"

"Yes, Daggers?"

I nodded toward the clock.

She took a peek. "Oh. Thanks for reminding me. Allison. It's been a pleasure, as always. Time for us to head out, though."

We said our pleasantries while making the rounds, shaking a few more hands and clapping more backs along the way. I asked Quinto about the bill, but he insisted he'd take care of it. I didn't pry. Maybe a close relative of his had bit the dust and left him a large inheritance.

We retraced our footsteps, back through the *Empress's* opulent entryway and out the gilded doors. We paused at the end of the red carpet, strokes of pinks and purples painting the sky despite the late hour. It was summer, after all.

"Now for the million crown question," I said. "You want to walk, or take a rickshaw?"

Shay didn't hesitate in hailing a cab. "I'm wearing heels. You should know the answer to that."

"Just thought it might be nice to walk off some of the six and a half pounds of food I'm currently giving birth to."

"If I'd packed flats in my purse, I'd be right there with you."

A rickshaw pulled up. We hopped in, Shay gave the man her address, and the cart clattered off.

"Thanks again for reminding me about the hour," said Shay. "I was having such a good time I might've forgotten otherwise."

"Well, my intentions weren't completely noble." I trailed a hand across her leg and gave her a suggestive squeeze, more toward the upper end of her thigh than the lower.

"Really?" Shay lifted an eyebrow. "After all that food?"

"Well, I did say I wanted to walk it off. Besides, I had three and a half cocktails, too. Those counteract the effects of the meal in the friskiness department."

Shay placed her hand over mine. "Jake, you know I'd be up for it most nights. But I have so much to do in preparation for my brother's business school graduation party tomorrow. My mom's expecting me at their apartment by seven, and it's not like I can just show up. I'm supposed to bake two trays of gingersnaps before I arrive, mostly because my mother insisted we order flowers from the florist rather than full arrangements. Those are going to take at least a couple hours to put together."

"I can commiserate," I said. "I'm cheap, too. It's why I almost had a heart attack when we arrived at the *Empress.*"

Shay smiled.

I gave her leg another squeeze. "Still. I could be quick. Just saying."

"I know you could." Shay gave me a wink. "But I've got more than one excuse, tonight. Mainly that I had fewer drinks than you."

I chuckled. "Fair enough."

Our rickshaw clattered along, the sky deepening in color. A slice of New Welwic passed us by at the speed of our driver's feet, a collection of the young and old, the rich and poor, the human and the not and everything in between. Compared to many of the couples that I saw, the mismatched pairing of Quinto and Cairny looked downright ordinary.

Shay must've been reading my mind. "I'm happy for Cairny and Quinto," she said, drawing my attention back into our cart. "I can't believe they're engaged, though. It seems like yesterday they started dating."

"It's been almost a year," I said. "Which isn't that long in the grand scheme of things, but it's enough to get the measure of a person."

"It is, isn't it?" The rickshaw wheels bounced over the cobblestones as we took a corner. Shay trailed her thumb over the back of my hand. "You ever think about our future?"

"Of course I do. All the time."

"And where do you see us?"

"Well...together, I hope. And you?"

She nodded. "I'd hope so, too."

I chewed on the edge of my lip. "And...do you think it's a realistic hope?"

"We're the ones who make the decisions about our futures, aren't we?"

Silence stretched for a moment, or at least what passed for it in a New Welwic rickshaw. Neither of us spoke amid the clatter of rickshaw wheels against pavement, the chatter of nearby pedestrians, and the angry shouts of a wine-soaked bum. Old me would've suffered a panic attack under similar circumstances, but present me felt oddly at ease with the conversation.

"You're not feeling...*pressured* by Quinto and Cairny's engagement, are you?"

"What?" said Shay. "No. I apologize if that's how it came across. I didn't mean it that way. It's simply that we've never discussed...you know. *Marriage*. And not between us, specifically. Rather our general stances on it. Given your previous marriage, I guess I don't know how you feel about it."

"I'm not jaded by the institution, if that's what you're asking. I'd be open to trying it again. I like to think I'd do a better job picking out the right partner this time."

The rickshaw slowed and pulled to a stop outside Shay's apartment building.

Shay leaned in and kissed me. I'd become so used to the slightly sweet taste of her lips, the scent of her lilac perfume, the feel of her warm breath as she exhaled through her nose as I kissed her back. The familiarity didn't diminish the experience in any way.

She pulled back. "The ceremony's at noon tomorrow, with the party and lunch afterward. I should be in the office by two or three at the latest."

"See you at work, then."

She hopped off the rickshaw, gathering and lifting her skirt to keep it from dragging. "Love you."

"Love you, too," I said.

She shot me one last longing look before heading through her building's front doors.

I sighed.

The rickshaw driver eyed me. He looked mildly sympathetic. "Women, am I right? Where to next, pal?"

I dug some coins out of my pocket and hopped out of the cart. "I'll walk from here. I've got food to digest and topics to ponder."

3

There was a time when the thought of turning down a rickshaw-based podiatric reprieve would've sent me into convulsions—roughly a year ago, if I was being honest. It seemed like eons past, though, and not merely because I'd overhauled my attitude toward burdensome activities and life in general.

Walking wasn't the chore it used to be. Thanks to Shay's culinary guidance and her unwavering encouragement regarding exercise, I'd shed a good forty-five pounds from my heaviest, recently weighing in at an unheard of one hundred and eighty. That alone eased the knee and ankle pain I'd once felt after long days spent on my feet, but it wasn't a mere lack of bulk that made walking more enjoyable. I'd actually started to *like* exercise. I felt better when I did it. More awake. More energetic. Sharper mentally and physically.

I'd asked Shay about it once and she'd laughed at me, citing the relationship as established callisthenic science. After pointing out to her that *callisthenic science* wasn't a thing, I'd relented, mostly because I could see regular exercise had produced the same effect in her. Not that either of us were in danger of becoming addicts, but we'd both derived enough ancillary benefits to want to keep active going forward.

Fact of the matter was I'd changed a lot about myself for Shay, more than I ever thought I'd change for another person, and yet I wasn't sure the changes were *really* as much for Shay as they were for me. Being healthier, more active, facing life with a positive attitude, tackling my personal demons of pride and jealousy and guilt. All of those things made *me* happier. The fact that they made Shay happier was a pleasant coincidence. And hadn't she changed for me as well? She'd grown more accepting, yet thicker-skinned. She'd torn down the exterior walls that had kept her isolated, and she'd learned to put up with both my lovable and more irksome quirks.

All those thoughts and more rattled around my head as I walked, heading up Layton Avenue before turning onto 3rd. The sky continued to darken following the sun's departure, now an inky morass of navy clouds hovering over a background of royal purple. Lights sprang to life outside the apartment buildings and businesses that lined the street, the newfangled electric ones installed by Sherman industries. They'd outfitted at least half of the city's streets by now, and last I'd checked they'd started retrofitting manors and statehouses with their electrical wires and glowing globes, too. Demand was high and kept soaring higher, which I appreciated from a progressive standpoint as well as a personal one. The hefty investment I'd made in Sherman Industries using the bonus I'd received following our gambling case had grown by an order of magnitude. If it kept on growing, I might have to find someone to help me with financial planning, not to mention to abandon my original retirement plan of begging on the street for scraps.

I paused outside one of the shops that had already been shuttered, a place with the uninspired name of Third Street Jewelers. Thick iron bars covered the windows, but shiny baubles glittered through the gaps, lit by the artificial light of the Sherman globes: necklaces with fine chains, ruby and emerald and sapphire pendants, pearl-studded earrings. Come to think of it, I'd never bought Shay a single piece of jewelry. Not that she'd ever complained. She preferred to spend her money on experiences over tangible things. Fancy dinners, tickets to concerts or plays or operas. Clothes and shoes were her one weakness, but that particular flaw seemed almost universal for her gender.

Perhaps I should buy her something. She appreciated surprises, at least ones that didn't involve unexpected medical diagnoses or gratuitous nudity. Purple was one of her favorite colors. Maybe a nice amethyst necklace or ring? I peered through the glass, trying to gauge what the jewelers had in stock. The reflected light was brighter than what a lantern would've provided, but it still wasn't enough. The necklaces hung at the back of the store, shrouded in darkness, and the rings all appeared to feature clear stones. Diamonds, most likely.

A chill ran down my spine as I gazed at them, but I wasn't sure why. Sure, Shay and I had finally discussed the prospect of marriage, but Shay had made it clear she wasn't in any rush to tie the knot, and I believed her. We'd passed the point in our relationship where either of us thought it necessary to lie to the other to avoid bruised feelings. Maybe it was hesitation on my end, but that didn't seem right either. When Shay had brought up the topic in the rickshaw, I'd felt surprisingly calm about the possibility. Besides, I'd been married before. A *failed* marriage, but that gave me experience in what behaviors to avoid. So why were the hairs on the back of my neck standing on end while staring at a set of diamond rings?

I looked away from the display, glancing up and down the street. The sidewalks were busy, not packed but far from empty either. Rickshaws bounced up and down the avenue, and all the bystanders seemed to be in motion other than me. *Seemed to be...*

I kept walking, heading toward my apartment by a more circuitous route than normal. I still felt the need to digest more of my meal, but that wasn't my only motivation. I kept an eye on my surroundings, acting casual as I processed the passersby. A couple out on the town, a businessman heading home, a group of rowdy young men well into their drinks. I glanced behind me when circumstances gave me reason, trying not to give away my suspicions. Despite my efforts, nothing caught my eye. And yet the prickly hairs upon my neck refused to settle.

Eventually I arrived at the foot of my building, still feeling unnerved but without any evidence to show for it. I'd been tailed numerous times, and tailed people myself even more frequently. I had a good eye for lurkers and miscreants, not to mention a sixth sense about when I was being watched. Right now, the latter had been engaged but without any of the other five senses backing it up. It unnerved me.

"Evening, Detective Daggers. Care for a nightcap?"

I turned toward the voice, belonging to one Mitch Murdock. His name, thick mustache, and workmanlike haircut all suggested he was a good cop in a world gone bad, but fate had dictated the man be a barista instead. A few months ago, he'd parked his coffee cart outside my apartment building. Apparently business was booming because he'd never left. I was partially to thank for that. I rarely brewed my own coffee anymore due to the convenience and quality of his.

Mitch gestured toward me with a half-filled carafe. "I know it's late, but that's never stopped you before. I know your type likes to burn the midnight oil."

"*Likes to* might be overstating things, but we do nonetheless." I stepped under his awning. "You trying to convert me into a twice daily customer?"

"I would've already if you weren't always over at your miss'us place. The usual?"

I nodded. "Straight, black, and boring, just like me. Except for the skin color, but you know what I mean."

Mitch poured me a cup. I paid him from the remaining change in my pocket.

I sniffed the brew, enjoying its earthy aroma, before taking a sip. Despite drinking it most mornings, the hints of chocolate and spice in the concoction took me by surprise. It beat the precinct's dirty dishwater by a country mile.

I sighed. "Someday, you're going to have to tell me where you get your beans, Mitch."

"And risk losing my best customer to a press pot? Not likely."

I snorted and took a look around. The evening crowds had started to thin—surely Mitch would pack it up soon—but the lessened foot traffic wasn't helping me identify the source of my unease. The breeze, until now non-existent, picked up, feeling deliciously cool as it ruffled my hair and wicked away the perspiration from under my suit.

Maybe I was wrong. Maybe the hairs on my neck had stood on end because I'd been surreptitiously approached by a cat or due to some invisible electrical field emitted by the newfangled Sherman Globes.

I saluted Murdock with my coffee mug. "Thanks for the joe, Mitch. Don't stay too late."

He smiled and nodded back. "As long as people are buying, I'll be here."

I took another sip of my drink and headed inside, worried the caffeine would keep me up all night even though I knew it wouldn't. Nearly two decades of swilling it had made me immune to its effects, if no less addicted to it.

Up the stairs I went to the third floor. I paused outside my apartment as I dug inside my pocket for the keys. With the sun having set, darkness enveloped the hallway. With the advent of the Sherman globes, it probably wouldn't be more than a few years before every building glowed with the light of day at all hours, if people willed it. For the time being, though, I had to remember where the keyhole to my padlock was.

As I turned the key in the deadbolt, I felt more than heard the rush of air behind me.

4

I ducked and spun as the fist flew past me, cracking against the wood where my head had been a fraction of a second earlier. I instinctively reached for my nightstick, Daisy, though I wasn't carrying her in my blazer. Not that it would've mattered if I had. A body crashed into me before I could blink, sending my coffee flying and me into the wood at my back.

The door groaned, cracked, and splintered, the lock on the handle no match for the force of my body being slammed into it by a much larger dude. Air escaped my lungs in a wheeze as I sailed into my darkened apartment, my assailant's shoulder driving into the soft spot under my ribs.

I stuck my leg between his as I grabbed the back of his shirt and twisted to the side. The end result was exactly what I'd hoped for. The guy's left foot bounced off my shin. He stumbled and fell, allowing me to rotate to the top. Somehow, I'd even timed it right. His head rebounded off the back of my couch with a thud as he toppled to the floor.

My fingers itched for Daisy, but she was still in my leather jacket in the closet. I'd have to make do without. I clenched a fist and aimed a knee at my attacker's neck when the second guy hit me, him even bigger than the first.

So *that* was how Topples had hit me so quickly after throwing a punch—because he hadn't thrown the punch. His partner had. All of which flashed through my head as Biggie slammed me into a bookshelf.

Pain lashed across my back, the shelves digging into my muscle and pressing against my spine. My collection of Rex Winters hardbacks cascaded over me and Biggie, battering the pair of us as we each fought to gain an advantage. Biggie shot a forearm at my neck, the stench of sour meat and garlic heavy on his breath, but I refused to hold still to accommodate him. I drove a knee into his midsection, once, twice. He countered with a downward chop of his free arm and a pair of coordinated mini-hops away from me. I tried to hook his left leg with my right, but he anticipated that, too, shifting his weight to his right leg and bracing against my swipe.

Shockingly, Biggie knew what he was doing. I would've figured a three hundred pound half-orc bruiser like him would've been attacking me in my own home for shits and giggles.

I kept him off balance with another knee aimed at his groin and managed to get a grip on his collar. As he batted away my knee and came in with his forearm again, I countered, pulling him in and dipping my head.

His jaw cracked off the top of my skull, which seemed to hurt him more than me. He stumbled back. I didn't hesitate, blasting my foot between his legs into his Mini Biggies as hard as I could. I would've followed it with a hard kick to the head if not for the fact that his partner had shaken off his mild concussion.

Topples rammed into me again with his shoulder, executing his signature move with the same grace as the first time. Luckily, he hadn't learned his lesson. I hooked his leg again as he drove me into the kitchen, twisting him around and using our combined momentum to slam him into the counter.

Behind me, I heard a crash as the bookshelf tumbled to the ground, likely taking one of my side tables with it. Topples shrugged off the counter's blast to his lower back and threw a weak, off-balance punch my way. I caught it with my arm and threw an elbow at his face, but gosh darn it if the thug didn't use my own move on me. As soon I had his arm in my grip, he lurched off the cabinets and sent us flying across the kitchen.

The opposite counter introduced itself to my spine, thankfully in a spot that hadn't already been savaged by the bookshelf. Topples snarled and slammed his body against mine, trying to free the arm that I held captive. His weight crushed into me, pressing against my already bruised spinal cord. It felt great.

I let go of him with my free hand, still trapping one of his arms in my pits. He took it as an invitation to choke me with his other hand. It would've been a poor choice on my part if I didn't know what part of the kitchen I was in.

I fumbled around on the counter behind me as Topples' fingers dug into the soft flesh at my throat, eventually finding the smooth glass neck I was searching for. A half-full bottle of Montvue special reserve whiskey. I'd had plans for it that didn't involve shampooing a snaggle-toothed criminal's hair, but such is life.

I brought the bottle crashing into Topples' face, where it shattered into a hundred razor-sharp shards. Topples gasped and fell back, the whiskey soaking his shirt as a dozen cuts in his face started to ooze.

I grabbed another bottle, but I lost it as Biggie put me in a headlock from behind. The bottle fell to the ground, shattering with a crystalline ring, and I knew right away I was in trouble.

Biggie's meaty arm wrapped around my neck, my windpipe right in the crook of his elbow. I reached up and clawed at his hand, but he'd secured it with his other. His fingers felt like iron, clasped together in a death grip.

I moved my fingers farther north, clawing at his face. Biggie chuckled. His teeth snapped and I felt his hot breath as he almost made a snack of my digits.

Topples stood, feeling the wetness on his face. He pulled his blood covered hand back and stared at it. "Son of a bitch."

My lungs screamed for air. I couldn't get more than a trickle through Biggie's grip. As dark as my apartment had been a moment ago, it was notably darker now and spotted with red.

I heard Biggie's heavy breath at my ear. "End this. Now."

Topples nodded. He whipped a six inch blade from under his belt loop and lunged at my midsection.

It was about the dumbest move he could've made.

With Biggie's arms locked on my throat, that left the rest of me free to squirm, and squirm I did. Engaging the abdominal muscles I'd gained after months of cross training classes, I brought my knees up and twisted to the side. Fabric tore as Topples' knife sliced through the side of my suit jacket, followed by a pained grunt and the sweet taste of fresh air as Biggie's grip loosened.

Even in the darkness I could see the whites of Topples' eyes. "*Shit...*"

I took advantage of the split second of confusion. I swung my arm down as fast as I could, chopping at Topples' grip on the knife. His fingers broke from the handle like chaff from wheat, and before either he or his partner could stop me, I slammed the knife further into Biggie's abdomen.

Biggie cried out and released me, clutching at his stomach, but Topples didn't panic. He slammed into me for a third time. My ribs groaned in protest, and when I went to hook his leg he twisted his body away from me. He reeked of my best whiskey, with blood coating half his face and his eyes showing a wild determination.

Together we careened across the room, both of us scrabbling for purchase. With my fingers wrapped around his soaked shirt, I managed to twist just before we slammed into the wall. It kept me from taking another full strength blow to my back, but my positioning lacked precision. Instead of hitting the wall, my shoulder plowed into the face of the grandfather clock I'd ironically inherited from my grandmother. Shards of glass pricked me through my coat, but my muscles didn't scream.

Topples, however, did. He emitted a guttural yell and swung a wild fist at me. I danced back as it cut the air a bare inch from my nose.

I was ready for the second one. As his right hook came flying in, I threw open the door to the grandfather clock's innards. His fist punched through the thin board, his arm caught to the elbow. As he tried to pull it out, I leveraged the clock off the wall. Both it and Topples toppled.

The pair slammed to the floor with a deafening crash. If no one had heard the commotion before, they'd be hard pressed to feign ignorance now. Topples lay face down with his arm trapped under the clock, groaning as he desperately tried to pull it out.

I stomped on the back of his humerus. Bone cracked. Topples screamed. Turns out having two nameless thugs try to murder me brought out the worst in me.

I ripped Topples from the shattered clock and drug him, half stumbling, toward the windows, hoping to get a good look at him. The light from outside barely illuminated the floor, much less his face, but there it was. Bloodied, ugly, and crisscrossed with faded scars. I'd never seen him before in my life.

The breeze picked up outside, rattling my windows in their frames. "Who are you?" I growled, my heart beating like a drum. "Who sent you?"

Topples cursed and threw himself at me, ignoring his shoulder as we slammed into the glass together.

It cracked but didn't give. I gripped Topples' upper arm in my fist and squeezed. He screamed.

"*Tell me,*" I said.

Maybe I underestimated the guy. Maybe more strength remained in his legs than I gave him credit for, and more strength of spirit in his core than his wild eyes gave credence to. Maybe he really did slam me through the shattered window, sending us careening into the cool breeze outside at the tail end of twilight. But it sure didn't feel like it. It felt like an explosion sent us both flying out the window, or an abnormally strong gust of wind had blown us out from the *inside*.

I didn't have time to ponder it. I simply twisted in midair, trying to keep Topples under me as I aimed for the awning of Mitch's coffee cart.

5

My world was pain. Everything hurt, but I guess that meant I wasn't dead. My ears rang, but beyond that I heard voices. Many of them. They sounded concerned. One of them even sounded familiar.

"*Detective?* Are you okay? Is anyone here a medic?"

Over the tingling numbness, I felt pressure at my neck. Fingers. Someone was taking my pulse.

I groaned and cracked my eyes. A good dozen faces swam within my field of view, lit by a lantern someone had procured from somewhere. Only one of the faces sparked my memory.

Mitch leaned over me, a look of concern showing through his thick mustache. "Detective Daggers? Can you hear me? Are you alright?"

I craned my neck to the side. It turned out to be a bad idea. My muscles ached, and my spine lodged a formal protest. It did give me a view of the aftermath, though. The remnants of Mitch's coffee cart lay splintered and broken around me, and around Topples' corpse besides me. Admittedly, he might've still been alive, but if so he wouldn't be for long. The broken wooden pole that stuck through his chest and protruded two inches out the other side would make sure of that.

"Holy crap..." I said, turning my head back toward Mitch. Thankfully the motion didn't hurt as badly in reverse.

"What the hell happened?" asked Mitch.

I cleared my throat. "I hurtled through my window and crash landed on your coffee cart. It seems to have broken my fall. That and the other guy." I tried to nod in Topples' direction, but my neck hurt too much.

The amassed onlookers continued to talk amongst themselves. An old lady even uttered a "My word!" Maybe she was an aristocrat.

"Are you okay?" asked Mitch. "Is anything broken?"

"Won't know until I try to stand. Not sure I want to try yet. How about you?"

Mitch blinked. "Me?"

"Yeah. I'm going to take a wild guess we didn't land on you. I promise I'll reimburse you for the cart. Either me or the department."

"I'm fine, Detective. Don't worry about me. It's a cart. I'll replace it."

I heard a whistle in the distance. Mitch looked over his shoulder at the sound, as did most of the other gawkers. The whistle blasted twice more, closer this time, followed by a stern voice.

"Alright, that's it. Back it up. Everyone. Make way."

A uniformed bluecoat burst through the crowd, a young man with blonde hair, a smooth jaw, and with a greater air of confidence than the last time I'd seen him.

His mouth opened as he recognized me. *"Detective Daggers...?"*

"Phillips," I said, grimacing. "Don't tell me you walk the beat around my apartment now? Are you ever *not* working?"

"Holy..." He trailed off as he took in the rest of the scene. "What the hell—"

"I fell out of my apartment," I said. "That guy helped me. That's the gist, anyway. You going to help me up, or what?"

"You sure that's a wise idea?"

I ran a mental check of my organs and extremities. They still hurt. "Not really, but I need to give it a shot sooner or later. Mitch?"

Phillips and the barista each took one of my arms and helped me into a sitting position. My head swam, but I didn't lose consciousness. No important body parts fell off, either.

I patted my ribs. They felt like a heavyweight champion had given them a once-over—hell, maybe a twice-over—but when I pressed harder, they didn't scream. I could also breathe without bursting into tears. Could I have gotten off that easy?

"Any broken ribs?" asked Phillips.

"I don't think so."

"And your neck?"

I rubbed it. "I sat up, didn't I?"

He whistled—the regular way, not with the pea whistle that hung from his neck. "You believe in miracles?"

"Maybe I should," I said. "Maybe I should also pick a church and start attending. Of course, if the gods favored me, they wouldn't have sent two hitmen after me in the first place."

Phillips glanced at Topples. "He tried to kill you?"

"Him and his buddy. Attacked me outside my apartment. Then *inside* my apartment. Made me spill my coffee. I'm still angry about that. I could use some right about now."

"Wait," said Phillips. "There's another? He's still up there?"

"Relax," I said. "I got him in the gut pretty good with the other guy's blade. He won't go far if he goes anywhere at all. We can follow the blood trail. Hell, I almost hope he tries to get away. Might lead us somewhere useful."

"You think someone sent them?"

"I sure didn't recognize either of them."

Phillips stood and pulled his nightstick. "I should check it out."

"Hold your horses. I may be alive, but I could use some back support. Can you find me a seat?"

"Right. Sorry."

Phillips and Mitch helped me to my feet. The crowd had swelled despite Phillips' orders, but it nonetheless parted as we stumbled toward the exterior wall of my apartment. My ankle hurt as I walked, as did every other part of me, and though I felt as if I'd spontaneously aged forty years, I could still move. A miracle, indeed.

Lacking a chair, Phillips and Mitch helped me sit with my back against the bricks.

Phillips gave me a nod. "I'll be back in a minute. Send backup if I'm not down in two."

"I don't have any backup to send, Phillips."

"Right. Well, I'll, ah...try not to die then." He disappeared into my building.

Murdock wrung his hands together. "Uh...is there anything else I can do for you, Detective?"

"You've already done plenty, Mitch. But you made the mistake to ask, so yes." I gestured toward the crowd. "I saw young faces among those gathered. I'd bet crowns to croissants there are runners among them. If not, find some. Send one to the Fifth Street Precinct. Another to the Empress of Welwic downtown, and yet one more to Shay's place. She's at four fifteen west Sixth. Apartment three-oh-five. Have the runners tell them more or less what happened and to get their asses here as fast as they can. All of them. Captain Knox, Quinto, Rodgers, Shay, obviously, and as many men as they want to send. Oh, and a medic, too. I feel like death warmed over."

"You got it, Detective. Whatever you need."

He hustled back toward the crowd, where he promptly started rounding up the youngsters. They all shot concerned glances my way, as did most of the adults. Not that I blamed them. People don't come flying out of third story windows often around these parts. Fewer still survive. Still not sure how I'd managed that.

The breeze, which had quieted since I'd regained consciousness, once again picked up. I closed my eyes, leaned back against the brick, and took a deep breath—or at least as deep as I could without my ribs screaming in protest.

I sighed as I opened my eyes back up. I had a feeling it was going to be a long night.

6

A half hour later, I still sat outside my apartment building. At least someone had found a folding chair for me to sit in, nothing more than a few sheets of canvas held together by wooden sticks. It felt like heaven.

"Very good, Detective. Now, could you follow my finger. First with your right eye."

The medic knelt in front of me, a young dark elven woman wearing a white smock and with her black as night hair in a tight braid.

"Am I supposed to be able to do that independently of my left eye?" I asked. "I don't think I could do that even before I fell out a third story window."

"Do your best, Detective. That's it. Good. Now your left."

I tried to do what she asked, sure that I was moving both eyes, but maybe that was her goal. She hadn't exactly told me what she was looking for as she performed her tests.

"Very nice," she said. "Now tilt your head back. Good. Forward. Excellent. And side to side? Nice. How does that feel?"

"Terrible," I said.

She didn't smile. "Please be honest, Detective. I can't help you if you're not. And if you're feeling pain, I need to know specifics. What motion caused the aches?"

I sighed. "It's worse when I move my head side to side than front to back. But it's more of a dull ache, not shooting pains. And the dull ache is everywhere. I think I've made that clear by now."

"Exceedingly." The medic stood and started plucking at my hair, like a monkey looking for lice to eat. "You said you head butted one of your assailants? His chin impacted the top of your skull?"

"That's right."

She kept inspecting my hair follicles. "Well, I don't see any lacerations. No external bleeding. Moderate bruising, but nothing significant. Unless you have any other concerns...?"

"I told you, my left arm hurts when I try to lift it over my head."

"I suspect it's a contusion, Detective, but we'll keep an eye on it. Make sure it doesn't get any worse. Now all that's left is to administer the concussion protocols. If you could—"

"Later, Thalia." Captain Knox stepped forward into the lantern light, Rodgers at her side.

The medic nodded. "Very well. He's all yours, Captain."

The Captain and Rodgers had been the first to arrive. The former stood there, wearing her green dress from our night at the Empress. To be fair, Rodgers still wore his suit, too, as I did mine. Of course, mine was torn, spattered with blood, and smelled of whisky, sour meat breath, and death. I wondered if the department would reimburse me for the expense of getting it cleaned and repaired.

The Captain watched the medic leave, her eyes slits and her jaw muscles tight. Her look didn't soften when she turned it onto me. "How are you?"

"Hurt, but apparently not injured. I'll live."

"You're lucky to be alive."

"I know."

The Captain chewed on her lip, the muscles in her jaw still bulging. She gazed at the coffee cart wreckage that had been cordoned off. "We're going to get these sons of bitches, Daggers. Whoever's behind it. You can bet your ass we will."

I stretched my eyebrows. I didn't think I'd ever heard the Captain curse. She must've been *furious*.

"I don't have any doubt we will," I said. "You going to pull me off the case?"

"Not unless you give me a reason to. You and Steele are the best we've got. No offense, Detective Rodgers."

"None taken," he said. "I came to that conclusion independently a long time ago."

I gave him a nod. He nodded back.

The Captain took a deep breath and made a conscious effort to loosen her jaw muscles. She probably didn't like the fact that she'd let her emotions get the best of her, but she wasn't a golem. Even the most hardened among us crack under pressure.

"Walk me through it," she said. "I want every detail. Everything you can remember."

"I could show you," I said.

Captain shook her head. "Later. Let Quinto and Cairny do their thing. Give me the story first."

The big guy and his now fiancée had arrived a few minutes ago. After checking to make sure I wasn't going to die on them mid-exam, they'd headed to my quarters alongside Phillips, who until then had been doing a bang up job keeping the assorted bluecoats who'd arrived on scene in line.

I licked my lips, wishing my coffee hadn't been so needlessly wasted, before diving into my story. I started it at the jewelry shop when I first sensed someone watching. I related the route I took back to my apartment, street by street. How many times I checked over my shoulder for tails. How long I spent talking to Mitch as I bought my java. How I dug in my pocket for my keys outside my door. And then I got to the good stuff.

I tried my best to relive every punch, every blow to my ribs, every lunging tackle, but I'm sure I missed a few here or there. Nonetheless, I was able to give a detailed account of the attack, down to the age of the whiskey I'd bashed into Topples' skull and the time at which I'd broken the face of my grandfather clock. I was a detective, after all. Observational prowess might be Shay's specialty, but I wasn't exactly a slouch.

The Captain didn't stop me until the end. "Hold on, Detective. I'm confused. Walk me through the last few moments again. You pulled that man—" She pointed at the crime scene surrounded by cops and yellow tape.

"—from underneath your clock, right after you'd subdued him with a tactical maneuver."

I'd told her how I'd broken his arm. She didn't seem upset about it. "That's right."

"Then you approached the window. He attacked you again. The window cracked. He attacked you a second time, and you fell through the window together. But you felt something else. A concussive force?"

I shrugged. The muscles between my shoulders protested. "It might've been Topples pushing me, but that's what it felt like. Phillips already told me my apartment didn't get firebombed, so I guess that's out. What can I say? It was toward the end of the fight. I was rattled. I probably still hadn't caught my breath from being strangled."

"You know as well as I do that details matter," said Knox. "I want to make sure I've heard it right. The windows were all closed, correct?"

I nodded. Throughout the exchange, Rodgers stood there with his arms crossed, a look that was part anger and part sympathy stretched across his face. I think he hadn't wanted to interrupt, either.

"And you didn't notice either of your attackers in the hallway when you arrived at your apartment?" he asked.

I shook my head. "I must've let my guard down once I walked through the ground level door. I hadn't spotted anything to confirm my suspicions that I was being followed. I wasn't as vigilant as I could've been."

Rodgers nodded, accepting my explanation. The breeze picked up again, fluttering the edges of the Captain's dress.

"You know how this works, Daggers," said Knox. "Our city may be full of knuckleheads and thugs, but they don't attack people at random. It's obvious this wasn't a mugging. Who were they? Do you have any idea?"

I shook my head again. The more I moved it, the less it hurt the next time. "None. Neither of the guys' faces looked at all familiar. And if you're thinking they might've let something slip, they didn't. Neither of them uttered more than two words our whole fight. I'll tell you what, though. They were pros. Maybe not the cream of the crop, but professionals nonetheless. If not for Topples' mistake with the knife, I'd be dead."

The Captain accepted that with a grim face. "So...who'd want you dead?"

"Conceivably, any number of people. I've put hundreds of individuals behind bars over the past dozen years, but most of them are still there. That's one of the perks of being a homicide detective." I shrugged. "Maybe a friend or family member of someone I helped incarcerate, but that would imply it's someone from a recent case. Those folks tend to have short memories after their loved ones disappear behind cinderblocks."

"We'll look into it," said the Captain. "Every case over the past year, at least, and we'll keep going back further if need be. What about personally? You have any grudges or debts? A mortal enemy?"

"*Mortal enemy*? Yeah, right. I do battle with him in his secret lair every other weekend."

"Don't screw with me, Daggers. This is serious. If there's anyone you know of who hates you, now's the time to let us know."

I took a deep breath. "Sorry. No, there's not. You know about Nicole, but we're good now. Our relationship's on the most solid ground it's been since our divorce. I don't owe anyone money. In fact, my financials are inordinately solid at the moment. This has to be work related."

Knox took her time responding. "Alright. We'll have to solve this the same way we always do. You okay to walk?"

I stood. "Should be, as long as you're not planning anything cross-country."

"Nothing that lengthy. As of now, you're officially on the case. Rodgers? You, too. Join me."

Knox crossed the stretch of sidewalk to the remains of the coffee cart, ducking under the yellow tape as she got close. Rodgers and I did the same. One of the blue-coats standing watch, a thick-necked, overweight bruiser by the name of Poundstone, gave me a nod as I entered the cordoned area. "Glad to see you made it in one piece, Detective."

"Me, too," I said.

Knox came to a stop over Topples' body. She stared at him, not an ounce of sympathy seeping through. "You check him for personal belongings?"

"Me?" I said. "I've been too busy trying not to die."

"I assume no one's touched him since his unfortunate encounter with the coffee cart's support beam?"

"Not that I know of. I missed part of it being unconscious and all, but you can ask Mitch. It's his cart. He'll be straight with us."

Knox nodded toward the stiff. "Rodgers?"

"My pleasure."

Rodgers knelt and started going though the guy's pockets. There weren't many. His shirt, still damp from the combination of whiskey and his own blood, clung to his skin, revealing a whole lot of nothing underneath it. I took an extended look at his face while I had the opportunity. Pale skin, battered and bloodied, probably in his thirties though he had enough scars for a man twice his age. His nose bent to the right, indicating he'd broken it long ago. I still couldn't place him for the life of me.

Rodgers emptied his pants pockets without success. "No wallet. No identification. No keys. Whoever this is, I'm guessing he was prepared for the possibility of being captured. Although..."

Topples lay on his back with his arms to his sides. Rodgers took his left arm in hand and rotated it so that his palm faced up. He pushed his sleeve up a few inches.

There, on the man's wrist, was a marking. A straight black line in the direction of his arm, flanked on either side by another pair of black lines, these inclined at fifteen degrees and separated from the first by a fingernail's width at the base. At the end where the lines diverged was another marking, a collection of four or five three-quarters circles and semicircles.

If I could whistle, I might've. "You saw that right off the bat? Good eye."

Rodgers smiled. "I'm no Steele, but I notice things every now and then."

Knox gave voice to what was on all our minds. "A tattoo. Anyone recognize it?"

Rodgers and I shook our heads.

"Someone will," said Knox. "I'll sic Detective Lamont from the gang unit on it first thing in the morning. If anyone's ever laid eyes on that before, we'll—"

An anxious cry cut her off. "Jake! Oh, gods, Jake!"

7

A rickshaw clattered up the street and out hopped Shay, having changed out of her yellow gown into a pair of simple black pants and a grey cotton shirt. She raced over, jumping over the police tape with the grace of a gazelle before enveloping me in a bone-crushing hug.

"Oh, thank goodness," she said with her arms wrapped around me and her face tucked into the crook of my shoulder. "The runner, he said... I mean...are you okay?"

"I'm tender everywhere, so you can ease up on the hugging. But to answer your question, yeah. I'm okay. Somehow."

Steele pulled back, eyeing the carnage for the first time. "Gods... The runner wasn't kidding. *You fell out your window?*"

"Well, I didn't exactly *fall*," I said. "I had help. From this guy. Topples. He pushed me out. Or I was blown out, one of the two."

Shay gave me one of those one eyebrow raised sorts of glances.

"Don't worry," said Knox. "He couldn't explain it to us any better."

"I'll give you the details later," I said. "I've already worn myself out telling the Captain everything. The short version is I was jumped. Outside my apartment, by this guy and his friend Biggie, who's still upstairs but isn't doing any better. I'm shy a half bottle of my best whiskey, my grandmother's grandfather clock is ruined, and with Topples' assistance, I got knocked out of my third story window. Luckily, my man Murdock's coffee cart broke my fall. Topples wasn't as lucky."

"And you're still in once piece?" said Shay. "No broken bones?"

"I've always told you the gods favored me."

"And yet they've cursed me with your presence." Shay smiled.

I did, too. "And you think life would be dull if I lost *my* sense of humor. Sorry to drag you out of bed. Your mom's going to be upset with me tomorrow when you don't show up."

"As if any of that matters right now, Daggers."

"Alright, that's enough," said Knox, undoubtedly sensing the sappy quality to the air surrounding us. "If it weren't obvious, you're on the case, Detective Steele. I'll put the entire department on this one, if need be. Time to do what you do best. What can you tell us about the body?"

Shay took a long look at me before turning to the corpse, as if she were trying to make sure I hadn't mind-controlled everyone into thinking I was okay when I wasn't. "I appreciate the vote of confidence, Captain, but even I'm not *that* good. You're more likely to learn the identity of Daggers' attackers through his recollection of the events than anything I might find on this man that you haven't already. Still..."

She knelt, flicking her eyes here and there over the stiff. "You noticed the tattoo?"

"We did," said the Captain.

"Face is pockmarked. Might've had a pox as a child. Also heavily scarred. I'd guess he'd been in his line of work for a while."

Knox nodded. "Noticed that, too."

"Guys!"

We turned in the direction of Quinto's booming voice. He and Cairny headed our way from the front door to my building, both of them still dressed in their matching cocktail attire. Phillips followed them closely.

We met them at the tape.

"Shay. It's good to see you." Cairny gave my partner a quick hug.

"You, too," she said. "Though I don't think I'm the one deserving of your sympathy tonight."

"I know," said Cairny. "I already gave Daggers a hug when I arrived, much to his vexation."

Shay shot me the eyebrow thing again.

"You can't blame me," I said. "The most contact Cairny and I ever have is shaking hands. I thought it would be weird."

"For the record, it wasn't," said Cairny. "Turns out almost dying has a way of bringing people closer together."

"We're just glad you're okay," said Quinto.

"As am I," I said. "Though I hate that this happened tonight of all nights. This evening was supposed to be about you and Cairny, not me."

"You're kidding me, right?" Rodgers snorted. "You go a decade never saying you're sorry, and here you've apologized three times in the last fifteen minutes. It's not like you planned on getting attacked tonight...*right?*"

Knox cleared her throat. "Detective Quinto. Cairny. You came down with information to share?"

Quinto's cheeks darkened, almost imperceptibly in the dim light. "We did. Better you come and see it for yourselves, you included Daggers. Assuming you're up for it."

"I don't think I'll suffer any post-traumatic stress from returning to the scene of the crime, if that's what you mean." I nodded toward the building entrance. "Lead the way."

Phillips stayed behind with the beat cops, while the rest of us went inside and took to the stairs.

In a series of events that would surprise no one, I turned out to be wrong. The moment I stepped through the splintered frame leading to my apartment, I suffered a strange sense of disquiet. It wasn't fear or even surprise, though seeing the devastation lit by a half-dozen lanterns did induce in me a modicum of that, too. But it did feel as if I were viewing a snippet of my life through a portal into the past.

"Holy harvest, Daggers," said Shay. "Are you—"

"I'm okay," I reassured her. "It's weird, but I'm okay. I promise."

The living room was a mess. Books littered the floor alongside shattered glass from the clock, the latter of which had raked a ragged gouge through the back of my sofa as it fell. The bookshelf I'd been rammed into had indeed fallen down, destroying not only the end table next to my couch but my coffee table as well. A wet stain slicked the floor near the kitchen, and more shattered glass glittered within.

The amount of blood surprised me, especially given I hadn't suffered any major cuts. It splattered the floor from the kitchen to the clock and further to the living room window, which itself provided another source of broken glass. The majority of the blood wasn't in aerosolized specks, though, but rather contained in a singular trail that led from the base of the kitchen to the wall where my bookshelf had fallen. Biggie sat at the end of it, a hand over his stomach, his mouth hanging ajar and his eyes wide open. A bloody, metallic gleam protruded from his side.

I followed Cairny and Quinto to him. One look told me all I needed to know. "He's dead."

"Indeed," said Cairny, kneeling beside him.

"I'll admit, I'm surprised by that," I said. "I know I got him in the gut, but I thought he'd at least make a run for it. Guess the blade bit deeper than I thought."

"Speaking of which," said Quinto. "How did he get stabbed?"

I was getting tired of repeating myself, but I knew how the process worked. I'd interrogated hundreds of johns myself over the years. "Biggie here put me in a headlock. Topples, who's on the street outside, came at me with the knife. Kind of a moronic thing to do, seeing as I'd have been unconscious in another thirty seconds anyway. I squirmed and made Topples miss. He nicked Biggie. That gave me the opportunity to break free and drive the knife further into Biggie's side."

"This was a knife that, ah...*Topples* brought with him?" asked Cairny.

"That's right."

Cairny hummed.

"What's that supposed to mean?"

Cairny looked up. "Your understanding of thanatology is improving."

"Thana-what?"

"Thanatology," said Cairny. "The study of death. You were right to suspect that a gut wound such as the one this individual suffered wouldn't have killed him so quickly. In my experience, given the width and estimated length of the blade, I'd guess this man probably would've lived at least a few hours before succumbing to this wound, maybe a day or more. Less of course if the blow lacerated a kidney or his pancreas, but from the angle of entry, I'm going to presume the blade is lodged entirely in his colon. And yet he's dead. Phillips reported him that way when he first came to your room following your encounter on the street."

I blinked. "What are you saying? The blade was poisoned?"

"There's always more than one possible explanation for any given set of facts," said Cairny. "But it would appear that way, yes."

I glanced at my torn suit jacket. The knife missed me by a hair's breadth. "*Damn...*"

"It gets weirder," said Cairny.

Shay, Rodgers, and Captain Knox had joined us after taking a brief tour of the carnage. "Weirder how?" asked Shay.

"Try to unclench his hand from the knife," said Cairny.

I glanced at the handle and Biggie's fingers wrapped around it, both of them slicked with blood as well as other gastrointestinal juices. "I'd rather not, if that's okay."

"Fine. Not that one. His free hand, then."

I stared at the guy, his visage much more evident in the light than it had been during our fight. Ratty, close-cropped black hair sprung from his skull, the hairline having retreated at least a few inches from where it had once started. His wide nose and sunken eyes were sure fire signs of orc heritage. He was ugly as a plucked hen, and he'd tried to murder me. Still, I hadn't meant to kill him in return. Him or Topples.

"I'm, uh...still good. Thanks."

Shay squatted next to Cairny and put her fingers on the guy's hand. She looked up, surprised. "Daggers. Really. You should feel this."

"Fine."

I joined them, reaching out and touching Biggie's free hand. It felt cold and stiff. "Okay. So he's a stiff. He's dead. We already established that."

Shay cocked her head at me. "He only died...what? An hour ago, Daggers?"

"Roughly, unless I passed out after my fall for a lot longer than I've been led to believe. What are you getting at?"

"That's awfully fast for rigor mortis to set in," said Cairny. "Normally it takes in the range of two to six hours to start, with the eyelids, neck, and jaw first to be affected. For his fingers to already be stiffened within an hour is highly abnormal, to say the least."

"Well, we've already concluded the blade was likely poisoned," I said. "Aren't there poisons that cause paralysis?"

"Of course," said Cairny. "Hemlock. Nightshade. Larkspur. All of those can cause paralysis of the nervous system. But rigor mortis isn't caused by that. It's caused by a depletion of oxygen in the muscles. Which isn't to say there couldn't be drugs that speed up that depletion process—although none immediately come to mind."

"So the guy died too fast, and his muscles locked up even faster," said Quinto. "It's like time sped up around him or something."

Rodgers snorted. "Alright. It's official. Daggers, you've been made obsolete. Quinto can provide all the crazy theories going forward."

"I still suspect a chemical compound is more likely to blame," said Cairny. "But it's odd, I'll give you that."

I eyed Biggie's stiffened arm. "You checked his pockets for identification?"

"We did," said Quinto. "He's not carrying a thing on him. Not even change."

Like Topples, Biggie wore a plain, long sleeve shirt and pants. His left hand gripped the handle of the blade. I wished it was the other way around.

Carefully, making sure not to touch the blade, I worked the cuff of Biggie's sleeve up his left arm. The same tattoo with three straight lines and bunched half-circles presented itself.

I grunted. "Well, we still have no idea what that means, but at least it's a pattern. Should help us down the line."

Cairny, Shay, and I stood. I stared at Biggie's corpse some more, wondering how I could feel sympathy for a man who'd nearly succeeded in killing me. It wasn't a new sensation. I'd been forced to end someone's life a couple times in my years on the force, and each time it left me hollow for days. I think it just meant I was a decent person on the inside.

"Alright," said Captain Knox. "I think I've already made it clear to everyone, but getting to the bottom of whoever tried to murder Detective Daggers is our number one priority. You're all assigned to the case. Cairny and Detective Quinto. On behalf of all of us, I apologize for the untimely nature of the assault. This was supposed to be your night, so please go home and enjoy what's left of it as best you can. I'll see the both of you bright and early in the morning.

"Detective Daggers. I'd suggest you spend the evening at Detective Steele's place tonight, and beyond that I'd encourage you to grab whatever things you might need from your apartment before you leave. CSU will be here shortly, and I'm going to ensure they stay as long as necessary to pry every last speck of evidence from the walls that might help us figure out who's behind this. It could be a day or a week, so plan accordingly. I'm also going to send a police detail to keep watch over your apartment, Detective Steele. Don't either of you dare complain. It's a safety precaution both of you should recognize as prudent, whether you like it or not.

"Detective Rodgers. That leaves you. As much as I hate to ask, I'll need your help overseeing our brothers and sisters in arms, at least until CSU arrives and we get the bodies loaded for transport to the precinct. I imagine it won't take more than an hour."

"My pleasure, Captain," he said. "Anything for Daggers."

I think he meant it. It was nice to know my friends had my back.

"The rest of you are free to go," said Knox. "But everyone? Be careful. We don't know why the attackers targeted Detective Daggers. Better to take a few extra precautions than to end up dead. I'll see you all in the morning."

Quinto nodded, and he and Cairny headed for the door.

Shay put a hand on my shoulder. "You sure you're okay? Physically, I mean. We can stop by a clinic on the way to my place, if you like."

I smiled. "A good night's rest and I'll be fine. Let me grab a few things from my room and we can be on our way."

8

The front double doors thudded shut behind us, blocking out the early morning sun as Shay and I stepped into the precinct.

Shay glanced at me. "You sure you're okay?"

"Would you please stop asking me that?" I said. "I've told you more times than I can count that I'm fine."

Shay smiled. "Yes, but you're a known liar."

I sighed. "I'm not lying. Last night, maybe a little, but not anymore. What previously manifested as a thousand small aches and pains has deadened into a nice full-body soreness. I've been through worse, trust me."

It was true. A night's sleep at Shay's place with her warm body at my side had cured more ills than the mightiest salve could've. I thought it might've been weird having a beat cop hanging around outside the door, but I slept sounder than a baby lamb swaddled in silk. Shay'd been forced to wake me as the clock approached eight.

"I'm just saying, if you needed more time to recover, I have no doubt the Captain would oblige you. You *did* fall three stories onto pavement less than twelve hours ago."

I snorted. "You think I'd take a breather on this case over tender ribs and a balky ankle? We're the same in that regard. It's not as if you're not making any sacrifices."

Shay glanced at her simple white sundress, knowing full well what I meant. "I think keeping you alive takes precedence over helping my mother prepare for the graduation bash. Besides, it's not as if I'm abandoning them entirely. I'm still planning to attend the ceremony at noon."

"I know," I said. "And like I told you, you're welcome to spend the morning with them if you'd like, too."

"I'd rather be here with you."

"Of course you would. Look at me. I'm irresistible, even when beat up."

Shay smoothed the shoulders of my leather jacket, which of course I'd snagged before leaving my apartment the night prior. Despite the summer heat, I felt better with it and Daisy protecting me.

"I know you're joking," said Shay, cracking a smile. "But you're right, you know."

"Aren't I always?" I gestured toward the end of the pit. "Come on. Let's get to work."

We headed toward our desks. Word must've gotten around, because everyone I passed acknowledged me in some way, either with a solemn nod or a friendly greeting or even the occasional "We'll get 'em, Daggers." Quinto and Rodgers weren't at their desks, but the Captain was at hers. She waved us in as she saw us walk past her office windows.

"Morning, Captain." I paused at the door. "Want me to close this?"

"No point. Everyone already knows, as you might've surmised from the gauntlet of officers you passed through on your way."

I took a seat, and Shay did the same. The empty mug on Knox's desk gave the impression that she'd been at her post a while already, and given her efforts last night with Rodgers, who knew how long she'd slept. Not that her demeanor gave that information away. She looked taut as a violin string, in a good way. Focused.

"How are you feeling?" she asked.

"Don't go all soft on me," I said. "I get enough of that from Steele. I'm here to work. That and drink second rate coffee." I already missed Mitch and his cart.

"Glad to hear it." Knox shifted her gaze to Steele. "What about you, Detective?"

"Don't get the wrong impression, Captain. I dressed this way so I could head straight to my brother's graduation ceremony when the time comes."

"I figured that out," said Knox. "It's not what I meant."

"Then what *did* you mean, Captain?"

Knox gave me a nod. "We all know about your relationship with Detective Daggers. Perhaps Captain Armstrong didn't know or didn't approve while he was here, but it doesn't matter to me. It does make things more complicated, though. He's become more than your partner. From personal experience, I've found it's easier to weather situations where you yourself are in danger over those where someone you care about is."

Shay's gaze didn't waver, and her answer came back forceful but controlled. "I'm as committed to solving this case as anyone in the department, Captain."

Knox nodded. I liked that she didn't ask either of us twice. It was a sign of respect.

"Let me fill you in on the state of affairs," she said. "The CSU team arrived shortly after you left last night. The report I received this morning shows they spent three and a half hours there last night, and I imagine they've been there for an hour already today."

"They find anything?" I asked.

"I'll inform you as soon as I know," said the Captain. "In the meantime, it's a game of wait and see. Detective Rodgers and I ensured the bodies were transported back here for study. I suspect Coroner Moonshadow is cutting into them as we speak. One of them, anyway. I requested an assist from the Grant Street Precinct, and they obliged by sending an additional coroner over. He and Cairny are tag-teaming the corpses."

I shed the unsavory mental image created by her turn of phrase. "The tox screens will take at least a day to go through, I'm guessing."

"At least," said Knox. "We'll try to expedite them, but there are physical and chemical limitations."

"If Cairny's in, I'm assuming Quinto is, too," said Shay.

"Not to mention Rodgers, but don't feel bad. As promised, we headed home within the hour last night. He and Detective Quinto are consulting with Detective Lamont from the gang unit upstairs. Hopefully he'll be able to provide leads on likely gang activity. For all I know, his team may have been on the trail of a suspicious group for some time. If so, I'll have a word with Lamont about the frequency of our communications, but for now I know as much as you do. Which leaves the two of you."

The Captain paused and stared at us.

I filled the void. "Where do you want us to start, Captain?"

"I don't know," she said. "That's why you're here and not already investigating the next lead. I'm open to suggestions."

I glanced at Steele. "Well...if I were investigating someone else's murder, I'd start by retracing the victim's steps, see what they were involved in leading up to the crime. In this case, I already know what I was up to, not to mention where I was, which makes the task trivial. But it might not be a bad idea to delve a little further into it. I sensed I was being followed even though I didn't lay eyes on Topples and Biggie until they jumped me. Could be someone else saw them before I did. Not that I enjoy canvassing street corners, but it could be worth a shot. Do we have sketches of the deceased yet?"

"Boatreng is downstairs as we speak," said Knox. "I imagine he has a copy of each ready. If not I'll lean on him until he does. Any other ideas?"

"We could follow the poison trail," said Shay. "Cairny already provided possibilities for the makeup of the concoction applied to the blade. We could locate known suppliers."

Knox gave her head the barest of shakes. "That's guesswork until we have the results of the tox screen.

I'd rather wait until we know the cause of death for certain. Anything else?"

"One other suggestion," I said. "Something more targeted than canvassing the entire path from Steele's apartment to mine. We hit tattoo shops. Show our sketches of the criminals. Maybe someone will recognize them."

Knox chewed the inside of her lip. "That one seems the most promising so far. Any better suggestions?"

Shay and I exchanged glances. She shrugged.

"Good enough for me," said the Captain. "Now get moving. I want the bastard responsible for this locked up before nightfall."

9

The door jingled as I pushed it open. A mix of scents greeted me as I stepped into the darkened shop: spicy day-old takeout, rubbing alcohol, and an 'herbal incense' that may not have been of the legal variety. The blinds across the front windows blocked a good portion of the midmorning sun, and what they didn't diffused into the smoky haze that hovered over the shop's worn wooden floor.

Yeah. *Incense, my ass.*

"You know, you could at least *try* not to look like you want to tear someone's head off." Shay stood beside me, having followed me into the shop.

"What if I *do* want to tear someone's head off?"

"Not the tattoo artist's we're here to talk to, hopefully."

I unclenched my jaw. "Sorry. Can't blame me, though. I'm starting to think we should've canvassed the streets after all."

"You know what they say," said Steele. "Third time's the charm."

"Only problem is this is our fifth tattoo parlor."

The sign above the door had read Thicker Than Water, which I gave a three out of five in terms of pun creativity. Sure, skin bled when tattooed, but the liquid most important to the process was the dye. I'd much preferred the name of the second shop we'd set foot in, Inked, Inc.

I took a look around. A quartet of leather barber's chairs populated the corners of the shop, each of them showing cracks in the seats, backing, and headrests. Cabinets loaded with bottles of ink, racks of sharp needles, and hand tools needed to insert ink under the patron's skin stood behind each station, but it was the artwork on the walls that caught my eye.

Each station had several pieces of art hung around it, no doubt representative of the individual artist's style. Based on the displayed pieces, one did traditional tribal designs, another ventured more into realistic depictions of animals and nature, though only in black and gray, the third focused purely on abstract, color works, and the last did something altogether unique. A quirky style of characters with oversized heads, exaggerated body dimensions, and the flair of a children's book illustrator. Hopefully the designs weren't actually intended for children...

A piece of furniture at the back end of the shop—more than a hostess stand but not quite a desk—stood a few feet in front of a bead curtain. The incense wafted over from that direction.

Shay approached the counter. Failing to find a bell, she knocked on the side of the stand and called out. "Hello? Anyone here?"

I heard coughing from the back, then the sound of something clattering to the ground. Footsteps followed.

A hand brushed the beads aside. A guy with long matted hair, sleepy eyes, and a braided goatee walked through. He wore baggy canvas pants, a colorful knit hat, and a vest over his bare chest. He brought with him a wave of fresh smoke.

I coughed, too, but probably not for the same reasons our host had.

The tattoo bum eyed the pair of us, but mostly Shay. "Welcome. My name's Dwayne. Sorry it took me a moment to come out. Didn't hear you at first."

"Really?" said Shay. "It's a small shop. That's the whole point of the door chime."

Dwayne blinked. "Uh...right. So what can I do for you? You've got sort of a yin and yang thing going on. Maybe a skull for the tough guy and a more delicate piece for you? A bird or a butterfly? Or are only one of you getting inked today?"

I took a wild guess that Dwayne specialized in the abstract color work, but who knows? Maybe he was the brains behind the swollen-headed marionette babies.

"Neither. We're here looking for someone. Two someones, actually." I reached into my coat and produced the sketches I'd received from Boatreng. I unfolded them and held them out.

Dwayne looked at them blankly. "Sorry. Those guys don't work here. You must have the wrong shop."

"We didn't expect them to *work* here," said Shay. "We were hoping they might be clients of yours."

Dwayne blinked again. I wondered if the habit was more chemically-induced or a product of his mental capacity. "Who did you say you were?"

"We didn't. Detectives Daggers and Steele. New Welwic PD. Homicide division."

"Whoa." Dwayne took another look at the sketches. "These guys are dead?"

I swallowed hard, recalling my role in that. "You catch on quick."

"Ever seen them around the shop?" asked Shay.

"Sorry," said Dwayne with a shrug. "Should I have?"

"Maybe," said Shay. "They had matching ink on the inside of their left forearms. A series of three lines, tight at the bottom, spreading out toward the wrist, with some bubbles or semicircles at the end."

Dopey Dwayne gave us a blank look.

I rummaged in my jacket, producing another piece of paper. Dwayne wasn't the first employee to look as if we'd described an engineering diagram instead of a tattoo.

"This," I said, holding the sketch forward.

Dwayne snorted. "Really? You think someone would come by Thicker than Water for *that*? Come on, man. We're *artists*. We take pride in our work. This isn't some two bit poke shop. That looks like the kind of thing someone got in a prison."

"We're not implying you *couldn't* do better than this. The wall art speaks for itself." *And not necessarily in a good way,* I thought. "But you run a business here, right? I'm sure people come in all the time asking for tattoos that aren't you or your shop mates' specialty."

"They do," said Dwayne. "And we turn them down. Because we have standards."

I glanced at the empty chairs. There seemed to be a clear inverse correlation between standards and business.

"Our apologies," said Shay. "We weren't trying to disparage your artistic talents. We're simply following leads. I'm assuming you have other artists who work here though, right? Next time you see them, could you ask if they've seen either of the individuals in the sketches?"

Dwayne held up a hand. His fingertips were stained yellow, either from his tattoo work or all the 'incense' he'd inhaled. "Hold up. I said I'd never seen the guys. Never tatted something so trivial, either. Doesn't mean I haven't seen the tattoo before."

My eyes widened. "You have?"

"Sure," he said. "A potential client from a couple weeks ago had one, same place you mentioned. Left forearm. Had a bunch of other tattoos, too. Skull on his upper arm. Knife on the inside of his bicep. Said he had a few others on his chest and back, too, but I didn't ask to see them. He was looking to get another one on his arm, of a warrior on a hill holding a hammer to the sky. Cool idea, but it needed a little work. I tried to convince him to—"

"Dwayne," I said. "We're not interested in the tattoo you gave him."

"*Didn't* give him," said Dwayne. "He and I couldn't come to an artistic compromise."

"Did he have a name?"

"Uh..." The smoke-infused tattoo artist blinked. "Come to think of it, he never mentioned it. I didn't get a chance to bond with him, you know, seeing as he left without getting anything. Maybe it was for the better. He seemed like a rough dude."

"What else can you tell us about him?" asked Shay. "Physical attributes. Any names he might've mentioned besides his?"

"I don't remember any, no," said Dwayne. "But I can tell you what he looked like. He was an ogre. A big one. Probably wouldn't have even fit in the chair, to be honest. Bald. Scary looking."

That wasn't the most helpful of descriptions. Most ogres were big and scary looking. "How well do you remember him? If we sent our artist over, do you think you could work with him to create a reasonable like-ness?"

Dwayne snorted again. "Dude. I'm an artist. I have an eye for that sort of thing."

"As long as you remember," I said.

"Why wouldn't I?"

In my experience, the particular type of 'incense' he reeked of didn't help with long-term memory, but I kept that bit of pessimism to myself. Instead, Shay and I thanked the guy for his help and assured him Boatreng would be right over.

10

When we arrived back at the precinct, Shay and I made our way to our desks. They were empty, as they should've been, but Rodgers' and Quinto's were, too. I acknowledged that fact with a grunt.

Shay noticed. "Hmm?"

"Nothing," I said. "Figured the guys would be done with Lamont by now."

"Maybe he had a lead for them."

I glanced toward the Captain's office. She was gone, too. I frowned.

Shay gave me a sideways look. "What's going on?"

"Captain's gone, too. Damn it, if they found something and didn't tell me... Do you think Knox ordered us to the tattoo parlors as a ploy? It would be just like to her send us on a wild goose chase to keep us out of harm's way."

"Actually, that feels more like a Captain Armstrong move," said Shay. "Captain Knox has always been straight with us. She wouldn't lie to cut you out of the action."

I refused to shelve my frown. "You're probably right. Doesn't mean that whatever came up isn't related to our case, though."

Shay gave me a once-over. "You sure you're doing alright?"

"Not this again. I've told you, I'm fine. The doctor gave me the a-okay, right?"

"That's not what I meant," said Shay. "You've been alternating between overly apologetic and terse all morning. You're worked up. Why?"

I snorted. "Isn't it obvious?"

"But why, exactly?"

I stepped closer to my partner and lowered my voice. "Do I need to spell it out? Someone tried to kill me. That's never happened before, not like this. I've been attacked, but always in the heat of the moment. Nothing premeditated. And that's not the only reason I'm on edge. The Captain was right this morning—about the stress of putting others in danger. What if I'm not the only one at risk?"

"We've been in far more dangerous situations and come out fine," said Shay.

"Sure, but prior success does not predict future results," I said. "Maybe it wouldn't be so bad if we knew what we were up against, but as of now? What if the attack on me last night was the tip of an iceberg?"

"I know you have an active imagination, Daggers," said Shay. "But don't let it get the best of you. One step at a time, okay?"

I knew she was right to preach calm, but I still would've argued with her if I hadn't seen Rodgers and Quinto entering through the front door at that instant.

I waited until they muscled their way through the cubicles before giving them a nod. "There you are. We thought you were talking to Lamont."

"We were," said Quinto. "About two hours ago."

"And?"

"And he didn't have much to tell us, which is why we didn't spend longer at his desk. You guys get lucky at any of the tattoo shops?"

"Captain filled you in, I guess?"

Quinto nodded.

"We did, as a matter of fact," said Steele. "No hits on the perps, but one of the artists had seen the tattoo before, also on someone's forearm. We're going to send Boatreng there to whip something up. What about you guys? What were you up to?"

"Plan B, according to the Captain," said Rodgers. "Canvassing the stretch between your apartments with more of Boatreng's sketches. We didn't get any leads."

"Not surprising," I said. "That's why it was Plan B. You really didn't get anything useful from Lamont?"

Quinto and Rodgers shared a look.

"Well...I wouldn't say we didn't get *anything* useful," said Quinto.

"What's that supposed to mean?"

Rodgers sat on the edge of my desk. "Lamont wasn't familiar with the line and semicircles tattoo, though he acknowledged it's almost certainly gang-related due to the simple design and uniform placement. He also said he hadn't heard any rumors of new gang activity. I don't know how odd that is, but he seemed confident he'd know about any new players in the game. Said the same five or six gangs have been skulking around New Welwic for the past few years and that the last major shakeup was when we busted the remains of the Wyverns and their dragon hatching operation."

"No offense," said Steele, "but none of that information seems particularly useful."

"It isn't," Rodgers said. "It's only the last bit he told us that might be. He prefaced this by saying it was a hunch at best, a gut feeling from spending so much time with his ear to the ground, but Lamont mentioned that if anything, gang-related activity had been abnormally low of late. He also told us he was getting minimal info coming through his channels."

"So, what?" I said. "The gangs are trying to stay out of the public eye? Or more so than they already do?"

Quinto nodded. "Could be there's something going on behind the scenes that Lamont and the rest of the gang unit aren't privy to. Could be a random lull, or exactly the opposite. That our gang units have been so effective of late that the remaining gangs aren't able to perform to the level of their predecessors. Or it could be they're concerned for some reason and don't want to overexert themselves."

"Because there's a new player in town?" I asked.

"Unlikely," said Rodgers. "Lamont was sure he'd have heard if there was. But in a case with as few leads as this one, a lull in gang-related activity is something to think about. After all, we haven't considered the timing of last night's attack. Why come after you *now*? We figure that out, and I'm sure we'll figure out who's behind the attack."

"Speaking of timing..." Steele glanced toward the nearest clock. "If I'm going to make it to Shawn's graduation on time, I should be heading out. The traffic through midtown is always rough this time of day." She smiled and squeezed my arm. I think she wanted to kiss me, but we were at work, after all. "It shouldn't take that long, even accounting for the afterparty. I'll be back by two, three at the latest."

I caught her hand before she had a chance to leave. "Shay?"

She turned. "Yes?"

"Be careful, okay?"

I thought she was going to lecture me on the improbability of being attacked in broad daylight at a university-sponsored graduation ceremony or the ensuing party, but she didn't. "Come with me."

"What? To the ceremony?"

"And the party for Shawn that my parents are throwing," she said. "Why not? You think the Captain would have a problem with it? She already approved my absence."

"That was before last night," I said.

"And she didn't rescind her permission this morning."

I glanced at my leather jacket. "I'm not dressed for it."

Shay gave me another smile. "It's okay if you'd rather not. I get it. But you're welcome to meet me at my parents' if you change your mind. I'll be with them the whole time. Promise."

I didn't stop her the second time she moved to leave, though I did keep my eyes on her until she disappeared through the precinct's wide double doors. When I brought my eyes back to the foreground, it was to find Quinto and Rodgers looking at me with concern.

"What?" I said.

"Nothing," said Quinto. "You sure you're doing okay?"

"Next person who asks me that gets socked in the mouth," I said. "Right now I need to deliver a message to Boatreng, and after that maybe talk to Cairny. See if she's found anything. Feel free to tag along if you like."

11

Despite the sour tone in which I delivered it, Rodgers and Quinto accepted my invitation. After dropping by Boatreng's desk with the tattoo parlor address, we all descended the steps to the morgue. The cool stone underfoot echoed the sounds of our footsteps, and a dim light suffused the equally cool, sterile air.

When I turned the corner into the cavernous investigation room, the usual suspects presented themselves. The shiny steel cadaver vaults along the room's far side, the examination tables laden with bleached white sheets, steel bowls, collections of scalpels, forceps, and pincers alongside the occasional clipboard, and our resident expert on all things deceased, Cairny. She'd replaced last night's little black dress with a pair of flowing black pants and a white lab coat, presumably with a black blouse underneath it, given her proclivities. Everything was as it should've been—except for the presence of Cairny's colleague.

He stood somewhere between Quinto's and my height, with close-cropped hair and cheekbones so sharp you could slice an apple on them. His ears were pointed as only a pure-blooded elf's could be, but even accounting for his race, he was on the gaunt side. His lab coat hung over his shoulders loosely, his clavicles a coat hanger of bone.

The pair of them stood side by side, up to their wrists in Biggie's chest cavity. I stopped a few yards shy. I didn't have any need to get up close and personal with the man's spleen.

"Cairny," I said.

She turned. "Hello, Daggers. I was wondering when you might drop by. Good to see you, Rodgers. And you, too, of course, Quinto."

She gave her beau a warm smile. Come to think of it, I couldn't recall her referring to him by his first name. Then again, I usually referred to Steele by her last name at work—not that the occasional given name or term of endearment didn't slip though the cracks. Usually only when we thought other people weren't listening, though.

"Who's your friend?" I asked.

"Coroner Larkspur," said Cairny, tipping her head toward the elf. "He's been lending me a hand most of the morning."

When the elf spoke, it was in an emotionless drawl, too high pitched to be pleasant. "Hel-lo."

What was it about the coroner profession that attracted individuals with severe social issues? At least we'd reformed Cairny. Mostly. "Right. Captain said you'd be here. From the Grant Street Precinct?"

"In-deed."

There was something about the man's eyes that gave me the willies. Nothing suspicious. Just your average, run-of-the-mill creeper mortuary vibe.

I nodded toward the body. "Make any progress, Cairny?"

She gave a waffling nod. "Yes and no."

"That doesn't sound promising," said Quinto.

He was right. Cairny usually brimmed with enthusiasm for autopsies.

"Larkspur and I already finished our examination of the first deceased," said Cairny, shooting a thumb toward a white sheet-draped exam table on the far side of the room. "His examination was straightforward, which isn't to say simple, mind you. We had to add more paper to his file to catalog his many injuries. Dozens of facial lacerations. Bruising to the ribs, stomach, chest, and back. The broken arm—which you did quite a number on, Daggers—as well as numerous other fractures he must've sustained during your fall. We counted sixteen, all told, including three ribs, a tibia, and his coccyx. And that's before getting to the severe puncture wound that ended his final suffering quite rapidly. The broken post from the coffee cart managed to tear open the lower portion of his right ventricle."

"That's part of the heart, right?" I said.

"In-deed," Larkspur said again. I was starting to question his vocabulary in addition to his social skills.

Quinto pointed toward Biggie. "I assume he's the one giving you trouble."

Cairny sighed. "To say the least."

I snorted. "Don't tell me you're stumped."

"In regards to what killed him?" said Cairny. "Certainly not, mostly because we haven't come close to exhausting our options yet. What we do have is an ever expanding list of what *didn't* kill him. The gut wound for one, as we already discussed last night. As it turns out, my initial guess was correct. The blade lacerated his bowels but nothing else. Larkspur and I have since ruled out a heart attack, which could've been triggered by an adrenaline surge induced during the fight. We haven't cut into his head, so we can't disregard a ruptured aneurysm, triggered by any number of blows he received, though we think that's relatively unlikely, too."

"An an-eurysm would've in-capacitated him quite rapidly," said Larkspur. "You would've noticed."

"Exactly," said Cairny. "It would've killed him too quickly. Which leaves my poison hypothesis from last night. I took blood and tissue samples from the cadaver. I've started what tests I could here in my lab. The rest I've sent for further analysis. I should have the results back by the end of the day tomorrow."

"And I imagine we'll have to wait on those for an explanation of his too rapid rigor mortis," I said.

"Most likely," said Cairny, "but...that's where things get confusing."

"I was confused when you tried to explain it last night," I said, "but go on."

Cairny shared a glance with Larkspur. "We talked it over, and neither one of us could come up with a toxin that would cause both of the effects we witnessed in the deceased. Either, sure, but a fast acting poison that also causes accelerated rigor mortis? If it exists, neither of us is familiar with it, which would imply that if this man were poisoned, it was with a cocktail of chemicals."

We stood there in silence for a moment.

Rodgers scratched his chin. "I'm sorry. Is there a reason we're supposed to be concerned by that?"

"Not especially," said Cairny. "But it begs the question of *why*? If the blade were intended for Detective Daggers, and by his own recollection it certainly was, then it's reasonable to assume it might've been laced with a fast-acting poison. But why also apply an additional chemical that affects the body's decomposition response? Why would that be a desirable outcome, either in the attempted murder of Detective Daggers or in the murder of anyone else? And it would have to be a desired outcome, otherwise why apply the second chemical?"

The combined weight of three sets of eyes turned my way, all except those of the skeletal Larkspur. "What are you looking at me for?"

"Isn't this sort of your specialty?" said Quinto. "The rest of us do the leg work, collect evidence, and you piece it together into a wild scheme only you have the creative chops to dream up."

"Hey, now," said Rodgers. "He's not the *only* one with creative chops."

"You want to take a stab at this, then?" said Quinto.

Rodgers shrugged. "Easy. Whatever made the rigor mortis set in quickly must be a preservative, right? It would imply the killers didn't just want to murder Daggers, they wanted to keep his body for some reason."

I gave the blonde charmer the old eyebrow raise. "Seriously? You're freaking me out. As if having two hitmen try to off me wasn't bad enough."

"You got any better ideas?"

I didn't.

"There is, of course, another possibility," said Cairny.

"That being?" I said.

"That Larkspur and I are entirely wrong. We tested the knife and didn't find any lingering poisons at the base of the blade. If it was poisoned, it must've only been at the tip, where the poisons entered and spread through the deceased's body."

"But if Biggie wasn't poisoned, then what killed him? And what made his body lock up like that?"

Cairny shrugged. "You're better at coming up with unfounded theories than the rest of us. It could be something completely removed of our realm of thought. Something magical in nature, perhaps."

"Really, Cairny?" I said. "You're usually not one to delve into the supernatural."

"I'm also not one to get stumped. Which I'm not. Yet."

I shook my head. "I'd love to indulge you, but I think poison makes the most sense. It wouldn't necessarily have to have been on the blade, either. It's possible Biggie realized he was a dead man and took a pill to put himself out of his misery, or to keep himself from being captured and interrogated. You find any evidence of elevated drug residue in his stomach?"

"We haven't bothered to look yet," said Cairny. "We'll take swabs, but those'll require additional toxicology tests."

"And more days of waiting. Wonderful."

Cairny crossed to an empty exam table and lifted a saw. "In the meantime, Larkspur and I are going to put the aneurysm question to the test. Anyone care to stay for the results?"

Quinto may have been engaged to Cairny now, but his feet carried him out the morgue and up the stairs as fast as Rodgers' and mine did.

12

I sat at my desk, plucking chunks of chicken, snap peas, and sauce-slicked noodles from a waxed cardboard container with a pair of chopsticks. I'd picked up lunch for Rodgers, Quinto, and myself at the nearest chow hut, a place by the name of Noodles and More run by an elderly gnome couple. A bare year ago I wouldn't have touched their noodles with a ten foot pole sprayed with industrial-strength noodle repellant, but apparently I wasn't the only one who'd changed in that time span. The noodles had improved from hellish to respectable. Perhaps the gnomes were taking night classes.

"Daggers?"

I looked up from my stir fry. A short, bald man stood in front of my desk, a smattering of stubble distributed unevenly around his rounded chin. "Hey, Boatreng. Just get back from the tattoo parlor?"

He dug into the satchel he wore over his shoulder, the one that contained his sketch pad and charcoals. "Why else would I be here?"

"It could be because you miss my charming wit and insightful social commentary," I said. "Or maybe because it's past lunch time and I'm holding something edible."

"One of those is more likely than the other." He pulled a sheet from his satchel and held it forward. "Here's the likeness I produced from working with that artist at the tattoo shop."

"Dwayne," I said, accepting the sheet. "He's a trip, isn't he?"

"He might be *on* a trip, that's for sure. I've worked with worse. He was able to describe the suspect pretty well."

I glanced at the drawing, which as promised by Dwayne depicted a big scary ogre, bald as a watermelon and with a head roughly the same size. He had all the traditional features of his race: dark skin, thick eyebrows to go along with wide set eyes, a wide nose, a wide jaw, a wide neck—hell, wide everything. To go along with that, the guy seemed to be clenching his jaw in the drawing.

"Did you intentionally make it look like the suspect was constipated?" I asked.

Boatreng shrugged. "Dwayne was insistent that he sported a perpetual scowl. As a fellow artist, he implored me to depict him accurately. I can whip up another with a neutral expression if you give me fifteen minutes."

I frowned.

"Something wrong?"

I looked at the sketch some more. There was something about the guy I couldn't put my finger on. "No.
It's fine. Can I keep this?"

"I need to produce duplicates," he said. "I can bring
you one in a half hour."

"Sure. That'll be fine." I handed the sketch back.
"Thanks."

I'd only gotten another couple bites of my chicken
and noodles down my gullet before Rodgers popped
over. "Hey, Daggers. Boatreng have anything?"

"A sketch. Same as always."

Rodgers looked mildly disappointed at my lack of ex-
position. "Right. Anyway, Quinto and I are headed out.
The big guy did some research and found a professor at
the University of New Welwic who's supposed to be an
expert on poisons. Seems like a long shot at this point,
but he might be able to make sense of Cairny and
Coroner Lurch's suspicions."

"Long shots are most of our leads right now," I said.
"Want company?"

"I've already got Quinto. Seems like enough."

"Rodgers, I'm sitting here eating chicken out of a
cardboard bucket. The Captain's still not back from
whatever crisis pulled her away from her desk, and
without Steele, I don't have anyone to bounce my crazy
theories off of. What else am I supposed to do?"

"Maybe something not work related?"

"In the middle of all this? You want me to take time
off?"

"Look, maybe it's not my place to say anything," said
Rodgers, "but Steele invited you to join her for her

brother's graduation thingy. Sounded like she might like having you along."

I snorted and waved my chopsticks. "Oh. That. She was only being nice. Inviting me because she thought I was unnecessarily worried about her."

"Well, seemed to me there was genuine interest on her part to have you by her side. But, hey, what do I know? I've only been happily married for seven years."

I chewed a chunk of bell pepper. "Point taken. But I'm sure the ceremony is at least half over."

"Perfect," said Rodgers. "You'll need the time to head back to your place to change into something respectable for the afterparty."

He was right. I'd get evil looks for wearing leather. "I don't know. Seems like a lot of wasted time…"

Rodgers gave me a look. "Daggers, for once in your life, take my advice. Go home. Put on something nice. Meet Steele at whatever shindig her parents are hosting for her brother. You won't regret it. You need to get your mind off the case. Right now we're spinning our wheels. Trust me. Lean on your team. Quinto and I can handle it, and if we can't, you'll only be gone a few hours."

I grumbled. "The CSU team is still probably combing through my things."

"You're running out of excuses," said Rodgers. "Come on, man. Go."

"Fine," I said. "As soon as I'm done with lunch. But if you die a horrible death at the hands of ruthless thugs, don't you dare haunt me in the afterlife. You can pester Quinto in the middle of the night and ruin his sex life, instead."

"Just the mental image I wanted, thanks."

Rodgers flicked his fingers at me and left. I horked down the last few lingering noodles in my carryout container and headed after him out the door.

13

When I reached my building's third floor landing, I found a friendly face waiting for me outside my door. "Phillips. They put you on guard duty? Please tell me the Captain let you go home and get some sleep last night."

"Not to worry, Detective," he said with a smile. "I didn't come in until ten. Captain's orders. You can save your sympathy for the officer who stood guard overnight."

"Captain Knox left a detail here, too?"

Phillips nodded. "Didn't want any interference with the crime scene after CSU left."

The door to my apartment stood open, though someone had strung another length of police-issue caution tape across the entrance. Inside, I could see a trio of white coat-clad technicians meticulously inspecting my living room's remains. "They're back."

"Ten o'clock, same as me," said Phillips.

I pointed at the open door. "You mind?"

"Not at all, sir," he said, stepping to the side. "Your apartment, after all."

I unpinned the tape and walked inside, careful not to step on any of the glass shards that still littered the floor. The CSU techs looked my way upon hearing my footsteps, but only the head tech bothered to give me a nod, a middle-aged woman by the name of Maribell or Marissa or something that started with an 'M.'

"Detective," she said. "I wasn't expecting you here."

I wondered if I could get through our conversation without admitting I'd forgotten her name. "I wasn't expecting to *be* back. Forgot a change of clothes for a ceremony I'm attending this afternoon. Well, I didn't actually forget, if we're being technical. My plans changed."

"Mmm-hmm." Mariwhatever turned back to her work of plucking hair fragments and mystery threads from the wall where Biggie's body had been recovered.

I could've gotten away scot-free, but I couldn't leave well enough alone. "Say, have you checked that area for traces of neurotoxins?"

Marisomething cast a glance my way.

"It's the guy who died there. Biggie, I'm calling him. Coroner Moonshadow suspects he might've been poisoned, but she didn't find anything on the blade. I'm thinking he might've taken a suicide pill to avoid questioning. Maybe he had more than one. Could've lost one, even."

Mariwhatshername lifted a brow.

"So you're looking into it? I can tell you're looking into it. Good. Great." I turned to one of the other techs, feeling like a heel. "It's fine if I grab something from my bedroom, right?"

"So long as you didn't fight anyone in there."

I nodded my assent before heading to my bedchambers. Once there, I sifted through the limited portion of my closet that didn't contain plain cotton shirts and denim, trying to think what Shay would've chosen for me if she'd been here. Eventually I plucked free a tan linen suit I hadn't worn in years and put it on. I felt naked in its silky embrace, and not because the linen breathed so well. Rather because I had to leave Daisy behind again. The thing barely had room for a billfold in the interior pocket, never mind a foot and a half long truncheon.

I was a master of avoiding eye contact as I left my apartment, making it back to the exterior door without so much as spotting any of the three techs in my peripheral vision. To be fair, I doubt any of them wanted to talk to me either. That didn't hold for Phillips, though.

"Looking good, sir," he said as I pinned the caution tape back into place. "Heading to another event with Detective Steele?"

"A reception for her brother. He graduated from business school today. Try not to die of boredom, Phillips." I gave the young guy a wave.

"Um...sir?"

I paused in mid-stride. "Yes?"

"It's really not my place, but ah...your shoes."

"What of them?"

"Black doesn't go with tan. Sir."

I blinked. "You're kidding, right? Am I the only one left at the precinct who's not fashion conscious?"

Phillips blushed. "No, sir. I didn't mean it that way. Forgot I said anything."

I glanced down at my utilitarian work shoes. They'd been black, once upon a time. Years of scuffs had turned them more of a dark gray.

I sighed. Phillips was right. Shay would notice them. She might not say anything, but she'd notice.

I blinked as I stared at my shoes. *Speaking of noticing...*

I knelt and peered at the floor. As with my shoes, the floorboards were covered with scuffs and criss-crossed scratches, decades worth instead of years worth, but there were a few that looked fresh, ones where raw wood unearthed by an errant boot had yet to oxidize and fade. Several scratches, actually. A set of three, all in a row.

I looked up and moved closer to Phillips.

"Sir, really, I apologize," he said. "I shouldn't have mentioned anything."

I found a few more scratches near my door. From when Topples bum rushed me? "You're fine. Don't worry about it."

"You're sure?"

I waved him off, swatting aside the tape on my way into my apartment. Sure enough, I found another set of scratches.

"Hey, Mari...er..."

The head tech looked my way, unamused. "Yes?"

"You catalog these scratches?"

"Already in my report."

I nodded and kept starting at them.

"I can strike them if you think they weren't caused during the skirmish."

I shook my head. "No. That's not it. Go ahead and leave them there."

I headed back to my bedroom before she could ask me what my issue with them was. It wasn't until I was halfway through changing my shoes that I realized there were two. The fact that there were so few scratches when Biggie, Topples, and I had darn near tangoed across my living room three times over was confusing, but the presence of a set of scratches in the hallway, where I hadn't fought anyone at all, was darn near baffling.

14

I knocked on the door and waited, muffled voices and laughter muted by the hardwood between us. I was getting ready to knock a second time when I heard the snap of a latch and the squeak of hinges.

"Ah, Jake. Glad to see you could make it."

Stephen Steele, Shay's father, stood behind the door, dressed in a cool grey suit that matched the streaks in his otherwise brown hair. He beamed as he waved me in with the hand that wasn't holding a half-full tumbler of brandy.

"Come in," he said. "Make yourself at home. You know where the coat rack is."

As glad as I was to see the man smiling, I wasn't naive enough to think it was because of *my* presence. Surely it had more to do with his middle son graduating from the prestigious UNW business program. Still, I could at least take heart in the fact that we'd all turned over new leaves since our disastrous first encounter, the one in which I'd accidentally turned a bottle of fine wine into an aerosolized spray and nearly killed their cat with an ill-timed karate kick. Since then, I'd apologized profusely, but more than that, I'd gotten to know him and his wife, not to mention their sons Samuel and Shawn. I wasn't sure if I could officially say they'd accepted me, but they were making a much stronger effort to make me feel welcome, no doubt in response to a talking to on the part of Shay, and in turn I was doing my damnedest not to screw things up.

"Thanks, Mr. Steele," I said, walking into the apartment. "How were the festivities?"

"You mean the ceremony? Well, I can't say it was the most exciting thing in the world. If you've been to one of those, you've been to them all, and seeing as Shawn is the last of mine to graduate from an advanced degree program, not to mention all the undergraduate ceremonies I've attended...well, you can imagine how it goes. I was more looking forward to getting home." He lifted his brandy. "But as graduations go, it was nice. Brenton Heimlich gave a speech on monetarism. Can't say I agree with the principle, but it was pertinent given Shawn's field. You're familiar with him?"

"Who?" I said. "Heimlich? Never heard of him."

"He's an economist. You can ask Shawn about him. I'm sure he could tell you much more about his theories than I could."

That sounded *thrilling*. "I'll be sure to do that when I see him. After I congratulate him, of course. Is he in the living room?"

"No, still at the university," said Mr. Steele. "Or rather, I imagine he's on his way back by now. He had to stay afterwards to sign the official yearbook, shake hands, and say his goodbyes. Not that he won't see his classmates again. He's already secured a good entry level position here in the city."

"That's great to hear. He'll be making more than me by the end of the week."

Mr. Steele chuckled. "Don't beat yourself up. He'll probably be making more than *me* soon. So, where's Shay? Don't tell me you left her back at the precinct."

I blinked. "I'm sorry. What do you mean?"

"Come now, Jake. She sent word that you were in a bit of a tussle last night, but it didn't affect your memory, did it? Shay. My daughter. Your girlfriend."

I blinked again, feeling pressure building in my chest. "Are you saying she didn't join you at the ceremony?"

Stephen cocked his head at me. "No. I was under the impression she'd be there, sure, but after she sent her note last night, I expected both of your schedules to be touch and go. I figured the two of you got caught up in something at work. What did happen last night, anyway?"

Darkness crept in at the edges of my vision. My heart started pounding, and I couldn't breathe. Blood pulsed through my head with each beat, making every artery, every capillary feel like a rushing river.

I swayed. Mr. Steele held out a hand to steady me.

"Jake, what's going on? Are you alright?"

"I'm sorry," I croaked. "I've got to go."

With Mr. Steele's confused voice ringing behind me, I turned and stumbled toward the stairs, fighting off the darkness as I forced my legs into a run.

15

My feet pounded on the stairs as I bounced off them, taking them three at a time to ground level. I blasted open the door to the street, throwing my bulk into it, nearly knocking a pedestrian to the ground as I took off at a dead sprint toward 5th Street.

A nauseating cocktail of emotions washed through me. Anger, fear, guilt, and despair, each of them fighting for control, each of them trying to drag me down to the ground, to make me decorate the sidewalk with half-digested chicken stir fry or to force me into a ball and shake with wracking sobs.

I elbowed them to the side and simply ran, faster than any rickshaw could go, partly because I wasn't pulling a cart behind me, more because I was fueled with desperation, a dying need to understand, to search, to find. A need to silence the crippling stew of emotions with undeniable proof that their distasteful influence was unfounded.

I ricocheted off foot traffic and rickshaw drivers alike as I tore through the streets, my breath coming in ragged gasps as the city blocks disappeared behind me. My heart pumped at a hundred and fifty beats a minute, now from exertion rather than blind fear. Sweat slicked my forehead and wicked my suit to my back. I might've ripped it at the seams in my haste, but I didn't care. Only Shay's wellbeing mattered. Nothing else.

I careened around the corner of 5th and Schumacher and made a beeline for the urchins clustered around the precinct's front steps. Some of the smaller ones looked alarmed as I barreled toward them at full speed, but most of them recognized me. They earned their coppers carrying messages for the department.

I skidded to a halt in front of them, speaking between gulps of air. "Detective Steele. Where... Where did she go?"

One of the oldest runners answered for the group. "Beg your pardon, sir?"

"Detective Steele," I said, still panting. "My partner. You know her. The pretty one. She left the precinct an hour and a half ago, two hours tops. Did anyone see her leave?"

The same runner gave me a nod. "Sure did, Detective. Took one of the rickshaws. Told the driver to head to the UNW auditorium, I think."

Then why the hell hadn't she met her parents there? I turned toward the rickshaws that waited at the foot of the steps, waiting patiently for patrons from the department, and hopped into the first in line.

"The UNW auditorium," I told the driver. "Hoof it. No. Scratch that. Go at a reasonable pace. I need to keep an eye on the streets."

The driver shot me a confused glance before shrugging and turning to his push bar. "You got it."

We took off east down 5th, the driver moving at a steady lope. I kept my eyes on the street, looking for something, *anything*. I wasn't even sure what. Sight of Shay, obviously, but anything that might signify signs of a struggle. An abandoned rickshaw. A large scary ogre with a gang tattoo on his left forearm. A pool of blood. Hell, I didn't know.

Gods, she couldn't really have been attacked, could she? Something must've come up. Maybe she forgot a present for her brother at her apartment and while there accidentally locked herself in a closet. Maybe she thought of something critical to the case while en route to the ceremony and made a last-second pit stop. She might still be chatting up a witness. Or perhaps she saw something on the street that caught her eye, not necessarily something related to our current case. A crime in progress that her sense of justice forced her to intervene in. For all I knew, she could be back at the precinct right now, booking some ne'er-do-well into the cages.

Except that the runners at the front would've seen her returning with the criminal in cuffs. And that Shay would've sent a runner to her parents at the first chance she got. She sent word last night. She wouldn't have neglected to do the same today.

My heart continued to pound, fighting back the weight of the invisible elephant sitting on my chest. A

thousand scenarios played through my mind at super-
sonic speed, trying to distract me from my job scanning
the streets. *Succeeding*, in fact. It took me a minute after
turning onto Briar Avenue to realize the driver's mistake.

"Hey," I shouted at the man. "I said the University of
New Welwic auditorium. Seventh Street's the most direct route."

"Yes, sir," he said in a rather annoyed tone. "Heard
you the first time. But there's a spill on Seventh.
Snagged me in a mess of traffic earlier. Not sure if it's
been cleaned up yet, but no point in tempting fate."

"*Spill?* What sort of spill?"

"A chemical of some sort, sir. City crews had the
area blocked off. It was a bloody mess trying to fight for
pass throughs to Sixth and Eighth."

"You didn't give a ride to a young half-elf detective
from the Fifth earlier today, did you?"

"No, sir. Got caught up in the traffic ferrying a
woman from Eleventh down to the southern end of the
Pearl. Hit the blocked area on the north side."

"Turn around," I said. "Go back. Take Seventh."

He glanced over his shoulder. "Sir, I think it'd be
better to—"

"I'll pay you for your time," I said. "Take Seventh.
The most direct route from the precinct to the auditorium."

He shook his head as he wheeled the rickshaw
around and headed back the way we came. An eternity
of minutes passed before we arrived at the scene of the
spill.

It wasn't as bad as it could've been. A quartet of city employees in bright yellow vests lingered around a makeshift barrier of yellow tape hung from temporary posts erected around a darkened, slick-looking section of road. One of the workers ushered pedestrians and rickshaws through a gap next to the buildings on the left-hand side while the other workers, all of them wearing cotton masks over their mouths, stood to the side, mops in hands but otherwise making no attempts to clear the spill.

I sprang from my rickshaw and burst past the crowd. Behind me, my driver yelled something about payment.

I nearly collided with the head worker waving people through. "You in charge here?"

"Whoa, there, pal," he said. "One at a time. Back of the line."

I ripped my badge from my coat pocket. "Detective Jake Daggers, NWPD. How long have you been here?"

"What?" He glanced at the badge. "I don't know. A couple hours, ever since someone called in the spill. Like I said, back of the line."

I snapped the billfold closed and jammed it in my pocket. "I am *not* screwing around here, guy. As of two seconds ago, this whole area is a crime scene, and I'm not talking environmental health hazard charges. I've got an officer missing and a suspected assault and kidnapping on my hands."

The worker's eyes widened. "Holy harvest. You serious?"

"Do I look like I'm joking? Get everybody back. Close the thoroughfare. *Now!"*

Maybe the head construction grunt got his job be-cause of his pipes. He bellowed with a voice that carried over the crowd. "Alright, everyone turn it around! Sev-enth's closed. Jerry, Paul, you guys get your asses on the other side of the tape. Push that crowd back to Eighth. Dunbar, help out, will 'ya? Come on everyone. Don't give me that lip. Let's go!"

The mop brigade abandoned their janitorial gear and hopped to it, helping secure the area and push back the rickshaws and pedestrians. My driver continued to bark at me.

"Take it up with the precinct," I told him. "In fact, head back there and tell them to send men. You'll get double the pay. Move it!"

I spotted a rickshaw breaking toward an alley and moved to cut it off. "No way! Back to Sixth. Alleys are off-limits!"

"They are?" said the laborer-in-chief.

"Yes. Get your men on it."

He shouted. The men moved. The crowds murmured some more.

I didn't give the head grunt any time to settle into a groove. I grabbed him by the arm. "Tell me what hap-pened here. Everything you know."

"Whoa. Relax. I'll tell 'ya. I got here a couple hours ago, like I said. There was a spill across the road. Not sure what. Was making a right awful smell. Maybe something for treating leather or making soap, beats the hell outta me. Whoever'd spilled it had taken off. Didn't hang around to file a report or nothing. Maybe they'd stolen it, I don't know. Me and the guys tried to clear everyone out, let the fumes blow away, but you know folks in this city. They kept pressing up on us. When the smell wasn't too bad no more, we opened up a little corridor, there on the side for folks to get through. We sent for a fire engine to help us wash down the street, but it hasn't showed. Not a high priority, I guess."

"And before you opened up that passage on the side," I said. "Were you turning people back to Sixth and Eighth?"

"I wasn't forcing them anywhere," he said. "Just kept them out of the hazard area, that's all."

"Some people took the alleys?"

He shrugged. "Sure, I guess. Probably. I wasn't paying 'em any mind."

"Did you see a young woman? Half-elf, wearing a white dress. She would've been in a rickshaw."

The man shook his head. "Sorry, Detective. Ain't ringing a bell."

The pot of emotions boiled within me, this time wrought with more rage than fear. *Gods, wasn't anyone paying any attention?* Didn't anyone care that Shay might've been attacked in broad daylight?

Rather than lash out, I rushed into the nearest alley, a narrow strip that ducked behind the clothing shop immediately below the spill. It hooked around and dumped me back onto 7th, so I picked another, this one wide enough for a rickshaw and with a couple ruts worn into the earth underfoot. I followed them to 6th, again finding nothing. Feeling frantic, I travelled back to the spill and picked another, this one with fainter ruts in the dirt.

I made it halfway past a group of faded brownstones before pausing at an intersection. The midday light cut most of the way across the homes' brick sides, but shadows still darkened patches of dirt at the base. In one of those patches, I spotted a rumpled tarp. In addition to the wheel tracks heading away from the spill site, there was another, moving from the discarded tarp and merging into the established ruts.

It could've been nothing—but maybe it was everything.

16

I slammed my fist on the Captain's desk. *"Gods damn it! How could I have been so stupid? I let her go. She's my partner, and I just let her...walk out,* without anyone to watch over her. *Shit!"*

Captain Knox stood behind her desk. She took a step forward, her hands held out before her. "Daggers, take a deep breath. I understand you're angry and upset. You have every right to be."

"You're damn right I do," I said. "This is Steele we're talking about. You know what she means to me. And they took her! In broad daylight! *Those sons of bitches..."*

The Captain took another step. "We don't know that."

I glared at her. "Are you serious? She didn't show up at her brother's graduation ceremony after telling me and her parents she'd be there. She didn't show up at her parent's apartment. She's not at her place, either. So where the hell is she, exactly? At the park working on her tan, or taking in musical theater?"

Captain Knox glared right back. "I'm on your side, Daggers. We're going to find her, but getting pissed off and acting like a bull in a china shop isn't going to help!"

"Gods, Knox, if I can't get angry, what am I supposed to do? I'm drowning here. I can barely breathe."

My ribs pressed against my lungs with the weight of ten thousand bricks, and a vein in my forehead threatened to pop. I was simultaneously on the verge of violence and tears. I turned to the window, not wanting the Captain to see me in this state. Not that she wasn't fully aware of my mood. The broken remains of the coffee mug I'd sent flying from her desk when I first arrived were a pretty good indicator of how I felt.

"I know it's difficult to stay focused in a situation like this, Daggers," she said, her voice at my back, "but think this through. We don't know for a fact if Detective Steele was kidnapped, but let's say she was. You looked through the alleys. You found a tarp at the side of a building, a cover for a cart that may recently have been moved."

"It had been."

"Fine. Let's say it had. Was there blood at the scene?"

"No."

"Sign of a struggle?"

"No, but—"

"Do you trust Steele to handle herself in a stressful situation? To not panic? To not lash out without thinking things through first?"

"Yes, damn it," I said, spinning from the window. "But we're talking about her possible abduction here, or worse! I was attacked by trained killers last night. If the same people behind my assault have her, what do you think the end game is?"

"Your assailants attacked you directly," said Knox. "The evidence suggests the same didn't happen to Steele, if it happened at all."

I held Knox in my focus. "Do you doubt me?"

"No, but whatever's happened to Detective Steele, you can be sure we'll get to the bottom of it. We've got twenty men on the scene as we speak, combing through those alleys, investigating the scene of the spill, talking to folks in the neighboring shops and apartments. Boatreng has the runners from out front, getting a likeness of Steele's rickshaw driver on paper. The city workers are on site, providing us every detail they can remember. We've put an APB out for the cart that caused that chemical spill. We've got more leads than men to follow them. Whoever's behind this won't be able to hide. Not for long."

The weight over my chest refused to lift. "We may not *have* long, Captain."

The gods took pity on me. Before Knox could force an awkward pep talk on me, Rodgers and Quinto burst through the door to her office.

"Captain?" Quinto shot a thumb toward the front of the precinct. "Is it true? The officers outside were saying—"

"We don't know anything at this point," said Knox, "other than the fact that Detective Steele is missing. As I've explained to Detective Daggers, we're going to get to the bottom of it as soon as physically possible. No one messes with the NWPD and gets away with it."

She affixed me with a glare that could crack granite before looking to the others. "What did you learn about the poison?"

"Nothing much," said Rodgers. "Certainly not in light of what's happened."

"Much isn't nothing," said Knox.

"My expert came to the same conclusion Cairny did," said Quinto. "He couldn't think of any poisons that have both of the effects we're searching for. In his opinion, we're looking at a combination of chemicals, which again doesn't explain why such chemicals would've been affixed to the weapon used to attack Daggers."

"Guys," I said. "The poison is the last of our concerns. We need to find Shay!"

"We *will*, Detective," said Knox with another piercing glance. "It's all connected, or it's likely to be. It doesn't matter which thread ultimately unravels the sail. Detectives Rodgers? Quinto? Keep an eye on Daggers. I'm going to grab him a coffee."

She left and headed toward the break room. Rodgers shot me a confused stare. "The *Captain* is getting *you* coffee?"

I paced at the far side of the room. "I'm a little on edge, in case you couldn't tell. She's trying to help. Either that or she's so frustrated with me that she's extracting herself from the situation before she does something she'll regret."

"You didn't insult her, did you?" asked Quinto.

"Come on," I said. "Of course not. But, gods damn it guys, this is Shay we're talking about. She's missing! She could be... She could..."

My throat closed up before I could get anything out.

Quinto took a step forward. "Daggers..."

I held up a hand. "I appreciate the sentiment, but save your hugs or pats on the back for later. Right now all I want is to break something. Preferably the face of whoever abducted Steele."

"What happened to her?" asked Rodgers.

I gave him the cheat sheet version.

Rodgers whistled. "So you think someone knew she was on her way to the ceremony, used a chemical spill to set up a road block, and diverted her into an alley to abduct her? Daggers, no offense, but that's—"

"Improbable? Unlikely? *Insane*? I know. But someone also followed me home last night and tried to murder me, all during a night where I didn't know what restaurant we'd be attending until Shay and I got there. But Shay knew. If someone's been spying on her, they might've known where we'd be heading. Just like they might've known her plans for today."

"Didn't she change her plans after you got attacked?" said Quinto.

"Her attackers probably changed plans, too. The chemical spill seems rushed. Haphazard. Maybe. I'm guessing. The point is—Shay's gone!"

"Then we'd better get down to the spill right away," said Quinto. "Start pounding on doors. Showing Shay's picture around."

"The department's already on that." Captain Knox returned with a steaming mug. She handed it to me. "Manpower we have in spades. It's brainpower we need. Daggers. Quinto. Rodgers. I need you to get me a lead, not to exhaust yourselves on legwork. We need a plan."

I gripped the mug of coffee tight, worried it might shatter in my grip. Anger coursed through me. Anger that someone had attacked me. Anger that someone had taken Shay, and most of all, anger at my impotence and inability to do anything about either of those. "Does pounding thugs' faces in until someone talks count as a plan?"

"Not unless you know whose face to pound," said Knox, taking a seat. "Think. What's the most productive angle we have? The best one gets all of your attentions, because don't think for a minute I'm letting you out of here alone, Daggers."

Quinto started in on something to do with tracing Steele's steps from the precinct, but I barely heard him. I was still stuck on something from a moment ago. *Not unless you know whose face to pound in.*

I left the Captain's office, mug still in hand, and headed to my desk, confused questions and calls trailing me. As I'd hoped, something waited for me there. A duplicate of the image Boatreng had shown me earlier, the one of the hostile ogre. *Could it be...?*

"Detective Daggers." The Captain's voice rung out over my shoulder. "Are you even listening to us?"

I turned toward her. "You said Rodgers and Quinto were with me, right?"

She narrowed an eye. "Yes..."

The pair of detectives had followed her out. Both looked at me with combinations of doubt and concern.

"Do you put much faith in gut feelings, Captain?" I said.

"Not under normal circumstances."

"This circumstance is anything but, though."

Knox eyed the drawing. She took her time answering. "You're free to follow whatever lead you wish, Detective. But you know the stakes."

"I do." I nodded to Rodgers and Quinto. "Come on, guys. We're taking a trip to Coldgate."

17

A balmy sea breeze blew as Rodgers, Quinto, and I approached Coldgate Prison's exterior wall, mortared granite six feet thick and reinforced with iron bars the size of a pure-bred giant's calves. It loomed over us, three stories tall not counting the sharpened iron spikes and barbed wire that adorned the top. The wall could incapacitate even the strongest of non-magical criminals, but given the city council's cautious nature and the populace's penchant for lawsuits, it alone had been deemed insufficient—which was why Coldgate perched on the tip of a peninsula jutting south into the Wel Sea, and why the surrounding land had been stripped of vegetation, littered with blockades and barbed wire, and surrounded with another ten foot fence.

A pair of guards who could've given Quinto a run for his money stood outside the massive iron gate in front, each of them wearing black fatigues and standing arrow straight. The one on the right held up a hand. "State your names."

"I'm Detective Jake Daggers."

"Detective Gordon Rodgers."

"Detective Folton Quinto."

I could've introduced my pals, but I knew from experience the guards wouldn't have any of that. Rules were in place for a reason.

"Identification?" said the guard.

We produced our badges and held them forth. The guard and his partner took them and inspected them, *thoroughly,* before handing them back. "State your purpose."

"We're here to interrogate a prisoner."

The guard rapped on the gate twice and called out, "Three officers coming through!"

"Three officers," someone confirmed on the other side.

I heard a scrape and a heavy clang, followed by a rasping squeal as the right-hand gate swung in, but only a few feet. Quinto, Rodgers, and I walked in, single file through the narrow opening.

A man in the same black uniform as the guards outside met us on the gravel path between the wall and the prison's front door. A patch with a bar across it adorned his shoulder. "Detectives? Sergeant Ezra Rios. What can I do for you today?"

"I need to speak with one of your prisoners," I said. "An ogre by the name of Dugruk. We put him away eight months ago for grand theft, aggravated assault, kidnapping, and attempted murder of a police officer. Also goes by the name of Bonesaw."

"Yeah, we get the best of the best here at the 'Gate," said Rios. "You trying to track down his associates?"

"Perhaps."

Rios nodded. "Fair enough. Come with me. I'll track him down."

We followed the Sergeant inside, past another locked gate and through an inspection station for family members and non-police personnel. Light trickled in through small windows set at the periphery. The walls were too close, too smooth, and despite it being summer, too cold. Guards stood at every entrance, always in pairs.

Rios ushered us past them into an interrogation room, one dressed with a metal table, a quartet of metal chairs, and nothing else. An additional door graced the wall on our right hand side, probably leading toward the cells.

"Be right back," said Rios.

He left, and we took our seats. They were cold, too. I'd hate to visit in the winter.

Rodgers cleared his throat. "Daggers...far be it from me to dismiss one of your hunches, but shouldn't we be at the spill? Or talking to someone from the rickshaw driver's guild?"

I plucked Boatreng's sketch from my jacket and slid it across the table. "You've seen it. Tell me that's not Bonesaw."

Rodgers didn't touch the paper. "I'm with you. It looks like him. But he's incarcerated. You think the correctional officers gave him a day pass so he could get some fresh ink?"

"We'll see."

It was a few minutes before anyone arrived. When they did, they came through the same door we had.

Another officer in a black uniform, a short, dark-skinned guy who was hairy as an ape and built like a bull—maybe a dwarf-orc hybrid, if I had to guess. Patches adorned his shoulders, too, ones that were wider and fancier than Sergeant Rios'.

"Detectives?" he said. "I'm Lieutenant Greyguard. I understand you're looking for an inmate. Dugruk Gruerot."

So *that* was his last name. I'd seen it on the sentencing paperwork but long since forgotten it. "That's right. Called himself Bonesaw."

"Indeed," said the lieutenant. "I'd be happy to let you grill him about whatever it is you're after, but I'm afraid I can't. Dugruk isn't at Coldgate anymore."

I practically growled, even though I'd expected the answer. "Gods *damn it*. What did I tell you, Rodgers?" I glared at the lieutenant. "What happened? How did he escape?"

Greyguard snorted. "Nobody escapes Coldgate. He was transferred. Down south, out of the city to Stinking Baths."

That caught me off guard. "Why?"

"Because he shanked another inmate and threatened several more," said Greyguard. "The guy was a menace. He should've been sent to the labor camps from the start."

"When was this?"

"A couple months ago. Why?"

"Who sent the order?"

"The warden, after we filed his assault report," said Greyguard. "Again, why?"

I pointed at the piece of paper on the table. Grey-guard picked it up. "Is this supposed to be him?"

"It looks like him, doesn't it?" I said. "That man was last seen soliciting a tattoo parlor in the city a few weeks ago. He's wanted for questioning in regards to an assault committed on me last night, as well as a kidnapping that took place today. You'll remember Bonesaw was incarcerated under both assault and kidnapping charges."

The Lieutenant put the sketch back down. "Well, whoever this is, it's not Bonesaw. I'm telling you, he was transferred. We put the paperwork in through the proper channels. The transport team came and picked him up, and we received a certified letter from Stinking Baths confirming his admission."

"Do you have this letter on file?"

"Of course we do."

"I'm going to need to see it."

Greyguard snorted. "Are you serious?"

I stood, feeling my anger seeping into my tense muscles. "What's your standard operating procedure for when one inmate kills another?"

"They get sent to the camps," said Greyguard. "Same as anyone else convicted of murder."

"And I'm sure Bonesaw knew that. It's not exactly classified information, is it? His buddies on the outside would've known that, too. They would've known how he would've been transferred. They probably even could've guessed *where* he'd be transferred."

Greyguard stared at me. "There was never any report of an attack on the transport, and we received confirmation of his delivery by letter."

I slammed my fist into the metal table, making it rattle and shake. *"And I'm telling you I want to see that letter!"*

A chair squeaked as Quinto stood. "Daggers..."

"Sorry," I said. "I'm stressed. That was uncalled for. But I *need to see that letter."*

Greyguard stared at me, his jaw tense. "Fine. Come with me."

He turned and left, leading us through another guard station into a less secure area of the prison. The walls remained as thick, the bars over the windows as solid, and the cold seeping through the stone as enervating, but there were fewer guards, and the occasional touch of color brightened a wall or two.

Greyguard unlocked a door using a keyring at his side and pushed forth into a room filled with filing cabinets, bookshelves, and desks whose surfaces had been beaten to hell. He snaked among the shelves, forcing me, Rodgers, and Quinto to follow in single file. He rapped his fingers along the sides of the filing cabinets, drumming out a metallic monotone, until he arrived at a cabinet at the end of the aisle.

He wrenched open the topmost drawer, flicked through the documents within, and eventually pulled one from the stack.

"There," he said, holding it forth. "Straight from Stinking Baths. Official seal's at the bottom right."

I took it and pushed past him, weaving my way to the nearest window. I lifted the document into the light. On initial inspection, everything looked appropriate. The paper felt thick and durable between my fingers, the ink dark, the stamp in the lower corner elevated and embellished with a flowing signature.

I heard Greyguard's voice behind me. "Satisfied?"

"You've sent other troublemakers to Stinking Baths before?" I asked. "Recently?"

"Last one before Bonesaw was a few months back," said Greyguard. "A goblin by the name of Gwarkirk who slit his bunkmate's neck while he slept."

"I'll need to see his letter, too."

I heard a snort. "You can't seriously think—"

"*I need to see it.*" I didn't even bother turning from the light.

Greyguard grunted. Another drawer slid open on squeaky wheels, and fingers flipped through paper. I heard the Lieutenant's voice again, more miffed this time. "Here. *You* take it."

Rodgers joined me, followed closely by Quinto. He held the additional letter.

"Thanks." I took the second sheet and held it next to the first. The pages looked identical, except for the contents. Even those only differed in the names of those transported, but the quality of the paper, the form of the seal, and the fluidity of the signature were a match. *Actually...*

"Guys." I nodded at the pages.

Quinto lifted an eyebrow. "What?"

I placed the letters over each other, held the stack to the window, and adjusted until the signatures overlapped. "See?"

Rodgers snorted. "A perfect match."

"We've signed our names a thousand times," I said. "How often do you think you've reproduced the *exact* same signature over those instances?"

"Excuse me," said Greyguard. "Are you suggesting Bonesaw broke into our records room, used that letter to forge his own, then slipped it back before making his escape?"

I eyed the lieutenant. "Better check your locks. Either that or the men who guard them." I held up the letters. "I need to keep these, by the way."

Greyguard shook his head. "I'll have to clear it with the warden. If you're right, and I'm not saying you are, we're going to have to launch an investigation into how this happened. We'll need those."

I glared at him. "I wasn't asking. Trust me, I'll get these to internal affairs once my partner's life isn't in danger." That shut him up. "Rodgers? Quinto? Time to go."

Greyguard looked on, dumbfounded, while Rodgers nodded. "Where to?"

"To find Bonesaw. Where else?"

Quinto might've looked even more dumbfounded than Greyguard. "You've got a lead on him already? And here I thought *Shay* was supposed to be the psychic."

"Not exactly," I said. "But if Bonesaw's out, I know someone who might have a bead on him. Let's go."

18

I knocked on the door, the lacquered hardwood smooth under my knuckles. The corridor I stood in matched the barrier before me in style if not in substance. Wood paneling down low, pristine white paint up high, floors clean enough to eat off of. It wasn't the sterile nature of the place that made it feel more like a hospital than an upscale apartment complex, though. It was the lack of discernible smells and sounds: no frying sausages or dried fish paste or concentrated garlic, no yelling or laughing or clumsy footfalls, no pattering feet or children's giggles. The last wasn't surprising. It wasn't the kind of place that tailored to families.

I could feel Quinto and Rodgers' gravitational pull at my back, a combined five hundred pounds of agitated police power. Despite the lengthy trek from the prison, they hadn't asked me where we were going. Maybe they'd figured it out for themselves, or maybe they'd taken a good look at me and realized engaging me in conversation could spark yet another murder attempt against an officer. I don't think I looked quite that dangerous, but I'd also failed to pass by any mirrors of late.

I heard the click and drag of a latch bar. The door opened slowly. Sensuously. The elf woman who opened it hung on the door's edge, her body stretched like a bowstring with all the same flexibility and accompanying snap. A pair of brown leather pants hugged her lean legs, and a white spaghetti strap camisole left a smidgen of her midsection bare. She swept a lock of honey-amber hair out of her face as she took stock of me.

"Well, if it isn't *Drake Baggers*." She looked me up and down me again and bit her lip. "You're looking good."

"I started working out. You're not looking too shabby yourself, Kyra."

She shrugged. "In my line of work, it pays to stay fit. Literally. What's it been? Seven months since our game of cat and mouse?"

"Eight," I said. "Though I wouldn't call our previous encounter a *game*, even if the guy in charge of putting it together treated it like one. Both of us almost died."

Kyra glanced at her left hand, which happened to be missing its ring finger. She filled the gap with her thumb. "Oh, it was definitely a game, though not without consequence. And I was definitely the cat."

"Can we dispense with the back and forth? We need to talk."

I took a half step into her apartment, but she stopped me with a hand to my chest. "Hold on there, cowboy. You got a warrant?"

I was too angry to be offended. "Are you serious? I'm not here to bring you in. I don't care what you've been up to, or who you might've robbed."

Kyra tsked at my mention of the last part. "Why would you say something like that? And if so, why'd you bring your goons?"

"*Goons?*" said Quinto. "You do remember Rodgers and I are the ones who saved you from Bonesaw's apartment before he made a snack of you, right?"

"On Detective Daggers' hunch, if I recall. But don't take it personally. You're not as handsome as him." Kyra glanced at Rodgers. "No offense."

"None taken," said Rodgers. "A lot of women tell me I'm too pretty for their tastes. Handsome yes, but not ruggedly so."

I glared at my fellow detectives. "*Guys...*"

"Sorry." Rodgers eyed Kyra. "He's telling the truth. We didn't even know where he was taking us. This is between you and him."

Kyra regarded me with a narrowed eye. "Is it? Alright. You've piqued my interest. Come in. Watch the rugs. I just had them cleaned."

Kyra stepped from her door and sauntered into her apartment. It said something about my mood that I barely noticed the seductive way she undulated as she walked. I did notice, though. I was furious, desperate, and as shaky as a guy with a central nervous system disorder who'd drunk too much coffee, but I wasn't dead.

Quinto, or perhaps Rodgers, shut the door behind me as I reached the living room. Afternoon light streaming through the windows, which reached from floor to ceiling across two full walls. I suppose when you lived in a sixth story penthouse, it made sense to take advantage of the views. At least that way you got something for your stair-climbing troubles.

Kyra had decorated the room sparsely, with a ten by ten foot lambskin rug, a pair of sofas with low backs and no armrests, and pristine coffee table, free of any and all mug rings. Everything in the room was modern, lean, and expensive. Kyra was no exception.

She sat in the middle of one of the couches, a cool gray in color, and threw an arm across the back, inviting me to take a seat beside her. *Almost.* "Don't get any ideas. Stick to the living room, Daggers."

"Pardon?"

Kyra kicked her bare feet onto the coffee table. "I recognize that look. Studious. Far-off. Tense. You're mentally cataloging everything you see. I invited you in in good faith. Don't test my limits."

I tried to soften my look. I failed. "It's not you. I act this way every time I arrive somewhere new. Even more so lately. It's a force of habit."

"Aren't we the cryptic one?" Kyra smiled, but just a hint. "But I'm not buying it."

I inspected a narrow side table, one that had been placed in front of the only section of living room wall not lined with glass. A decanter sat there alongside a few glasses. "You're not buying what?"

"That you always act this way. Last I saw you, you weren't ready to chew rocks and spit gravel."

"Ever think there might be a reason for that?"

Kyra's smile expanded. "Believe it or not, I did. I'm smart like that."

Rodgers and Quinto had stopped at the mouth of the room, out of respect I guess.

Kyra flicked a hand toward the free couch space beside her. "Lighten up a little. Have a seat."

"No thanks."

She lifted an eyebrow. "That's no way to treat your host. All I'm asking for is a little levity. I know you deal with grizzly murders on a daily basis, but—"

I slammed my fist against the side table, rattling the glasses and almost toppling the liquor. *"Damn it, Kyra! They have her."*

Kyra drew her arm slowly off the back of the sofa. Her face lost its mirthful aura. "Your partner?"

"You *are* smart, aren't you?"

Being angry didn't give me the right to be an asshole, but she let it slide. "Who's they?"

"Remember when we last parted?" I asked. "After Rodgers and Quinto saved you, after you got patched up, when you ran after me on the front steps of the precinct?"

"I remember. I gave you a kiss on the cheek. Said I owed you one."

"Did you mean it?"

Kyra's gaze hardened. She drew her feet off the coffee table and back onto the plush rug. "I keep my promises. What's going on, Daggers?"

My teeth clenched. "Bonesaw's out. I don't know how. I just found out."

Whatever mirth lingered in Kyra's face vanished. Her eyes widened. She rubbed at her missing finger reflexively. "You're serious."

"Deadly. He seems to have engineered a prison escape. Stabbed a guy to force a transfer to Stinking Baths and managed to arrange for a fake transport to pick him up from Coldgate. But he had help from the outside. Whoever sprung him had the resources to make it look legit. Nobody at Coldgate had any idea anything about the transfer had gone amiss until I started sniffing, and even then I wouldn't have known to look if not for a chance sighting at a tattoo parlor."

Kyra looked me over again. "You're working out *and* getting inked?"

"Give me a break, Kyra. I was canvassing shops looking for the guys who tried to kill me last night."

"Your sour mood is starting to make more sense."

My hand hovered over the tumbler on the side table. I wanted to pour myself a glass, maybe two or three, but at some point over the past year my self-resolve had hardened. I settled for clenching my fist as I skirted the sofa and took a seat on the couch opposite Kyra.

"I need to call in that favor," I said, rubbing my fist with my free hand. "I need you to help me track down Bonesaw, Kyra."

"*What?* You've got to be kidding. You do remember what that psychopath did to me, right? He tied and gagged me, cut off my finger, and probably would've raped and murdered me if you and your police friends hadn't come along. As it was, he..." She shivered. "Well, he got plenty."

"Which is why I need you to help me find him," I said. "Someone came after me last night. Evidence suggests it was his buddies. Now Steele's gone, and while I don't have a scrap of evidence to support it, I'll be damned if he's not behind it, too. You think he's going to treat her any better than he did you? All you did was catch his eye and piss him off. She and I put the bastard in jail. Besides, who's to say he won't come after you again after he's done with us?"

Kyra looked into my eyes. Hers were amber in color to Shay's azure pools, but they were captivating nonetheless. "You love her, don't you?"

I didn't hesitate. "I do."

Kyra regarded me for a little longer before snorting and looking away. "Can't say I'm surprised. I had my hopes for you, but you were always too much of a do-gooder."

I caught a snippet of something from Rodgers and Quinto's direction, a hushed *"Are you kidding me?"* if my hearing wasn't failing me. If so, this was *so* not the appropriate time for that.

"Are you going to help me or not, Kyra?"

She sighed. "You sure know how to pull on a gal's heartstrings. Like I'd abandon your partner to a fate worse than I went through after you tell me *that*. But I'm not sure how helpful I can be. I haven't seen Bonesaw since you dragged him off to jail."

"But you knew him beforehand," I said. "When I first met you, Bonesaw was there. When we all tried out to join the Wyverns. You spoke to him with a level of familiarity. You guys worked together at one point?"

Kyra shook her head. "We'd heard of each other, that was it. I never did a job with him, thank goodness."

"But you're still in the game. You have contacts."

Kyra leaned back a little. "I'm not entirely sure what you mean by *game*."

"Gods damn it, Kyra, I'm not playing around! I told you I'm not here for you. You could tell me you have five thousand golden crown from the city's strategic reserve in your bedroom, and I wouldn't bat an eye. I'm here for Shay. Are we clear?"

Kyra had the wherewithal to look chagrined. "Yeah. Right. Sorry. I'll do what I can. Ask around. See if anyone knows anything. You got anything else to go on other than a suspicion that Bonesaw's out and that he's behind everything?"

"He might be in a new gang. The guys who tried to separate my guts from my stomach last night had tattoos on their inner forearms. Bonesaw has one, too." I stuck a hand in my jacket pocket for one of the sketches before remembering they were still in my leather jacket at my place. "It's a simple design. Three lines, the outer ones at a bit of an angle from the inner one, with some bunched half-circles at the end. I can draw it if you like."

Kyra didn't say anything, but her brow furrowed slightly, and the tiniest of gaps opened between her lips.

"—or, I'm guessing I don't have to draw it. You've seen it before."

"What?" The confused look disappeared. "No. It's not that."

"Then what is it?"

"The new gang part. I've heard a rumor."

"Just one?"

"None, if we're being honest," said Kyra. "More like a scrap here, two-fifths there, and brain power on my end to fill in the gaps. But you might be right. There may be a new gang forming. Let me look into it, and I'll get back to you."

That was probably my cue to leave. I didn't. "I don't have a lot of time."

"You presume you don't, rather," said Kyra. "But I know what you mean. I'll work as quickly as I can."

Now I stood. "Send for me as soon as you know anything. Preferably within the next few hours. Any more than that..."

I couldn't bring myself to finish the thought.

I think Kyra understood. She stood and put a hand to my elbow, just for a second. "Go. I'll be in touch."

I turned and nodded to Rodgers and Quinto. They led the way out.

Rodgers gave me a nod as I closed the door to her apartment behind me. "Think she'll uncover anything?"

"I have no choice but to believe she will."

Rodgers swallowed hard. He got my gist.

"What now?" said Quinto. "The Captain left you in charge. Unless you don't feel fit for the task."

I gave him the fisheye. "What are you implying?"

He shrugged, as innocently as he could. "You've looked better."

I realized I was still clenching my fist. I shook it loose. "I'm fine. Tell you what though. I need to get the hell out of this suit. After that? I'll think of something."

I led the way down the stairs, mostly because I knew the best route to my apartment, but also because Rodgers and Quinto would've been suicidal to get in my way. Not that I'd ever hurt them. Not on purpose.

19

The CSU team had cleared out of my apartment by the time I returned, and a heavyset, bearded cop by the name of Gorman had spelled Phillips—thankfully. If he'd still been there I would've had a word with someone about his workload. Not that Phillips had seemed annoyed about putting in extra hours when I'd seen him earlier. On the contrary, he'd been only too happy to assist, and that was before Steele went missing.

I shook my head as I crossed into my bedroom. Here I was, still recovering from a near-lethal three story vertical plunge less than twenty-four hours ago, wracked with anger, fear, and guilt over Steele's disappearance, and I couldn't keep myself from worrying over Quinto and Rodgers' feelings or Phillips' free time. It wasn't long ago that Rodgers and his cart-sized partner were the subjects of my constant ribbing, and as for Phillips? I spent the first year of his tenure calling him Phelps. What had Shay done to me? Drugged me? Put me under a decidedly non-psychic spell? Turned me into a better person?

Maybe too good of a person, I thought as I stripped off my suit and slipped back into my work attire, making sure to take the prison letters from my sport coat before hanging it. I threw my leather jacket over my shoulders and checked the pocket. My fingers wrapped around Daisy, the cold from the metal seeping into my fingers.

They tightened. A better person, yes. But not too good to bash a face or twenty in if necessary. Whatever it took to get Shay back in one piece. *Whatever it took.*

Quinto and Rodgers met me in the hallway, and together we headed toward the precinct. I got about three-quarters of the way there before surprising them, hooking a right onto 7th.

Quinto was brave enough to call me on it. "You come up with a new avenue you want to pursue?"

I pointed a half a block up the street to a three story brick building flanked on one side by a bakery. "I wouldn't say new. Zaldane and Associates, unless they've changed their address. Remember them?"

"The authentication firm," said Quinto. "You planning on having them look at the forgeries from Coldgate?"

"What else am I going to do with them?"

Quinto shot me a reproachful look. "I was under the impression you'd hand them to internal affairs. If anyone, they're the ones who might be able to trace a path from the cop who assisted Bonesaw to the forger and back to Bonesaw."

"I'll give the letters to internal affairs as soon as I let Zaldane and company look at them."

"What are you hoping to get anyway?" asked Quinto. "Confirmation that Bonesaw's letter is a forgery?"

"Something like that. Look, if you don't want to come, that's fine. I can meet you back at the precinct. Or you can pursue a different avenue after Steele and my attempted murderers. Divide and conquer."

Rodgers cleared his throat. "That's going to be a no-go, Daggers."

I glared at him, too. "Look, I know the Captain put me in charge, but you're not babies. Use your brains. With Steele gone, we have more threads to pull on then men to do the pulling."

"You think we're tagging along because we're out of ideas?" Rodgers snorted. "And you're telling us to use *our* heads. Daggers, you were nearly murdered last night. We're all hoping for the best with Steele, but... Look, the point is the Captain made it clear we're not to let you out of our sight."

"When?"

"Before we left. You might've been too much inside your own head to notice."

If so, that wasn't good. I grunted to confirm I'd heard him and made my way to the offices.

I found them on the third floor. The front door, a frosted glass and wood affair that would've felt at home at either a law firm or a private detective's office, swung open at my touch. Inside I found as orderly and symmetric an arrangement as one could hope for. A square room with a neatly trimmed potted tree in each corner, a quartet of desks, and moveable dividers organized in the middle, all aligned neatly in parallel with the walls.

To be fair, I could only see the front two desks from my vantage point, but given the symmetry of what was visible to the eye, I rather doubted the two cubicles in back contained avant-garde furniture, colorful shag rugs, and a collection of tribal instruments.

A woman's head popped up from behind one of the partitions at the sound of our entrance. It was a rather birdlike motion, quick and precise and with a sharp turn of her head. Her short spiky hair, thin bifocals, and sharp features didn't make her any less avian, though her navy suit was on the mundane side. Then again, it was male birds who tended to have elaborate plumage, weren't they?

"Can I help you?"

"Ms. Clure, right?" I rounded the nearest cubicle to get to hers, Quinto and Rodgers following me.

"That's correct," she said. "You're with the police department?"

I nodded. Turns out we were all on our deductive game at the moment. "You worked with us a year back on a forgery case. Got a pair of new items I need your expertise on." I pulled the letters I'd confiscated from Coldgate Prison out of my jacket and held them forward.

She adjusted the glasses as she brought the pages toward her. "More suspected forgeries? Hopefully part of a different case."

I couldn't tell if she was joking or not. "Indeed. I'm not here to test your memory, just your professional skills. Both of those letters were delivered to Coldgate Prison upon completion of prisoner transfers. I have reason to believe the one on your left, the one that references a prisoner by the name of Dugruk, is a fake."

Ms. Clure kept her eyes on the letters. "And you're here, what? For confirmation?"

"At a bare minimum, yes," I said. "Hopefully much more. Understanding the art of forgery is your specialty. Part of understanding and recognizing forgeries is to also recognize *forgers,* and I'm in the market for names. I need to know who was responsible for this forgery yesterday, and find out where they live even sooner than that. I'm hoping someone at your firm can help me with that."

Clure turned her cold, piercing eyes on me. "What was your name again, Detective?"

"Daggers."

"Right. Detective Daggers, first of all, let me point out that our firm doesn't operate on a drop in, drop out basis. We schedule appointments in advance. It makes the accounting easier and ensures we give each case its due attention."

My teeth clenched. "Ms. Clure, I don't have—"

"—but I'm willing to cut you a little leeway because you're clearly agitated, and my experience with men in your profession who come in with scowls rivaling yours and teams of backup behind them is entirely negative. I should point out, however, that I'm not as familiar with forgers as you seem to think I am. None of my firm's employees are. We're familiar with the classical examples, the famous ones, but I can't be of much help in locating individuals who are currently *in the game,* so to speak. Not that you need to find any forgers, at the moment." She held out the letters.

I blinked. "Excuse me?"

"The letters." She gave them a shake for emphasis. "They're not fakes. They're copies."

I took them back slowly. "I'm not following you."

"They were made with a polygraph."

Rodgers gave the question voice before I could. "A poly-what?"

"A duplicating device," said Clure. "A combination of two or more pantographs, or mechanical linkages, that can be used to write two or four or perhaps eight copies of an identical letter at the same time. That's why you assumed these were forgeries, I assume. Because the scripture is nearly identical. As it should be."

"*Scripture...?*" I organized the pages one over the other and held them to the nearest window as I'd done at Coldgate. The signatures overlapped perfectly, but so did much of the rest, with the exception of Bonesaw and the other prisoner's name, the date, and a brief closing line at the end of the letter. How hadn't I noticed?

"You mentioned these are prisoner transfer letters? Confirming receipt of the prisoners in question?" said Ms. Clure.

"That's right."

"It's not surprising then that a polygraph was employed," she said, pointing at the writing. "Imagine writing so many of these letters, all stating the same thing. Much easier to write them four or eight at a time. Then the scribe in charge of the letters can come back and fill in the pertinent details later, along with a signature. It's a simple time saving maneuver."

"So…you're saying the letters are legitimate?" I said. "That Bonesaw *was* transferred to Stinking Baths after all."

Clure shook her head. "Detective Daggers, I can't say anything to their legitimacy. The letters are pre-prepared. Someone could've taken one and added this individual's name to it after the fact. And before you ask, no, I can't say with any certainty whether or not the warden, bailiff, or clerk who wrote these filled in both sets of names and dates. Both sets of hand-added text are similar enough in nature, but I need more of a sample size to make a definitive estimation."

"Daggers."

I turned at the sound of Quinto's heavy voice. "Yeah?"

His face was drawn. "This could be even worse that we'd originally thought. If what Ms. Clure says is true, then not only do we have a security problem at Cold-gate, but Stinking Baths might have a similar problem. We need to involve internal affairs immediately."

"You may be right, but internal affairs isn't going to help us find Steele, Quinto."

"Maybe not," he said. "Or maybe not right away. But this goes deeper than we thought. We're not just deal-ing with forgers anymore. Bonesaw or not, whichever group is behind this has roots that burrow deep."

"Fine." I pocketed the letters. "Not like we're going to get much else out of this. Ms. Clure? Thanks for lending us your eyes."

"Oh, it wasn't a loan, Detective. Your department will receive an invoice shortly."

Of course they would. My subconscious felt like it should complain, but money was the absolute last thing on my mind at the moment.

20

After arriving at the precinct, Rodgers, Quinto, and I headed to the top floor, skirted the tightly packed morass of desks and dividers in the middle, and headed for the only real office on the floor, squirreled away in a corner and out of the way. Unlike the Captain's on the main floor, this one wasn't fitted with a barrage of windows, rather just one. Its blinds were drawn.

I knocked on the door. After a few seconds, I heard a voice. "Come in."

I cranked on the knob and let myself into Jameson Hunt's office. Technically, Hunt wasn't a detective, at least not a capital 'D' Detective under the jurisdiction of the NWPD. The internal affairs unit operated under a jurisdiction independent of ours, one that encompassed police, fire, and corrections and ultimately answered to the chiefs of each of those departments and to a board of civilian deputy commissioners appointed by the mayor. Only the military branches had a separate set of internal investigators, which I'd discovered several months ago after an encounter with one Agent Blue.

Hunt sat behind his desk, pen in hand. He was a square-shaped man, with broad shoulders, a straight up and down neck, and a jaw with three distinct sides. His flattop only added to his boxy nature, and the horseshoe mustache he wore, shaved with right angles, seemed like a bad joke. Maybe the man had a secret, unresolved love for cubism.

He flicked his cool blue-grey eyes up only long enough to identify us before turning them back to his page. "Daggers. Quinto. Rodgers. What can I do for you?"

Hunt didn't fraternize with the guys at the precinct—I'm pretty sure if he did it would be grounds for his expulsion—but he still knew everyone in the building by name. By contrast, I'd been around for over a decade and still didn't recognize half the officers I bumped into. Then again, I wasn't a cold lump of inhuman flesh masquerading as a person.

"We've got a serious problem, Hunt," I said.

"Correction. *You've* got a serious problem."

"Excuse me?"

He refused to look up from his page, scribbling away. "Or so I assume. But you have to understand that *your* problems are not *my* problems. We're under different chains of command, or did you forget?"

The anger brewed inside me, restless and hot. Any other day I could deal with Hunt's raging indifference, but *today?*

"I'm not in the mood for this, Hunt. Are you even aware of what's going on outside?"

"Should I be?"

"It's your damn precinct. You tell me."

"Again, different chains of command. I shouldn't have to keep explaining this."

The anger continued to brew, bubbling inside me like a pot over a stove ready to spill. "Are you even going to look at me?"

Scribble, scribble. "I'm perfectly capable of multitasking."

Quinto's deep, stern voice cut the air. *"Hunt..."*

The man finally looked up. He sighed and set his pen to the side. "I'm listening."

I took a deep breath, forcing down the emotions inside. "Are you aware of what's gone on since last night?"

"You'll have to be more specific."

"Come on, Hunt," said Rodgers, his tone no more pleasant than mine or Quinto's. "Daggers got attacked. Two thugs tried to kill him. Now Detective Steele's missing. You can't tell me you managed to avoid mention of either of those things?"

Hunt crossed his arms. "It's my job to maintain a level of impartiality between my investigations and yours. So no, I didn't." He glanced at me. "Sorry to hear about it."

"Sorry to hear...?" My teeth squeaked as they ground together. I'd nearly been murdered, Steele was missing, and that was the best he could do?

"Look," said Hunt. "Is there a reason you're in my office?"

Quinto must've noticed the look on my face, because he answered quickly. "Potential corruption at multiple prisons, one municipal and one federal. We were at Coldgate earlier today on one of Daggers' hunches, following a dangerous prisoner by the name of Bonesaw. We have reason to believe he escaped with the help of prison personnel both at Coldgate and Stinking Baths."

Hunt's gaze narrowed. "You have any proof?"

Quinto gave me a nod. "Daggers."

I ripped the letters from my jacket and tossed them on the desk. "Bonesaw faked his transfer paperwork, or at least the letter confirming his delivery to Stinking Baths."

"Thanks. I'll look into it." Hunt picked up his pen and nodded, as if to shoo us.

"Excuse me?" I said.

He glanced up again. "I said I'll look into it."

I took a step forward, feeling the frothing anger creeping up my throat. "Maybe you don't understand what's going on, Hunt. Bonesaw is out of prison. Chances are he's the one who sent people after me. I almost died. Now my partner is missing. You think that's a coincidence?"

"I have no idea," Hunt said, "but it's also not my place to investigate it. As I've made clear several times, my role is internal affairs, which is why I *will* be looking into these corruption allegations you've brought before me in good time."

"*In good time?*" I whipped my arm forward, slapping the pen from Hunt's hand. "Do you think this is a godsdamned game, Hunt? My partner's out there!"

"How dare you." Hunt shot out of his seat, a scowl stretching his face. "You—"

I'm not sure when my hands shot forward, but the next thing I knew I was latched onto the front of Hunt's shirt, and he was grappling me right back over his desk. Hunt grunted and cursed, and I realized I was screaming.

"Gods damnit, that's my partner! Shay! She's out there! Do you hear me!"

A shadow drenched me. Quinto enveloped me in his arms, ripping me off Hunt and bear-hugging me all the way to the back of the office. Hunt's angry shouts trailed me. Rodgers swooped into the path between us as Quinto shouldered the door open.

He kicked it shut behind him as he released me outside Hunt's office. His gray skin had adopted a distinctly crimson glow. "Holy hell, Daggers! What in the world is wrong with you?"

My face radiated heat, and my heart raced. I felt dizzy and short of breath. "Shay is gone, Quinto! We need to find her now. NOW. And that asshole in there... I mean, are you serious? What's wrong with me?"

Quinto stepped into my personal space, looming over me despite my considerable height. "Daggers, we're all aware of the situation. I may not understand what you're going through right now, but I can take a guess. That's still no excuse. You need to get a grip. Rodgers and I have been trying to let you run this show, but you've been sullen, distracted, and uncooperative ever since Steele went missing. We're all on the same team here. Those letters may just be one avenue toward Bonesaw, but if you piss Hunt off and get us all reported, how it that going to help Steele? You think the Captain's going to leave you on the case if she sees you like this? You want to help find Shay, right?"

"Of course I do, but—"

"No buts," said Quinto. "Get a hold of yourself, now, or you won't have to wait for Hunt to ask the Captain to suspend you. I'll ask her myself."

He shook his head and stepped back into Hunt's office, closing the door behind him. Through the office walls, I could hear Hunt and Rodgers going at it verbally. Quinto added his voice to the fray, booming but reasonable, as was his method.

I stood there a moment, seething, my muscles twitching, my fists and jaw equally clenched. I wanted to burst back into Hunt's office, to tackle him and rain punches into his face, at him, at Quinto, at *anyone*. It didn't matter who, at this point. I needed to lash out. To vent the violent energy coursing through my veins and pounding through my head. I needed to hurt someone, preferably not one of my friends or any of my coworkers if I valued my career prospects.

Without thinking I turned and headed to the stairs, taking them three at a time. A few officers passed me in a blur, some of them probably nodding their heads or saying hello, but I couldn't be sure. I didn't hear them as I stormed to the basement, headed down the hall, and burst into the station's modest gymnasium. My jacket flew to the floor as I made a beeline for the standing bag in the corner.

I cut loose with a roar as I slammed a fist into the bag's leather exterior, a savage punch with the entire weight of my body behind it. First a right, then a left, each of them hard enough to send a ripple down the offending arm, then another and another. I hopped on the balls of my feet as I slammed my fists into the bag over and over, using my leg drive for maximum effect. The chain holding the bag screeched and squealed, the entire harness holding it up shaking, but I drowned out its complaints with my own. I grunted with each of my attacks. Sweat beaded on my brow and my breath quickened, but I kept on punching, kept going faster, harder. My grunts turned into yells as I envisioned Bonesaw's face on the bag. I refocused on that spot, punching it over and over and over, beating his face into a battered pulp. A bloody mass that existed only in my head.

I'm not sure how long I kept it up. Maybe a minute, two at most, but it was enough. When I stepped back, it was with legs and arms shaking, chest burning, sweat pouring off my face, and breath rasping through my throat in ragged gasps. I bent over, holding my knees for support, but I wasn't getting enough air doubled over, so I gave up and lay on my back, stretching my arms overhead as I closed my eyes.

Shay waited for me behind them, smiling at me through the back of my eyelids. She laughed, her eyes sparkling, and I half-expected her to chide me with some witty barb. She didn't, though. She just stayed with me while I sucked air into my screaming lungs.

I'd find her. She was smart. She was strong. She was in trouble, but she'd make it. I had to believe that. There wasn't any future where she wouldn't break through. She'd punch her way through all comers, through Bonesaw's belly back to the land of the living if she had to, just as I would. To get back to her.

"Detective Daggers?"

21

I cracked my eyes open. Another detective stood over me, but only barely. He was a dwarf and short for one at that. He looked concerned.

"Hey, Lamont," I said, still sucking air down like it was going out of style. "What brings you down here?"

"Exercise, same as you," he said. "You know we have gloves, right?"

"*Gloves?*"

He pointed at one of the cubbies along the far was. "You know. For boxing? Keeps the pressure off your knuckles."

I sat up and rested against the nearest wall. "Right. I'll be sure to remember that next time."

Lamont lifted an eyebrow. "You feeling alright? You know, Rodgers and Quinto came by my desk this morning. Told me about yesterday, and then I heard about your partner..."

I swallowed back a lump, or maybe just a thickened glob of saliva. Hard to tell which following my burst of activity. "I've been better, but I appreciate your concern. More than some have offered."

Lamont snorted. "You serious? I didn't offer much."

I gave him a look. "Hunt."

Lamont's face hardened. "Oh. That asshole. Don't pay him any mind. I'm not sure he's filled with the same organs as the rest of us."

"I know, right? Nice to know I'm not the only one who thinks so."

Lamont nodded. "Take care of yourself, Daggers. Let me know if I can do anything for you."

"Wait." I held up a hand before he could leave. "Give me an update."

"On what?"

"The gang situation. That's what Quinto and Rodgers came to talk to you about, right?"

"Sure," said Lamont. "They neglected to relate what they learned? I swear, ever since Quinto started dating that coroner, his mind's been a little foggy. Not that I blame him."

I wiped sweat off my brow and waved him off. "No, they told me, but it wasn't much. Said you weren't familiar with the tattoos we found on the pricks that tried to whack me. Also said you hadn't heard any rumblings about new gangs, but that you weren't totally sure about that last part."

"Sounds like they covered the bases, then."

I'd recovered enough to stand, but I wasn't in any hurry. Lamont was so short it might've seemed like a slight if I rushed into it. "Come on, Lamont. There has to be more. Something else you can tell me. Something to get us on the right track. I have reason to believe Steele's in serious danger."

"Look, Daggers, it's not like I'm holding out on you. The idea of some upstart gang coming after our own pisses me off as much as it does you." Lamont glanced at the punching bag. "Well...close, anyway. The point is, I don't have any proof to back up my suspicions. Do I suspect there's something brewing underneath the city? Sure. Things have been too quiet for weeks. Now a pair of thugs try to kill you? And you say Steele going missing is tied to that? It's too organized to be the work of a few malcontents and lowlifes."

Too organized... Somehow that struck a chord with me. I hadn't given it much thought until now, but how had Bonesaw, or whoever it was who'd abducted Steele, known where and when to go after her? It wasn't a secret among her friends and family that she was going to attend her brother's graduation ceremony, but it wasn't exactly knowledge someone on the street would have. It would take a certain amount of planning for someone to take her, what with the chemical spill and all. Even the attack on me last night hadn't been slapdash. I'd been followed, probably all the way from Steele's apartment. Who'd organized that? Bonesaw? He'd been in prison until recently. Obviously he'd had help getting out...

"Daggers?"

I blinked and looked up.

"You sure you're okay?" asked Lamont.

"How common is it?" I asked.

"How common is what?"

"This whole silence on the ground thing," I said. "The gangs taking a bit of a breather. When has that happened before?"

"Fairly often, I suppose," said Lamont. "Happens now and then in the winter if we have a prolonged stretch of bad weather. Sounds stupid, but it's true. Even criminals hate the cold. Happens for a day when there's a big sporting event. But when you're looking at several weeks, it's usually due to a power vacuum."

"You saying one of the local gang leaders might've bit the dust?"

"Possible," said Lamont, "but again, I haven't heard anything. If so, it means we might be in for something big. Power vacuums only last until someone realizes they have the strength to make a move."

"And when was the last time that happened?" I said. "When we took down the Wyverns?"

"You mean the bust that took Captain Armstrong down with it?" Lamont shook his head. "The Wyverns weren't powerful enough at the time. We didn't even know they were back. The first time, a couple decades ago, when they went down—that spawned a crapstorm that lasted months."

I sucked on my teeth and nodded.

"Daggers, if you don't mind my asking, what's this have to do with you and Steele? Don't get me wrong, there's often overlap between gang and homicide, but not *that* much. Who did you two piss off?"

I stood, shaking my head. "I don't know, Lamont. But I'm starting to think I need to give that more thought."

I gave the guy a wave and headed toward the gym door, grabbing my jacket along the way. As I headed up the stairs from the basement, I found Rodgers and Quinto on their way down from the top. Neither of them looked any cheerier than when I'd left them.

"Hey, guys," I said. "You, ah...smoothed things over with Hunt?"

"More or less," said Quinto. "Would've been easier if you hadn't laid hands on him. I mean, seriously. I know you're on edge, Daggers, but—"

"I know. I get it. I was out of line, and I'm sorry. Not so much to Hunt. He's a prick, but I am sorry for you two. I shouldn't have put you in that position. And I won't again. You were right, Quinto. We have too much work to do. I can't be screwing around, letting my temper get the best of me. Shay helped me shelve it, and I'm sure as hell not going to let it get loose and trash my life at the worst moment possible."

Rodgers peered at me quizzically. "Are you feeling okay?"

"Why does everyone keep asking me that? Of course I am. Why wouldn't I be? Because I'm acting rationally for once? I'm telling you, I've got my anger under control. Won't happened again."

"It's not that," said Rodgers. "It's that you're *flushed*. And sweating. Did you go for a jog?"

"Close enough," I said. "It's not important. What's important is we stay focused. Productive. Once I found out Bonesaw'd sprung himself loose, I got caught up in the *how*. That's my fault. It was the anger talking, narrowing my focus, but following that loose thread isn't going to get us anywhere, certainly not fast enough for it to make a difference. Let Hunt deal with it."

"So what *is* important, then?" asked Quinto.

"The crime scenes. My place and the site of Steele's disappearance. There are still plenty of pieces of evidence that don't add up. Take my apartment, for example. When I went back there earlier today, I noticed numerous scratches in the floorboards. Deep gouges, both inside my apartment and in the hall outside."

"Scratches?" said Rodgers. "From your fight?"

"Inside, maybe," I said. "But I found them in the hallway, too, where I didn't battle anyone. You guys know as well as I do that unexplained oddities often have logical explanations behind them. And we've talked about Biggie's mysteriously rapid demise and subsequent stiffening. That's another element that doesn't make any sense. Drugs don't seem to explain it. So what caused him to die so quickly and his body to lock up?"

"I don't know, Daggers," said Quinto. "But so far, his bizarre death hasn't provided any leads, and it's not likely to until Cairny gets the results of her tox screen back. The CSU teams have already gone over your place with a fine-toothed comb. Your apartment is a dead end."

I chewed on my lip. "Right. Which means we should head back to the site of the chemical spill."

Quinto tilted his head. "You sure? Captain's already got a dozen officers there, and you've searched the place yourself. What do you expect to find?"

"The officers at the scene don't know Bonesaw is involved. We do." I dug his likeness out of my jacket, the one Boatreng had drawn upon the tattoo artist's description.

"Good point," said Rodgers. "We could show his picture around. Might be able to get some leads."

"I thought you said Bonesaw was unimportant," said Quinto.

"I said figuring out *how* he broke free from prison is unimportant," I said. "Finding him is anything but. All signs point to him being the beating heart at the center of this."

"That may be true," said Quinto, "but even *if* Bonesaw if behind this, there's no reason for us to believe he personally executed Steele's abduction. He didn't try to kill you himself last night, Daggers. We might pound the pavement and get nothing for our troubles. Tracking those chemicals from the spill on the other hand..."

"We're in a time crunch, Quinto," I said. "If we can find Bonesaw, we'll find Steele. Trust me. It's worth taking a shot at him directly."

Quinto put a hand to my shoulder. "Daggers, I know you think if you find Bonesaw you'll find Steele, but you don't know that for a fact. I'm not trying to rain on your parade, but what if he's only tangentially involved? Yes, he had the same gang tattoo your attackers did. *Probably*, if we can believe the tattoo artist you talked to. But you can't focus on him to the exclusion of every other clue we have at our disposal."

The big guy had a point. I assumed Bonesaw was behind everything, but I didn't know for sure. It was the same thing I'd told myself minutes ago in the gym.

"Okay," I said. "We'll make it quick at the spill. Keep the radius of our net tight as we show the picture around. We'll hit the chemical companies next. Fair enough?"

My two detective pals nodded their agreement. I tossed my jacket over my shoulder, still too hot to put it back on. "Alright, then. Time to get to work."

22

I wish I could say Quinto's concerns were unfounded, but the big guy proved to be more prescient than me. Officers swarmed over 7th Street a block in either direction of the spill, most of them looking as nasty and disgruntled as I felt. They combed through the alleys, noses to the ground, doing their best detective impersonations as they looked for hair and bone fragments or whatever it is they thought us real detectives based our judgments on. They'd gathered bystanders into groups, asking them questions and showing images of the thugs who'd attacked me—which apparently Boatreng had scribbled together multiple copies of, the threat of carpal tunnel be damned.

We took advantage of the officers' efforts, tackling the groups one at a time and showing them Bonesaw's sketch. Unfortunately, none of the witnesses could give definitive answers about the ogre's presence. Most of them didn't recognize him at all. A handful did, or so they claimed, but upon application of pressure, our best witnesses ultimately admitted they couldn't be sure they hadn't seen some *other* large, bald ogre earlier in the day. None of them got a good look at his face, and none of them got close enough to see if he'd sported any tattoos on his arms. As if those vague replies weren't dispiriting enough, nobody had any idea if the ogre had been present at the time of Shay's disappearance.

It was the worst possible outcome we could've received: enough to make me think we were on the right track with Bonesaw, but without any verifiable evidence to show that we were and no additional path for us to follow as a result of our efforts. I even pushed the envelope a little, widening our beaten path to include more businesses to the north and south in an attempt to get a positive ID, all to no avail.

Needless to say, I was fading toward despondency as we headed back to the precinct, intending to grab coffee and dive into the robbery reports in hopes of finding a chemical vendor who'd reported a stolen shipment, but I never made it past the front doors.

One of the kids loitering outside the station waved us down as we arrived. "Detective Daggers?"

"Yeah?" I said with all the warmth of a day old fish.

"Runner came by five minutes ago. Said a Miss Kyra needed a word with you."

My heart skipped a beat. I hadn't expected her to get back to me so fast. In fact, I'd half expected not to hear back from her at all. Not that I didn't trust her, but...well, actually I didn't trust her.

I gave Rodgers and Quinto a nod, we flagged down a rickshaw, and off we went.

The ride flew by in a blur, either because our driver employed superhuman speed or because I was lost in thought. Maybe a little of both. The driver was on the wiry and youthful end of the spectrum.

Either way, I wasted no time tackling the stairs at Kyra's apartment. My impromptu boxing match earlier hadn't drained my reserves, as I beat Rodgers and Quinto to the top by a full thirty steps. I knocked on the door while I waited for the others to catch up.

I still stood there when Rodgers arrived, panting. "Gods, Daggers. You training for a race?"

"You know that's not why I ran."

"I know. Just trying to lighten the mood."

I knocked on the door again as Quinto joined the fray. "Kyra? It's Daggers. You there?"

Quinto's breath was more measured than Rodgers', but he'd taken the stairs slower. Probably to avoid looking as foolish as his partner. "Think she's out?"

"Why would she be out?" I said. "She just sent for us. The kid outside the station said the runner arrived five minutes before we did."

Quinto shrugged and didn't say anything.

I tested the doorknob. It gave.

A sense of dread settled over me. I reaching inside my jacket and pulled out Daisy as I pushed the door in. I motioned for Rodgers and Quinto to be silent as I crept inside. "Kyra? You there?"

Her voice ricocheted off the walls. "Hey. Back here, Daggers. In the bedroom."

I breathed a sigh of relief as I returned Daisy to her home. Maybe I should've taken a shot from Kyra's decanter earlier after all. I needed something to take the edge off.

"Great," I called back. "Are you, ah…decent?"

"*Decent?*" I heard her call. "Oh, give me a break. Get over here, will you?"

I followed her voice into the nearest hallway, leaving Rodgers and Quinto in the living room. As I turned a corner, I found Kyra standing at her bed, notable for its enormous size, its crimson red silk sheets, and the equally enormous mirror overhanging it from the ceiling.

Thankfully, Kyra hadn't lied. She was decent, more so than she'd been earlier in the day thanks to the addition of a teal blouse and a pair of knee-high boots. She *was* bent over with her back to me, however, though I don't think it was meant as a come on. The furious pace with which she stuffed garments into a portmanteau tipped me off.

"What are you doing?"

Kyra glanced at me. "You're the detective. What does it look like I'm doing?"

"If you're trying to hide incriminating evidence, the time for that would've been *before* you sent word for me."

Kyra snorted and rolled her eyes. "Come on, Daggers. I was joking earlier. If I *had* been a naughty girl, do you really think I'd leave anything in the open?"

"Only if you were trying to tempt me."

Her lips curled. "I'd be willing to try, but I got the impression you didn't want me to."

"Why are you packing, then?"

"Why else?" she said, turning back to her clothes.

I joined her by the bed. "You're leaving town?"

"I hear the mountains to the north are lovely this time of year. All the winter snows melted, the flowers in full bloom—"

I reached out and grabbed her by the arm, spinning her toward me. "Damn it, Kyra, *stop!* This isn't the time and you know it. You said you were going to help me. You sent for me at the precinct. Please tell me you're not screwing with me for kicks."

She dropped a folded pair of pants on the bed. "Sorry, Daggers. I can't help playing. It's the way I am. But I did find something." She glanced at my hand reproachfully.

I let go. "Tell me."

"Something bad is afoot. It wasn't that hard to discover once I asked the right people. The gangs are trying to keep a lid on it, but it's going down tonight. That's why I'm getting the hell out of here. The buyers I work for aren't going to be paying for the sorts of services *I* provide anytime soon."

"What are you talking about?" I said. "What's going down?"

Kyra shook her head. "I don't know exactly. It could be nothing. But in my experience, meetings like these never lead to anything good."

"*Meetings like these?*" I ground my teeth. "Kyra, *what are you talking about?* Please tell me you have something concrete."

"I do," she said. "There's going to be a meeting tonight between the five most powerful gangs in New Welwic. The Blacks, the Razors, the St. Kerry's Street gang, the Seasides, and NWX. They're all descending on the King's Theater in a few hours."

"The old abandoned place east of the Earl?"

Kyra nodded. "The meeting's supposed to take place after dark. Around ten is what I heard."

I glanced toward the nearest window. What time was it? Four? Five? The afternoon had flown by in a blur. "What's happening at the meeting?"

Kyra shrugged. "That's where the concrete portion of the information ends. Normally, when the gangs get together it's to set citywide boundaries or call a truce."

"But there aren't any gang wars going on now," I said. "Lamont said things were all quiet on that front."

"I don't know who Lamont is, but yeah. Exactly."

"So?"

Kyra sighed. "I don't know, Daggers, but I have a bad feeling about it. Not just because they're getting to-gether. More because I hadn't heard about it before. The gangs are keeping this quiet. And honestly, given the fact that you've been attacked and your partner is missing, I'm worried my neck will be next on the chopping block now that I've been pulled into this."

"But Steele and I don't have any beefs with the gangs," I said. "Not more than any other detectives."

Kyra lifted an eyebrow. "Do you believe in coinci-dences?"

"Only as a last resort."

"Then you're involved, one way or another," said Kyra. "And so am I. Which is why I'm getting the hell out of here."

"Hold on," I said. "What about Bonesaw? What about Shay?"

"I don't know," said Kyra, turning back to her clothes. "I didn't manage to find out anything about the former, and I didn't ask about your half-elf squeeze."

"*You didn't ask?*" I could feel the anger I'd tried to punch away earlier creeping back. "Why do you think I asked you to track down Bonesaw? For kicks?"

"Daggers, don't you get it? You said it yourself. Bonesaw's in a gang now. The guys who came after you are in the same gang. There's a gang meeting tonight. Don't you think it's all connected?"

"*Connected* doesn't help me find Shay!"

Kyra avoided my gaze. "I'm sorry, Daggers. I really am. I've done what I can."

"*Done what you can?* Are you serious? My partner is in danger of being raped and murdered, and all you've given me is info about a gang meeting. *I saved your life.* What kind of deal is that?"

"I told you, I'm sorry. It's all I can get without exposing myself."

"*Without exposing yourself?* So that's what this is about? You're willing to help, but only if you don't have to put your own ass on the line?"

"*Yes!*"

Her sudden outburst pushed me back a step.

"Yes," she said again, in a more measured tone this time. "Are you happy now that you got me to admit it?"

"No, I'm not happy," I said. "I want your help like you promised. I *need* your help."

She looked me in the eyes, her amber globes deep and sorrowful. "I'm not like you, Daggers. A warrior with a heart of gold. I'm a thief. My number one priority has always been myself. It still is. I've told you what I learned. It's time you go."

"But Shay—"

"The King's Theater. Ten PM."

I took a step back, disappointment overwhelming my anger. "If that's how it's going to be..."

"Daggers. One last thing?"

I stopped at the door to the hallway. "Yes?"

"My source didn't think it likely the police would show up at the meeting. Didn't think they knew about it."

"We didn't."

"My source also implied they'd know if you did."

I had a flashback to the precinct's gymnasium, where I wondered how Shay's and my attackers had known where and when to find us. "You're saying we have a mole?"

"You're probably lucky if it's only one."

I might've growled. "Great. Just what I needed."

23

"Excuse me? Captain?"

Captain Knox looked up from an inch-thick report, tossing it aside when she saw me. "Daggers. Come in. What have you got?"

"A whole lot of nothing, a few maybes, and one probable something." I waltzed to the nearest chair, gripping its worn smooth back with anxious fingers. "We can discuss it later. In the meanwhile, what are you doing for dinner?"

Knox leaned forward, looking at me keenly over the tip of her nose. "You're asking me...*to dinner*?"

I nodded. "I know a good place not far from here. Best burgers this side of the Earl. Steele took me there once upon a time."

Knox rapped her fingertips on her desk. "Detective, I'm aware it's difficult to work on an empty stomach, but has it crossed your mind that we might have better things to do with our time? You of all people should understand what we're up against."

"All the same, Captain, I think it might be worth-while. It would give us an opportunity to talk. *Alone.*"

"We are alone, Detective."

I didn't say anything. I stood there gripping the chair.

Knox was bright enough to read between the lines. "Come to think of it, I could use a bite. Lead the way."

Knox stood and waved me through the door. By some miracle, nobody descended upon us as we wove our way through the pit and out the front doors. Then again, everyone in the station knew of the situation with Steele by now, even perpetual shut-in Hunt. They knew better than to get involved.

Once in a rickshaw, the driver hauled us to The Bleating Goat, a gastropub not far from the station. Shay had taken me there for dinner one night early in our partnership. We'd talked about relationships. Mine, mostly—when we could hear each other over the din. A stiff breeze battered our rickshaw as we rode, bring-ing with it an unnatural coolness given the season. I was almost glad for my jacket.

When we arrived, I pushed through the front doors, reflexively clenching my jaw in a futile attempt to shield my eardrums from the noise. Even though it was early for dinner, patrons packed the booths and tables and stools at the bar, orcs and giant half-breeds with booming voices that couldn't quite drown out the higher-pitched giggles of over-served gnomes. Glasses clinked and laughter roared, all while a grill spat and taps gurgled with the flow of beer.

A cute hostess wearing a form-fitting black top and pants noticed us and grabbed a pair of menus. "Table for two?"

"We should already have one," I shouted over the noise. "A big guy, grayish skin, and his friend? A blonde dude with a disarming smile?"

The hostess replaced the menus. "Back right corner."

We moseyed over, finding Rodgers and Quinto seated on opposite sides of a booth, sandwiched between a group of dwarves and what appeared to be a pixie bachelorette party. Their shrill laughter and the bride-to-be's minuscule veil gave it away.

Captain Knox sidled in next to Quinto, and I took a seat next to Rodgers. The detectives each had a pint glass in front of them, two-thirds full in Rodgers' case, though Quinto's had little more than suds left.

Knox eyed the glasses. "And here I thought this was a work trip. Apparently we *are* springing for dinner?"

I had to speak up to make myself heard—as intended. "Might as well multitask while we're here. I have a feeling we're going to need the energy later. I didn't say anything about beer, though. That's on these guys."

"It felt justified after today," said Quinto. "Don't worry. I'm only having the one."

"You guys order?" I asked.

"Already on its way," said Rodgers. "Burgers all around. Hope that's okay, Captain."

"It'll do," she said. "Anyone want to tell me what the hell is going on?"

I glanced at the door, checking for familiar faces. Snippets of fairy laughter and bawdy dwarf jokes swirled around me in the bar's cyclone of noise. I lowered my voice nonetheless. "Sorry, Captain. I have reason to believe it's not safe to speak freely at the precinct. There may be prying ears."

"Given that our first and only time dining together was last night and that was initiated by Detective Quinto, I figured as much," she said. "Who's the snitch? One of the runners? The support staff? Or one of our own?"

"I'm not sure," I said. "I don't have a name. But a cop. Maybe more than one."

Knox's eyes hardened, and the muscles around her jaw tightened. "Who's your source?"

"A friend. A thief. Someone who works for the gangs. She owed me a favor."

"That elven woman you saved during the Wyverns case?"

I blinked. "Yeah. How'd you know?"

"Please, Daggers. I know your file, and that case better than most given it's the one that forced Captain Armstrong's retirement and landed me at the Fifth. When you stormed off toward Coldgate Prison without expressing your intentions, I was forced to assume you'd visit a criminal you previously incarcerated. There are several folks there who you've put away but only one who matched the sketch Boatreng Davis showed me earlier. It was a small deductive leap from assuming you wanted to speak to him to you seeking the other member of your previous undercover competition. Besides, there can only be so many female thieves working for New Welwic gangs that you list among your acquaintances."

"Dang," said Quinto. "Remind me never to lie to you, Captain."

"Or to leave anything out by omission," she said. "But noted. Detective Daggers?"

"That's right," I said. "It's Kyra. And I did go to Cold-gate in search of Bonesaw, who we have reason to be-lieve broke out of jail while in transport to Stinking Baths. He's on the loose. Sorry for not telling you right away. I was in a bad place. Too angry. Too agitated. Too focused on who might be behind Steele's disappearance and not focused enough on finding her."

"I understand," said Knox. "But don't let your emo-tions get the best of you again. I can't force Hunt to shut his mouth if he chooses to make a stink about your actions."

"You know about Hunt? Of course you do. The point is I asked Kyra for a favor, and she delivered, at least to an extent. She suggested we might have one or more moles among us, which confirms my suspicions. Some-one knew where and when to attack Steele. Someone with insider knowledge."

Knox frowned. "We've had dirty cops in our midst, and we will again. We'll find them and squash them. But our focus is on finding Steele. Did your contact give you a lead on her?"

"Not exactly," I said. "The best she could provide is that there's a meeting tonight between the most power-ful gangs in New Welwic, around ten o'clock in the old King's Theater. She didn't know the purpose of the meeting, or who called it."

"But you suspect the gang who attacked you last night might be behind it? The same gang responsible for Steele's disappearance?"

I nodded. "Kyra had a gut feeling about it, too."

Knox glanced at Rodgers and Quinto. "Detectives?"

Rodgers shrugged. "We don't know for a fact that the ogre in Boatreng's sketch is Bonesaw, or that Bonesaw escaped prison. We don't have hard evidence tying Steele's disappearance to the attack on Daggers last night, or know if her disappearance is gang related. We also don't know why the city's gangs might be calling a meeting. But if we assume the tattoo artist positively identified Bonesaw with the gang tattoo belonging to Daggers' attackers, then everything starts to fall into place."

Quinto nodded. "He's extremely violent. He threatened Daggers and Steele during the Wyverns case, and he tried to kill Daggers. If he's out, its not surprising he's coming after them."

"And he's smart," I said. "He might not look it, but he is. I learned not to underestimate him during the Wyverns case. If he could organize his own escape from Coldgate from behind those walls, I have no doubt he could've put together the attacks on myself and Steele."

"Excuse me? Four burgers?"

A waitress came by with a tray. She distributed the food and left, but none of us dug in right away.

"So we assume Bonesaw's involved in tonight's meeting," said Knox after she'd left. "Why, exactly, is unclear. Maybe he's called a meeting to talk to the other gangs, or the gangs are meeting to discuss his actions. Or something else we haven't considered."

"Exactly."

"Well, that's good," said Knox. "Especially if Bonesaw is attending the meeting himself. Get him and we'll get Steele, or at least get a bead on her—assuming she hasn't broken free by then."

Quinto snorted. "You're optimistic."

"I'm pragmatic, like Detective Steele. You realize she's not sitting around, waiting for us to save her, don't you, Daggers?"

"I do," I said. "But this is Bonesaw we're talking about. We need to act, and soon."

"My thoughts, exactly," said Captain Knox. "I'll send our best to scout the theater. Then I'll pull most of our officers from the scene of Steele's disappearance. Spread the word that nobody's going home until we find her. Once the scouts let us know the gangs have arrived, we'll move in."

I shook my head. "Will all due respect Captain, no."

She looked at me keenly. "Why not?"

"Because we don't know who's reliable and who isn't," I said. "If word slips to the wrong set of ears, the meeting's off, and then what? We're at square one. Worse. The gangs will know we're onto them and Bonesaw will grow angrier. And I'll bet you anything that if we *were* to capture Bonesaw, he wouldn't talk. He'll probably have put in place measures to leverage Steele's capture against us should anything happen to him. We can't risk it."

"I understand your concern, Detective," said Knox, "but what would you have me do? Not put surveillance on the meeting you've argued is a focal point in Detective Steele's abduction? Not make any move at all?"

"Of course not. I'm saying I should make the move alone."

Knox glanced at Rodgers and Quinto. "Neither of you seem surprised."

"He's not done," said Quinto.

"You mean this idea get crazier?"

"Hear me out, Captain," I said. "What we need isn't to barge into this meeting, nightsticks swinging. We need information. We don't know where Shay is, what Bonesaw's goals are, or even why the meeting is taking place. I can sneak in and get a measure of what's going on. Before you scoff, ask these guys. Ask Captain Armstrong. I'm one of the best tails in the department, I can lose just about anyone who's onto me if I sense them, and I can be surprisingly quiet when motivated. Trust me, *I'm motivated*. I'm also the one with the most on the line. If anyone should stick their neck out, it's me."

The Captain snorted. "Honestly, Detective, why are you telling me this? I know you well enough. If you thought this was the best chance you had of obtaining intel on Steele's whereabouts, you'd do it without telling anyone, especially if you're concerned about word getting out. So why *are* you telling me?"

"Because if things go sideways, I'm going to need help," I said. "And because I care too much about Rodgers and Quinto to ask them to risk their necks in a futile effort to save me, especially one that would almost certainly get them in the deepest of crap with you if they were to go along."

"For the record," said Quinto, "I think the idea's nuts. But he's right about needing knowledge, knowledge we won't get other than by spying on the meeting. And yes, Daggers, I'd happily put my neck on the line to save you. Steele, too."

"Not me?" said Rodgers.

Quinto snorted. "You go without saying, pal."

Knox eyed her food, her face inscrutable. "I understand the need for secrecy. But no matter how much the three of you care for each other, that won't do a lick of good against a building full of hardened thugs. We need boots on the ground. I'll get in touch with SWAT. Get a couple teams together, see if we can't get a spellcaster on our side. I'll keep it discrete. Go through alternate channels. Nobody will know. We'll have to come up with a detailed plan. Times. Routes. The works. That way I'll know when to move in if you don't come back. Speaking of, how in the world do you plan on infiltrating a meeting between hostile gangs? Because if you think they won't be guarding against intruders at a clandestine meeting, regardless of their intel, you're crazier than I already thought."

I smiled and picked up my burger. "With one of my most hated weapons, Captain. Research."

24

It occurred to me as I crept along one of New Welwic's three century old sewers, a lantern in hand and a tactical pack strapped tightly into place over my leather jacket, that Quinto was right. I was completely insane—or at least my plan was.

I still couldn't figure out how I'd managed to convince Captain Knox of its worth, especially considering I wasn't totally sold on it myself. I knew it was the right course of action, without a doubt giving us the best chance at discovering crucial information as to Shay's whereabouts, but the imminent threat of death or capture that might result from it put a damper on its overall merit. Rodgers and Quinto and the Captain's strike teams, who lingered aboveground in the unnaturally blustery late summer evening, could only do so much to assuage my nerves.

At least I had preparation on my side. So often in my past I'd barreled headlong into danger without sparing a thought for my own skin. Not this time. I'd cut it close on timing, but thanks to the efforts of sundry speedy rickshaw drivers, I'd paid visits to a host of old friends and acquaintances: fire mages, doctors, and semi-legal weapons distributors. I patted my belt, taking note of the various begged, borrowed, and bought implements I'd secured there, the ones I'd need quick access to in the event of a skirmish.

I hoped I wouldn't need them. My plan, which I'd gone over with the Captain, Rodgers, and Quinto so many times that there was little more than a nub left, involved stealth and speed, not combat. I was to get in quickly, quietly. Stick to the shadows and make less noise than a laryngitic mouse wearing moccasins. Listen to anyone within range, ideally one or more of the gang bosses, should I find them. I wasn't to push too hard, and I was under strict orders not to expose myself. Even stricter were my orders to return within the hour, otherwise Knox would be sending the strike teams after me, one of them through the sewers and another through the front. At least the former would have access to the sewer blueprints to help them find me.

Having borrowed the blueprints from the municipal library's restricted document's section (under the Captain's orders of course), I'd memorized the directions from a sewer access grate southeast of the King's Theater to the maintenance hatch underneath the abandoned building, drilling it into my brain until I could recite it by rote. Head east, third right, straight until the five-way intersection, take a hard left, straight again until the T, then right, third right again and the first left, up the ramp to the theater's hatch. The problem was remembering which of the steps I was on.

I stopped at an intersection of the underground canals, thankful for the two foot wide walkway at the edge that kept me out of the effluent underneath. How many passages had I walked past since I took a right after the T? I visualized them in my mind. Yes. This was the third.

I shuttered my lantern and set it at the ground at my feet. I'd have to go in blind from here. I couldn't risk being seen. Hopefully I wouldn't be smelt either. I'd donned a black cloth mask over my face, both to keep unwanted smells out and to hide my otherwise pasty skin, but it wouldn't do much to keep the sewer's unique aroma off me. I couldn't smell any worse than most of the gangbangers on staff, though, could I?

I walked carefully, trailing my hand along the wall until I felt it open. I turned, knowing from the blueprints it would be about a hundred and fifty feet until I reached the ramp. I counted steps in my head, more to make sure I wouldn't be caught off guard by the angle of the floor than out of fear of missing it.

Around the count of fifty, I noticed a light, in front of me and at roughly double my eye level. There should've been a grate separating the sewer access from a maintenance subbasement in the back of the theater. I assumed the light leaked through the grate from somewhere far above, but as I neared it I grew concerned.

The grate hung open, the light shining from a lantern set inside.

I paused at the foot of the ramp, wondering what to do. For all the planning I'd done, all the talks I'd had with the Captain, all the decisions regarding the positioning and timing of the SWAT teams, I'd never considered the possibility that the sewer entrance would be compromised.

Of course, compromised though it might be, it didn't appear to be *guarded*. As I hesitated at the base of the ramp, holding my breath and straining my ears, I didn't catch sight of any motion beyond the grate, nor hear any footsteps or mumbles or grunts. Not so much as a whisper reached me, which begged the question: why was the lantern there? Did someone plan to use the sewer system in the event of a quick getaway? Was someone waiting for the arrival of someone through the tunnels? Had someone *already* used it to enter the theater? If so, who?

I crept forward, one step at a time up the ramp, and gazed into the subbasement beyond. There wasn't anyone there.

I wouldn't call it luck. Luck would've been finding the place dark and abandoned as expected, and to have a clear route to the gang meeting open in up in front of me as if by the whims of the gods. Still, I'd take it. As long as I could find a way in without being seen, I could find a way back out. I knew what I was risking when I stepped foot in the sewers.

Quickly, I crossed the last stretch between myself and the grate, slipping into a theater subbasement full of moldy canvas sacks, decaying wood, and more mouse droppings than I cared to count. A rusted metal ladder hung bravely to the wall, leading to a hatch overhead.

I put my ear as close to the hatch as I dared and listened. Still nothing.

Hoping for the best, I pushed it open and slipped through into another basement, or so I thought. Instead of ending a few feet overhead, darkness shrouded the ceiling, probably a good three stories above me. Ropes stretched down from the rafters, many of them hanging from pulley systems and tipped with hooks. Stacks of wooden pallets and crates dotted the floor, as did several lever-laden stations that must've been tied to the rope systems.

I slipped behind one of the stacks of crates as I oriented myself. Based on where I'd entered, I should be in the back of the theater. Perhaps in the loading and storage area where props had been stored during the King's heyday? A ramp on the far end of the open area led to a pair of oversized doors secured with heavy chains. Windows set in the walls above flickered with lantern light from the outside, and somewhere in the distance, I heard a chortle. Apparently, the gangs didn't trust the chains alone.

The chortle turned into a snort, and I realized it wasn't coming from outside. I slipped deeper into darkness, between a massive coil of rope and a stack of old set pieces, faded trees and dull brown mountains.

I heard footsteps, two pairs of them, and voices. Quiet ones, one deep and another with a lazy drawl.

Lazy Drawl reached me first. "—and I know that. But you can't tell me it's a good idea to parlay with these guys."

"I'm not so sure," said the deep voice. "They want to talk, let 'em talk. What's the downside?"

"The downside is you legitimize them by listening. You give them a seat at the table once, they're going to expect it going forward."

Deep chuckled. "Then they'll be all the more surprised when we pull the chair out from under them."

The footsteps got closer.

"You're not taking this seriously."

"Maybe. Or maybe you're taking it *too* seriously.
You're acting like we're not the ones with the muscle.
Anyone screws with us, we gut them. We're the gods
damned Seasides. These Winds of Change chumps are
nothing but ants waiting to be squished."

"The boss doesn't think so."

"The boss is being careful. And smart. You don't get
to be in charge by ignoring opportunities to make bank,
even if they do seem on the crazy side."

The footsteps started to recede.

"What if it's a trap, though?"

"*A trap?*" Deep snorted. "Yeah, for those Winds of
Change chumps. They're the ones who invited us here
with twenty of our best. Same for the other gangs. Unless an army's coming in through the cracks in the
floor, I think we'll be fine."

"Hey, you're the one who called them ants."

"Give me a break. It's a metaphor. You know, like if I
was to say—"

The voices faded. *Winds of Change?* Was that the
name of the gang that had come after me? I wracked my
brain, but I couldn't recall hearing of them before. More
importantly, there were a *hundred* gangbangers at the
theater? If so, I needed to be quick. The Captain's
SWAT teams were eight men apiece. Even with Rodgers and Quinto on their side, they'd be outnumbered
five to one if they came in after me. I couldn't let that
happen.

I hopped out from behind the props and climbed to the level where I'd heard the guards making their loop. Their path around the perimeter of the theater suggested the meeting was taking place in the center, confirming my suspicions. Probably the bosses were meeting on the stage itself, or maybe underneath in the orchestra pit. Either way, that gave me some direction.

With the King's blueprints front and center in my mind, I worked my way inward, using old stage pieces, hanging curtains, and piles of discarded rubbish as hiding spots. Another pair of guards pacing through the backstage area forced me to slow, as did a few other times I caught snippets of conversation in the distance. Eventually, I worked my way far enough inside to catch a glimpse of the stage.

It stood there, dark, bathed in glimmers of moonlight and reflected shadows cast from lanterns at the mouth of the auditorium. Empty, though. The orchestra pit it was, then.

My internal clock ticked as I waited for another pair of guards to pass by. How long did I have left? Forty minutes? And that was to get out and back to the Captain. It didn't give me long to listen, even if I could find the meeting. I needed to hurry.

With the guards gone, I slipped down a stairwell to the basement level. This time, whether through luck or perseverance, I caught a break.

At the edge of my hearing, I caught snippets of conversation. Not like those from the guards above. Shouts and bellows among more measured tones. The meeting, probably.

I slipped around a corner and caught a glimpse of lantern light, distant but bright. A doorway stood open. Two guards stood outside it. The voices echoed from within.

I slipped across the hallway, settling in behind a set of old crates that smelled of must and onions. It was as close as I could get to the meeting without risking being seen. I stretched my ears yet again, wishing I had Shay's natural physiological advantages. Truth be told, the Captain should've sent an elf in my stead, but nobody in the precinct possessed my combination of craziness and moxie. One of the SWAT team could've taken my place, sure, but they didn't have my same headstrong determination to save Shay.

I slowed my breathing, letting my heart calm. Snippets of conversation reached me.

An old voice. Creaky. "He's serious, isn't he? This guy's *actually* serious."

A younger voice. Headstrong. "You've gone crazy if you think any of us are going to agree to that. Why would we?"

I missed the next part over a surge of mixed voices. Someone tried to calm everyone down. "Please, gentlemen. Relax. Hear me out."

The last voice was cold, even, and smooth. It carried a threatening note and flowed like oil over water. It was also somehow familiar.

It continued. "You know me. I wouldn't bring you here on a whim. I'm dead serious in everything I've retold. I've given you my demands. It's up to you to meet them."

Another chorus of loud voices, some angry, some filled with mirth.

"Are you kidding?"

"This guy's funny. I'm almost laughing."

"You dare make demands?"

The voices quieted again, shushed by a new voice. An old one, weathered, raw, and barely audible. "I've heard enough. The Blacks decline. We heel to no one. Count yourself lucky that we agreed to this parlay, otherwise I'd be decorating my home with your entrails. As it is, I'll give you twelve hours to make your leave from the city. Are we clear?"

The oily voice cut through the air, slicing it like a knife. It laughed. *Charles... Are you sure you want to go that route?*

The old voice snarled. "You will address me by my title, *boy,* or I'll cut the truce to the time it takes you to reach the door."

I shivered, and the hairs on the back of my neck stood on end. I knew better than to think it was the gang boss's tone. As I spun, I fumbled at my belt for a knife, the illegal one the Captain had turned a blind eye to as I was getting ready, knowing I'd have only seconds to silence whoever'd spotted me before they raised an alarm. That in turn would surely alert the guards. I'd have to run before anyone could identify me, make a bee line to the sewer grate, hopefully without encountering more resistance, and...

I couldn't see anyone. Darkness suffused the hallway, drenching it in shadows. I could make out the edges of a few other piles of scrap, stacked chairs, and coils of rope—always rope—but I didn't spot the whites of any spying eyes. And yet as I crouched there, coiled and tense with knife gripped tight, my sense of disquiet only grew. I shivered again, a full body tremor that started at my shoulders and shot into my toes. My heart thumped heavy in my chest, and despite the lack of anyone glancing my way, I wanted to run.

That's when I noticed it. A *clack-clack-clack* of nails tapping on tile, followed by a long squeak, like rubber boots being dragged across a floor. It cut through the distant commotion from the meeting room, monotonous and repetitive and even.

It chilled me to the bone.

I should've stuck my head out, tried to catch glimpse of its source, but the sound had such a nebulous quality to it. I couldn't tell if it was coming toward me or away from me, from the hallway I hid in or farther past the guards, or even if the damned noise was all in my head. But I couldn't force myself to look. Something inside me screamed to stay hidden.

So I listened. I was here for information, not to stick my neck out, not to get captured or die. What use would I be to Steele then? Risking life and limb without a reasonable chance of a reward wasn't courage but stupidity.

From down the hallway, I heard a strangled shout, then a thump, followed by another. Voices drifted from the meeting as the commotion lessened.

"What was that?"

"AJ? Knuckles?"

Then the oily voice. "Men. It's time."

Another *clack-clack-clack*, another long squeaky drag.

"Holy—"

"What the hell is—?"

The room fell into silence. Not a man spoke, but I heard more thumps, crashes, and a haunting peal of laughter from that same voice, the one that was so familiar but wouldn't ring a bell.

A new voice, a deeper one laced with self-assurance and menace. One that I recognized right away. Bonesaw's. "Is it safe, boss?"

"It is," said the oily voice. "Go now. Give the word. Let a few escape, to spread fear."

A set of heavy feet receded. Then the oily voice again. "Come, my pretty. There's so much work yet to be done. Follow the sound of my steps."

The clack and drag receded into the aether, leaving a void in its wake.

I exhaled and filled my lungs with air, realizing only now I'd been holding my breath. It was Bonesaw's voice I'd heard, no doubt about it. I'd recognize his deep rumble anywhere, words spoken like the wrenching of necks and gnashing of teeth. The mere thought of his voice filled me with anger and purpose and fear at the same time, and yet the other voice. The unctuous one. I couldn't place it, yet I was sure I'd heard it before.

A crash drew me out of my reverie, followed by shouts. Bangs, thuds, more shouting, cries of fear and anger and pain followed. They cascaded through the ceiling, peppering me from overhead. The oily voice— the head of the Winds of Change I had to assume—had given Bonesaw an order. Were his men attacking the guards? It sounded like a war had erupted over the stage.

I swallowed my fear and took my chance, heading from behind the crates, down the hall, and toward the makeshift meeting room.

25

The two dead guards in the hallway provided me a warning as to what I'd encounter, but I still wasn't prepared for the scope of what I found.

My jaw dropped as I took stock of the situation. The orchestra pit had been transformed into an impromptu meeting room, the far side having been barricaded and hammered together with spare planks and nails. The orchestra seats had been torn out, replaced instead with a sprawling table that looked as if it had been slapped together out of whatever pieces were too good for the barricade. A dozen chairs had been assembled on either side of the table. It was on and around those that the carnage lay.

A quintet of men, dwarves, orcs, and half-breeds sat in the chairs, slumped over or leaning back, some of them with looks of horror carved into their faces, all of them with limp jaws and glassy eyes. Around each of them sprawled several thugs, some having collapsed onto the table or onto spare chairs, others to the ground, clutching their chests or doubled over into fetal positions, some with weapons in hand and other with clenched fists.

Seventeen men, all told. All of them unmoving. Unflinching. Dead.

I crossed to the nearest seated body, that of a dwarf with a wild, bushy beard, a crown shaved clean as a whistle, and a slew of dark tattoos encircling his eyes. I vaguely recognized him. The head of the Razors, a guy by the name of Redmace who'd taken over after I'd helped put the previous head, Occam Silvervein, in jail on drug charges. I placed a couple fingers against his neck, hoping to feel a pulse, but I might as well have been holding my digits to a slab of beef. A warm slab, but a stiff one nonetheless.

A stiff one... I knelt down and tested Redmace's arm, trying to flex it at the elbow. It resisted—vigorously.

I flashed back to Biggie's corpse in my apartment, sitting there, eyes open, clutching his stomach. Cairny had been baffled at how he'd undergone rigor mortis in an hour or less, but Redmace had been dead for, what? Three or four minutes? I checked his elbow pit for tract marks, then his neck, but I didn't see anything. Not that it could've been drugs. Injecting one man with a cocktail to force his body to seize was plausible, if firmly in the realm of the bizarre. Administering it to an entire room of drug lords, dons, and bodyguards simultaneously was nigh on impossible. It would've taken an army of ninjas to inject everyone. Unless a chemical had been administered through drinking water, or aerosolized in the air.

I pulled the mask off my face and took a tentative sniff, taking note of an odd, musky odor in the air, like that of a pet ferret. A cold dread filled me, and I briefly wondered if I'd already been exposed before realizing how stupid of an idea that was. Anything potent enough to drop a dozen and a half men in their tracks would've knocked me to the ground as I'd made my way down the hallway. Besides, Bonesaw had been in the room, as had his boss with the cold, fulsome voice, and they'd been unaffected.

Even though logic reigned supreme, the cold dread didn't dissipate. It only grew stronger, because if drugs hadn't been to blame for Biggie's death and subsequent rigor mortis, then what had? What could cause a score of bruisers and badasses to keel over mid-breath? When I'd delved into the sewers hoping to catch word about Shay, I'd known full well I might be faced with violent psychopaths, murderers, and thugs for whom cruelty was second nature, but *this*? Something powerful had torn the life force from everyone in this room. Something evil. Something...*with claws*.

I knelt down further, casting my eyes to the ground. The years of decline hadn't treated the King's Theater's floors well. Between the removal of the orchestra seats, the construction of the barricade, the carpentry of the table and chairs, and the heavy boots of countless thugs and homeless people who must've called the room home at one point or another, it was hard to find a scrap of wood that hadn't been scratched, scuffed, or dented. But there were sections here and there with fresh scuffs, fresh scratches. Some in sets of three. Just as there'd been in my apartment.

A werewolf or griffin subservient to Bonesaw or his boss would've been terrifying enough, but not one motionless thug had been torn open at the throat or had his entrails littered upon the floor. Not one man was soaked in his own blood. They all simply lay there, frozen but warm.

And yet at least two people had survived it.

I just had no idea how.

I kept gazing around the room, unable to process the scope of what had happened. Redmace, dead. An old guy wearing a black suit, clutching a cane and with an eyepatch over the right side of his face. The head of the Blacks. The orc contingent from NWX. Two other gang bosses. All dead. The underworld would be thrown into chaos. There'd be infighting for weeks. Months, probably. People would die, not just gang members but the more vulnerable members of the city, those at the bottom of the pecking order who'd be easy pickings for whoever filled the power vacuum—unless Bonesaw and his Winds of Change gang could consolidate everything.

From the sounds of fighting trickling through the walls, they were trying. I heard more shouts, more slams and crashes and whumps, more cries of pain.

It occurred to me I should get out while the fighting raged. I couldn't have more than twenty minutes until the Captain would pull the cord on her strike teams, and even though the infighting would weaken the gangs, I didn't want to subject my fellow police officers to crazed knife-wielding hooligans and mysterious dark magic if I could avoid it.

And yet... I wasn't any closer to finding Shay. I had a name—the Winds of Change—and a vocal assurance that Bonesaw was involved, and that was it. I hadn't heard mention of her. No mention of any prisoner at all. I hadn't caught so much as a whiff of her lilac-scented perfume, just a weird acrid stink that faded with every passing moment.

I wrinkled my nose, sucking in more of the off-putting scent. I hadn't noticed it until I stepped into the room. I stepped back toward the hallway and took another sniff. Nothing. I crossed to the far side of the orchestra pit and did the same. There I smelled it. Kneeling, I searched for claw marks and found them, outside in the adjacent hallway.

Come, my pretty, he'd said. *Follow the sound of my steps.* I was too late for that, but I could follow tracks and a scent. And if Bonesaw was working for the man with the voice of a greased fish, then he'd be the one with knowledge of Shay. He was the one I wanted.

And pet gargoyle or not, I'd find him.

I sent a prayer to the gods to keep the Captain, Rodgers, Quinto, and the rest of the tactical strike officers safe when they inevitably came after me before setting off into the hallway. The pervasive darkness outside of the meeting room made tracking the claw marks difficult, but I did the best I could, hoping beyond hope that my nose led me in the right direction.

I followed the faint, weasel-like aroma more or less in the direction I'd come from, up a spiral staircase to the theater's backstage area. I paused in the shadows as a pair of panicked thugs raced by, shouting for help before exiting stage right, then kept going, using my nose and the power of insincere prayer to guide me as I hopped from shadow to shadow, taking refuge behind everything from a wooden cutout of a pirate ship to a grove of faded pine trees. The darkness of night enveloped me in its quiet embrace as I slinked by, hiding the claw marks but also myself. It was all I could do not to bumble into stacked boxes, giving myself away.

I stopped as I broke free of the backstage curtains and props, pausing at the edge of a warm glow radiating from two lanterns in the center of the storage and loading room. I would've welcomed the light if not for what it illuminated: eight thugs, all pacing in the center of the space. Two dwarves, four men, an orc, and an ogre—not Bonesaw, though. His complexion was too light, and his head too narrow. They carried bats, clubs, and knives, some of them bloodied. Rival gang members lay prone here and there, surrounded by pools that glistened in the near darkness.

And wouldn't you know it, at the center of the group of eight was the subbasement hatch, thrown open, lantern light illuminating it from within.

I glanced at the loading doors, which remained chained from the inside. I'd been right, in a way. Someone had planned on using the sewer entrance, same as me. It must've been how Bonesaw's gang had moved their men in, allowing them to take the rival gangs by surprise.

I sniffed the air. Maybe it was my imagination, but I swore I could still smell the ferret stink. And there. Near the hatch. Were those scratches? Was the sewer the gang's escape route as well?

The thugs wandered around the stacked crates and coils of rope, some of them serious, others chuckling. They probably thought they'd eliminated their threats, and in terms of the gangs, it looked as if they'd succeeded.

But I was still here.

I hadn't planned on plunging myself into danger. I liked living. My life had sucked once upon a time, but it didn't any longer. But the only reason it didn't suck, the *only* reason my life was full of joy and laughter and good cheer, was because of Shay. She'd been the one to pull me back from the brink, to sit through my blatant sexism and asinine jokes, the one to nurture the good that lingered inside me, the one to push me to rekindle my relationship with my son and my ex-wife and father, to put down the bottle of whiskey and limit my beers to meals. She was the shining light in my life.

If she wasn't worth risking my neck for, who was?

I took a deep breath to settle my nerves. I was outnumbered eight to one, locked in a hostile abandoned theater with backup too far away to make a difference, chasing a man who commanded the power to stop twenty men's hearts with the snap of a finger.

At least I had the element of surprise on my side.

26

Hiding behind the edge of the curtains at the tail end of the backstage, I took off my pack and lay it down before me. From it, I retrieved a bottle of water, which I used to soak the cloth mask I'd been wearing, a trick to keep out smoke that I'd learned long ago while fighting a serial arsonist. I slipped the mask back on and double-checked my belt and jacket. I'd filled my pockets and pouches as best I could, so I tucked the backpack behind me on the floor. It would only restrict my motion during the coming fight, and if I survived I could always come back for it.

When I survived. No need to be morbid.

I stared at the assembled thugs, trying to burn the surroundings into my memory. The crates. The ropes. The barrels. The location of the hatch, the placement of the two lanterns. I'd need to know where to go instinctively if I was to make it. My gadgets would only serve as a hindrance if I wasn't prepared.

I fingered the knife at my belt. I'd brought it for a reason, and the Captain wouldn't blink if I told her I'd been forced to end someone's life to save Steele. And yet...barring the occasional filleting of a fish or whittling exercise, I'd barely ever used one. I'd probably be as liable to cut myself as someone else.

I reached into my jacket and withdrew Daisy, which I slipped into a belt loop at my right hip. She was bent, battered, and dented, a dull implement of pain best suited to guys with two word vocabularies, not senior homicide detectives, but I knew her. Her weight, her heft, her balance. I'd been blasting thugs in the cranium with her for over a decade. I knew how she danced, and I wasn't sure I could learn a new set of steps on the fly. I'd have to roll with her and hope for the best.

From the safety of my hiding spot, I took one last look at the assembled gangbangers, trying to craft the order I'd take them in. The dwarves I'd deal with first. They were small, but squat. Their kind had wrecked havoc on me before. Best to incapacitate them. Then maybe the orc. Being a human myself, I knew how to handle the men. And the ogre? Well, if I got that far, I'd bring whatever I had left.

I closed my eyes and thought of Shay. *Here goes, babe. Wish me luck.*

My eyes snapped open and I reached into my utility belt, pulling a couple of sealed glass bottles filled with white powder. The fire mage I'd secured them from, the subject of Shay's and my first murder investigation, said all I'd need to do was throw them hard to make sure the glass broke and they'd start smoking like a fire full of wet leaves, no ignition required—or rather, they'd ignite themselves, which sounded like a useful bit of fire magic if ever there was one. The old mage had countered, saying it was chemistry, not magic, though the magic certainly helped in getting the chemicals into the bottles in the first place.

All I cared about was them working. I burst from behind the curtain and darted toward the thugs, hurling the first bottle toward the feet of the dwarves sixty feet in front of me. I had the second bottle airborne, headed toward the orc, and a third in hand before anyone noticed me.

One of the men pointed a finger and shouted "Hey!" as the first bottle hit the ground. I heard a crystalline crunch and a crackle, followed by an unexpected puff. White smoke shot out in a cloud, sending bits of broken glass flying with the force of its expansion. I threw the third bottle at the quartet of human thugs as the second bottle broke and sent more smoke flying, then dove into the first cloud.

White smoke hung thick in the air, creating a screen far more dense than I could've imagined, and I was immediately thankful for the mask. My eyes itched the moment I stepped inside the cloud, and I could hear the two dwarven skull-crackers hacking and coughing from somewhere within the smoke.

Even having surveyed the storage room from above, I'm not sure I would've found them without their barking. I slipped a syringe from a custom made wooden block tied into my belt loop and sprung toward the first source of hacking coughs, barely spotting his doubled over form before I crashed into him. With all the grace of a first year medical student, I plunged the needle into the side of his neck and slammed on the plunger.

One.

The dwarf grunted, spun, and took a swing at me, but I'd already danced back into the smoke. I heard him gurgle as I turned to the next source of coughing. I counted the seconds in my head as I searched for the next cougher. One. Two. Three. *Thump.* Cairny had said it would take about five seconds for the sedatives to take effect, but dwarves didn't carry as much mass as us full-sized folk.

The second dwarf saw me coming a half-second too late. He brought up a hatchet handle to ward off the blow he assumed was coming, but it didn't do anything to block my downward needle chop. I plunged the syringe into his shoulder and moved on.

Two.

I burst from the cloud of white smoke, my eyes watering. An eerie yellow lantern glow suffused the cloud to my right, shouts and coughs emanating from within. I heard another bellow behind me, as well as heavy feet and curses.

I hopped over a crate and sprinted toward the third cloud, the spot where I'd last seen the orc. He stumbled out from the smoke as I arrived.

I slammed into him hard, driving the last of my syringes into his chest as we tumbled to the ground.

Three.

He looked at me with a mixture of confusion and anger, trying to grab me by the coat as I scrambled to my feet. His shout turned into a gurgle as I pulled Daisy from my belt loop and ran back to the last of the clouds—which, as I now saw, were coalescing into a single large cloud. Were the bombs still smoking? I hadn't considered the full implication of using them indoors. No matter. My throat felt only a minor tickle thanks to the moist rag covering my mouth and nose, and the room had high ceilings. The smoke would rise. Hopefully I'd sneak away through the sewer before it got too thick.

I heard another angry bellow in the smoke behind me as I plunged into the eerie yellow glow. Though the smoke continued to expand, it did seem to be thinning ever so slightly. I saw the first thug from almost three feet away.

He growled and swung his spiked club in an over-hand smash, but I stepped into him, planting a fist square in his gut. He grunted but didn't go down, instead latching onto my jacket, but thankfully not my arm. I let him yank on the leather, pulling my left arm from my sleeve as I tucked and spun, planting a hard elbow into his ear. He stumbled back, clutching his head as I slipped back into the sleeve and whipped Daisy toward him at high speed, catching him in the jaw. Bone cracked, and he went down in a heap.

Four.

That's when someone leapt onto me from behind, wrapping his arms around my neck and chest. Maybe the sounds of fighting had given me away. Either way, I got lucky. My attacker came at me too high.

We stumbled forward, but feeling his weight pressing on my shoulders, I tucked into a roll, flipping my attacker over me and onto his back. He landed with a thud. I aimed a heavy foot as his face, but he rolled out of the way, grabbing my exposed boot in the process. He yanked, and I fell, but I refused to let my gravitational energy go to waste. I landed on top of him, driving an elbow into his midsection. He heaved and groaned, trying as best he could to roll away, but I was ready. Scrambling to my knees, I slapped him across the temples with Daisy, one, two, three times. His eyes rolled back into his head. Somewhere in the background I heard another angry bellow.

Five.

"There he is! Get the bastard!"

The last two of the human thugs came at me together, materializing out of the smoke several feet in front of me. One of them walked in a half crouch, holding a long knife, balanced carefully like he knew how to use it, and the other one, a big musclebound bruiser, held a piece of lead pipe about a foot longer than Daisy.

Topples and Biggie had already shown me what two gangbangers working together were capable of, and based on first impressions, Topple's knife skills paled in comparison to Crouchy's.

I turned tail and ran.

"Hey! Get him!"

I leapfrogged a stray crate, darted around a stack of boxes, and spun around a massive spool of rope, weaving this way and that, barely knowing where I was going. I tried to access the mental picture I'd taken of the storage room, but whether because of a lack of landmarks, a failure to memorize the room's assorted junk, or the adrenaline shooting through my veins, it came back as a blur. The smoke didn't help. Though it had diffused a bit, it still permeated the space, scratching at my eyes, obscuring every turn.

Again I heard the bellow, followed by a decidedly angry roar. "He's over here."

I turned back the way I'd come. A figure dove out of the smoke at me, pipe whistling as it swung through the air. I couldn't get out of the way in time. All I could do was turn.

Pain lanced across my back and the upper portion of my left arm as the pipe thwacked into muscle. I tried to ignore it and drove forward, throwing my bruised shoulder into my attacker.

It didn't do much damage, but it knocked him off balance enough for me to run past him. At least I was prepared for the moment his buddy tried to knife me.

I swung Daisy, trying to knock free the knife from my attacker's hand, but Crouchy was too quick. He danced back, pulling his knife out of harm's way. He lunged in for a quick jab. I slapped him away with Daisy, catching him with a glancing blow.

We lunged and swiped and parried a few more times, me managing to get a decent whack on the guy's free elbow and Crouchy managing to slice my jacket open at the bicep, but not doing much real damage. We danced backward, toward the flickering yellow glow of one of the lanterns, each of us growing more wary with each strike. Neither one of us could get the upper hand.

Then Pipehands lunged out of the smoke, I tangled my foot in a coil of rope, and everything went to shit.

I toppled backwards and fell, crashing into the crate that held the lantern. Wood shattered underneath me. Daisy flew from my hands, clattering across the floor and disappearing into the smoke. The lantern toppled to the floor, the flame dimming as oil spilled from its reservoir. I rolled away from the wreckage, expecting an attack from above, but a tug at my leg kept me tethered. The damn rope had looped itself around me.

Before I could move, Crouchy and Pipehands were on me. I curled up, trying to protect myself from the rain of blows. Ribs, back, hips, and arms all blossomed with pain as pipe blows, kicks, and punches rained down on me.

I tried to banish the pain by thinking of Shay. I couldn't give up. Not now.

I kicked out, trying to get someone in the legs, but it was no use. I was too far away. Too exposed.

"Son of a bitch," said Crouchy. "I'm going to cut his damn nose off."

Pipehands dove on me, smothering me, and I caught a glimpse of Crouchy coming toward me, knife drawn with a wicked sneer stretching his face.

Pipehands had me pinned at the shoulders. I couldn't get any leverage. But I could still reach my belt.

I slipped a vial into my free hand and mumbled a veiled threat.

Crouchy's face loomed large. "What was that, asshole?"

The guys from the SWAT team had said to throw the bottle from a distance. Not like I had any choice. I held my breath, shut my eyes tight, and whipped the glass vial into Crouchy's face.

The broken glass bit into my hand as the vial shattered, then I heard a growl of anger followed shortly by an inhuman shriek. "Ahh! AAAAAHHHH! *Get it off me!*"

I heard Pipehands' voice next. "Dude, what the—? Ah! Oh, *it burns!*"

With my eyes and lips still shut tight, I shoved with all my might. Pipehands grunted and cursed as he fell off me, all while Crouchy continued to shriek incessantly.

"Son of a bitch! *Son of a bitch!*"

I opened my eyes, hoping the pepper extract I'd smashed into Crouchy's face hadn't gotten onto my own.

Instantly they started to burn and water.

Crouchy clawed at his face. "*Ahh!* I'll kill you!"

Half blind, he lunged at me, knife still in hand.

I fought back with the only thing in reach. I grabbed the lantern and cast it at Crouchy's face. The glass shattered, sending shards and oil flying. Then a fireball ripped through the air, engulfing the entire side of Crouchy's head in flames. He cut loose with a bloodcurdling scream and fell to the ground, rolling and slapping weakly at the inferno.

I hadn't known the pepper concoction was flammable. Still...*six?*

Pipehands growled and launched himself at me. I should've seen it coming, but with my eyes watering, I couldn't see much of anything.

He slammed into me, and we fell to the floor. With both of us having lost our weapons and the light of the flames dying, Pipehands and I resorted to good old fashioned wrestling. He pushed. I pulled. He tried to get on top of me. I twisted. He grappled. I rolled.

Thanks to my police training, I had the better technique, but Pipehands had me on strength and size, and gosh darn it, I was getting tired. Sweat poured off my face and soaked my shirt. My breath came in ragged gasps through the wet mask, and my throat burned.

I tried to slip free, to break away, to give myself a fresh angle of attack, but Pipehands was too tenacious. He grabbed me around the thigh, lifted, and drove me backward, through a makeshift curtain of hanging ropes. Pain shot through my spine as he slammed me into one of the panels of levers. The things cracked and shuddered, or maybe it was my ribs.

Pipehands jabbed an arm into my neck and grappled at my face, trying to gouge my eyes. He was dumb enough to leave his thumb hanging there for the taking, though.

I chomped down on it, feeling the hot, metallic taste of his blood flow into my mouth. Pipehands cried out and recoiled, stumbling into the hanging ropes.

Ropes...

I feinted to the left and darted to the right as Pipehands dove for me. It only gave me a small window, but I took advantage, slinging one of the hanging ropes around his neck and jumping on his back.

Pipehands tried to buck me, as I'd done to my attacker earlier, but the rope wouldn't let him. It tightened as he struggled against it, attached as it was up in the rafters. I pulled on my end of it, adding more pressure to Pipehands' neck.

I'll give credit where credit is due. I thought I finally had him, but Pipehands didn't panic. He drove me backwards, slamming me into the panel of levers. Bruises sprouted upon my bruises, pain streaking through my battered body, but I held on anyway.

He slammed me again, and I cried out. My grip slipped. The lever panel shuddered and shook. The rope around Pipehands' neck, now taught, vibrated, and despite the pain, an idea sprouted.

Pipehands readied another backward slam, but before he could shatter my spine, I hopped off, raking my arm across the levers. They responded with a series of clunks and a whirr. Pipehands grunted as he was lifted off the ground, clutching the rope as it whisked him into the rafters.

I may not know much about theater, but I know enough about physics to know that what comes up must come down. I danced out of the way as a half-dozen sand-filled canvas bags thudded to the floor in front of me, most of them followed by whizzing sections of rope that had slipped their pulleys and undulated down to the ground atop the pile.

I bent over, pulling my mask off as I sucked smoky air in through my mouth. *Gods. Seven. I did it.*

I would've jumped if not for the flicker of light that gave him away.

A nebulous shadow loomed behind me, and I heard the menacing voice from before. "Got you. Now you're going to pay."

I glanced back to see the ogre from before setting the second lantern down at his feet. He cracked his knuckles and hunched into a fighting stance, beckoning with his fingers.

Right. There'd been eight.

27

I reached down to my belt, grabbed another pepper vial, and flung it at the ogre's face, but he ducked his head to the side, sending the projectile sailing into the darkness beyond. I'd already used all my smoke bombs. My syringes hadn't lasted much longer. I'd even lost Daisy. I didn't have anything else.

Then I remembered the knife.

Of course, Tall and Scary stopped playing fair the moment my vial of toxins went whizzing past his face. As I realized stabbing the guy in his fleshy bits was a worthwhile endeavor, he slammed into me, picked me up, and chucked me into a pile of barrels.

My entire body cried out as I hit the aged oak. If I'd yet to break any bones, it was only through sheer luck and my heavy consumption of milk as a child. Every muscle ached, reminding me that getting beaten to a pulp after nearly dying in a three-story fall wasn't the healthiest of exercises.

The ogre pulled me from the pile. I tore into him with every ounce of strength I had left, blasting him in the chest with punches, driving knees and kicks into his gut and shins.

I think it surprised him, sort of in the way a boulder is surprised when you try punching it to death, too. He grunted and tossed me again.

I flew like a wet rag, hitting the floor with a slap. I skidded to a stop near the lantern. Somewhere in the distance, I heard footsteps and voices.

The ogre approached me, flexing his fists. "Playtime's over, pal. Time for me to have some fun."

I strained my ears, praying for a miracle, ideally one outfitted in riot gear and with an angry 5th Street Precinct Captain bringing up the rear guard.

My heart deflated when I heard the noxious, oily voice from the meeting, quiet and distant. "Go, my darling. End this."

The ogre stepped over me. In the background, I heard the same *clack-clack-clack, drag* from before. The sweat on my arms and face went cold, and goosebumps rippled across my arms.

The ogre heard it, too. "Uh...boss?"

He looked into the smoke, past the pile of old crates at my back, his eyes narrowing. Then they widened. He froze, and like a statue, fell over with a crash.

Fear gripped me in an icy embrace. I trembled as the *clack-clack-clack* of the claws closed in on me, wanting to run but unable to get my legs to obey. Images of Shay laughing, smiling, lying naked in my arms flashed before me, as did the horrifying images of death from the last two days. Biggie. The room full of gang leaders. Now Tall and Scary. What would the Captain and Rodgers and Quinto do when they found me? Had Shay already suffered the fate that awaited me?

The click of the claws raked trails of fear into my heart. I forced myself to think back, to remember that Bonesaw and his boss had survived whatever lingered behind me, but I couldn't tear my eyes off the ogre's body.

My eyes.

I lashed out, smashing the lantern Tall and Scary had brought with him. The flame within flickered and dimmed. I slammed on it with my arm, smothering it and plunging my surroundings into darkness. Then I squeezed my eyes shut tight for good measure.

Perhaps I was wrong. Perhaps the beast I *thought* approached was an old wives' tale and I was about to dying a horrifying death regardless, but why take any chances?

The *clack-clack-clack, drag* sounded once more, incredibly close, so close that I thought I might be able to reach out and touch the source of its haunting tenor. In the distance, I heard the oily voice. "Come out, come out, wherever you are."

I stretched my ears, searching for nearby breath or motion, but I couldn't sense any, in part because of my body's betrayal. My heart beat heavy in my chest, blood pounded in my ears, and I couldn't still my heavy breathing. In addition, rather than making my senses more acute, my self-imposed visual depravation made me hyperaware of my aches and pains. The stabbing sensation in my lower back, the itching in my throat, and the burning in my eyes, to name a few.

I reached out my left hand, wondering if the sounds had been all in my head, a physical manifestation of my fear. Maybe I'd been wrong. Perhaps Biggie and the gang leaders had died through a dark ritual, an obscure bit of black magic. Perhaps I wasn't being stalked by a cockatrice or basilisk or medusa. If so, I'd have to re-think my strategy, because—

I heard a nearby hissing, a long slow exhale, then cried out as a dozen sharp teeth latched onto the flesh of my hand. I tried to pull back, but the powerful bite held me in place. Whatever manner of beast held me in its jaws yanked, sending me crashing into it.

My first instinct was to protect my eyes with my free arm, but as I fell, off-balance, into the creature, I think I smacked it in its face with my elbow. It hissed again, refusing to let go of my hand. It must've tossed its head, because my arm wrenched violently to the side. I skidded across the floor, feeling the shattered remains of the lantern's glass globe crunch underneath me. My hand screamed in pain. Then I woofed as a hundred and fifty pounds of beast landed on me.

I gasped, trying to refill my lungs following the body slam. A noxious wave of ferret stink filled my nostrils, hot and moist and putrid. The creature growled again. Its rough tongue scraped against my hand, lapping up the blood that seeped into its mouth. Claws dug into my shoulder, pricking me through the thick leather of my jacket.

I punched with my free hand, and I think I landed a blow to its head.

The creature didn't even grunt.

I pulled back and slammed another punch into the creature's skull, then another, but the beast's thick, scaly hide deflected my blows. I might as well have been punching a bag of wet sand. The creature simply growled again through its clenched teeth.

Maybe it was my imagination, but I thought I caught a malevolent, satisfied tone in the growl. My arm pressed forward into my chest. The acrid odor intensified. Hot breath caressed my face, and my eyes began to burn. Not as they had from the pepper bomb. Much more than that. A searing sensation, like my eyes might self-combust. I wanted to pull back, but the floor wouldn't let me. Then I saw them. Two orbs of light, murky and indistinct but visible all the same through my eyelids.

I turned away as I rained more blows at the creature's head, knowing my waning strength, the beast's thick skin, and my compromised position made them as effective as a toddler's blows, yet still I tried. *Thump.* Maybe if I hit it in the neck. *Whump.* The eyes. *Thwack.* My hand ached. I gasped for air.

What was the definition of insanity again? Trying the same thing over and over and expecting different results? I had to try something new. *Anything.*

Ignoring the pain in my hand, I kicked up as hard as I could, trying to toss the creature over my head. I maybe lifted it an inch off the ground. It may not have outweighed me, but it had all the leverage, not to mention an inhuman strength.

The murky eye glow intensified. I tried again, kicking with all I was worth. Something dug into my thigh:

a sharp, directed prick, not like the pincer grip of the claws.

My knife!

I slipped my hand to my belt, managing to tear the blade from its sheath despite the creature's bulk atop me. My eyes burned with an impossible fury, feeling as if I'd plunged my face into an inferno.

I drove the blade into the creature's back. It slipped and skidded off the monster's skin.

I tried again. This time the blade bit for a fraction of a second before slipping.

The creature growled, pushing its hot, fetid snout into my face, still refusing to let go of my hand. My face boiled, and yet I kept my eyes shut.

One last try. I flipped the blade over and plunged it with all the strength I could muster into the beast's belly, right at the side where it lay atop me.

The creature's skin ripped, and I felt the blade drive to the hilt. The creature hissed and roared, letting go of my hand, causing a fresh wave of agony to ripple down my arm.

I took advantage of the moment, pushing off with my free arm and pulling down on the knife with the other. Flesh tore. Hot blood slicked my knife hand. The beast reared. I rolled, and my knife pulled free of the wound.

I stumbled to my feet, my eyes still closed but suddenly free of their supernatural burning, back instead to their more mundane pepper-induced anguish. I didn't dare open then, and I'd lost all sense of direction as soon as the beast had latched onto me.

Apparently, it could still see, despite the darkness. It could also still move, despite its wound. It slammed into me low. I toppled backwards, stumbling into a taut rope. I burned my mangled hand as I scrambled for purchase before tumbling into a soft pile—the sand-filled canvas bags I'd sent crashing down on their pulleys.

I heard another *clack-clack-clack*, followed by a drag like before, this time right in front of me. I scrambled back and tucked my legs. A whoosh of air and a snap of jaws nearly ensnared my foot, catching me instead on the pant leg, but I ripped them free.

Grunting, I flipped over backward, rolling over the bags, using the one taut rope to steady myself. The sand bags shook as the creature slammed into them a fraction of a second later, hissing and growling in anger.

My heart pounded, my hands were slick with blood, and I could hear concerned shouts in the distance. I needed to kill the beast and get out while I could, but how? The creature's belly was its weakness, not its back. It would take a blow greater than I could deliver to damage it.

My musings on the nature of physics came back to me in a rush. *What comes up must come down.* The only question was, on which side of the sand bags?

Oh, well. A fifty-fifty chance was better than none at all. I fumbled for the rope with my wounded hand, found it, then delivered a sweeping slash at it with my knife.

It sliced through with barely a hitch. I heard a whirr of a pulley, and I threw myself backward in desperation.

I managed to crack my head against something in the process, but it was worth it. A bone-crunching crash and an inhuman cry rewarded me in recompense.

I tried to steady my breathing, counting to ten before opening my eyes. In front of me, shrouded in
darkness but visible against the smoky background, lay
Pipehands' broken body, twisted at an unnatural angle.
Underneath him was a creature unlike any I'd ever
seen, an enormous lizard, covered in dark gray scales,
with powerful legs and three inch claws. Its eyes lay
closed, but it appeared to be breathing shallowly.

I closed the distance in a long stride, pulled up on its
head, and drove my knife into the underside of its jaw,
averting my eyes as I did so. It whined and gurgled
weakly, its life force mostly spent by my slash to its
stomach and Pipehands' dying blow.

I stood and looked around, trying to orient myself in
the lingering smoke and the darkness. Footsteps approached, and I needed to get out. I had nothing left to
fight with, no weapons, no energy, no desire.

I stumbled around the edge of the crates through
which the ogre had tossed me, hoping it led to the
sewer entrance.

I guessed both right and wrong. The sewer hatch
materialized out of the smoke in front of me as I ran, lit
by the flickering glow of the lantern in the subbasement, but another form appeared alongside it. A huge
one. Six feet eight inches tall and four hundred pounds,
with a glistening shaved head, tattoos staining his
chocolatey skin, and a menacing grin stretching his
face.

"Well, well," he said, stepping forth. "If it isn't Jake
Daggers. I should've known this was all 'cause of you."

My heart sank and I took a deep breath. "Bonesaw. I
was hoping to find you, just not right now."

The oily voice cried out behind me. "No! NO! *You killed her! HOW?*"

"Over here, boss," called Bonesaw.

I glanced at the smoke. It was rapidly dissipating. I could try to run, but I couldn't hide. Also Bonesaw was quicker than his four hundred pounds would suggest, if memory served me right.

"Nice job at Coldgate," I said, stalling for time. "You fooled the guards there, if not me. Winds of Change, eh? How're you liking your new home?"

"I'm loving it," he said. "Though it's not as new as you think."

The befuddlement must've been evident on my face, but I didn't get a chance to ask him about it. I heard footsteps behind me, and saw the glow of a lantern.

"You," said the oily voice. "You murdered my pet."

I turned and blinked as I took stock of the man who stood there, a lean, wiry sort with medium length wavy brown hair and the limber, agile stance of a dancer. An aura of menace surrounded him, but the air of indifference I remembered was gone.

"*Sebastian Cobb?*" I said.

Suddenly, it made sense. The leader of the Wyverns, the gang Steele and I had busted at the start of winter for dragon trafficking. We'd taken down Bonesaw, not to mention a gang-bought electromancer by the name of Left-Eye Lazarus, but Cobb had escaped. I'd always suspected he was more than the gang's recruiter, and I still suspected him in the murder of my ex-partner's friend, Randall Barrett.

"You," I said. "So the Winds of Change...you're the Wyverns? That's how you got the basilisk?"

Cobb panted and snarled, like a rabid dog testing the edge of his leash. "*Daggers.* You think you've won? You think I can't get another basilisk? She served her purpose. You're too late. All you've succeeded in doing is making me angry, and I have plenty of other tricks up my sleeve, *believe me.*" He looked up at the sounds of distant fighting, and a sudden gust of wind rattled the windows high above in the rafters. "The Wyverns... *Please.* The Winds of Change have arrived. And they're blowing."

He served me up a retort on a silver platter, but before I was able to explain who exactly was doing the blowing, pain blossomed at the base of my skull and my world went dark.

28

When I awoke, it was to comparable bliss. Don't get me wrong. My back ached, my hand throbbed, my eyes itched, a dull ache pounded at the back of my skull, and I desperately needed a throat lozenge and a dozen glasses of water, but on the bright side, I wasn't immersed in smoke, surrounded by weasel stink, or actively being punched, kicked, beaten, bitten, clawed, or bored into with petrification-strength demon eyes by a monster out of legend. And I was alive, so overall, it was a win.

I winced as I sat up, taking stock of my surroundings. I was in a small room, dark but with an outward facing window that let in a smidgen of moonlight. I sat on a steel-framed bed—not an uncomfortable one, to be honest—but other than that, my furnishings were limited to a narrow washbasin pushed against the far wall.

I stood, my legs complaining but working as intended, and crossed over to it. I plunged my hand into the basin, but no cool water met my touch. I sighed.

I moved to the window, or as close to it as I could get. The glass panes were recessed, kept out of reach by a thick iron grating. I tested them, but they didn't budge.

I gazed through the glass. Clouds covered the majority of the sky, but enough moonlight got through for me to get a gist of where I was.

Wind whistled through trees two stories below me. I spotted a gravel path, dark vegetation, snippets of tile and carved stone. It reminded me of the view from the vast expanse of the Aldermont, the luxurious estate belonging to the Vanderfellers where Shay and I had been tasked with the mysterious disappearance of the home's matron. It wasn't as big as the Vanderfellers' place, or didn't appear to be in the darkness, but it was a manor nonetheless, not an underground dungeon. That surprised me.

I held my left hand to the window, trying to inspect it in the moon's dim glow. Dried blood coated most of it, and I could vaguely make out puncture wounds set in a neat curve. I couldn't have been lucky enough to avoid breaking any bones, could I? I flexed my hand and stopped halfway, the pain nearly crippling me. *Guess not...* I'd need to sterilize it. Who knew what germs resided in a basilisk's mouth?

I looked around, once again wishing for water in the basin. Or even better, a drink of the alcoholic variety. Not that I was lapsing to a darker period in my life, but the alcohol would dull the pain and help clean my hand.

I crossed to the door at the front of the room and tested the handle. It rattled, but didn't budge.

I tried knocking. "Hello? Anyone there?"

A not-too-nice voice responded, muffled by the wall. "Best be quiet lest you want a beating."

I heard another voice, this one quieter, then a chuckle from the first voice. Two guards, it would appear?

I checked my belt only to find it gone. Surprisingly enough, Cobb and Bonesaw had left me my jacket, though they'd cleaned that out, too. I thought back to Daisy, lying in the back of the King's Theater, cold and alone.

I blinked the thought away. I enjoyed anthropomorphism as much as the next guy, but now wasn't the time to be worried about a truncheon.

"You with the Winds of Change?" I called.

"Told you to shut it."

I lifted the corner of my mattress, but there wasn't anything of use down there, either. I couldn't pull the bed apart in search of a makeshift weapon. It was welded steel and brass.

I glanced at the washbasin. It was mostly wooden, but I wouldn't be able to pry it apart with my bare fingers, not with my left hand in its current state. I'd be defenseless if I antagonized my jailers into coming in after me, but what choice did I have? I needed to get out, and I couldn't do so through the window. Besides, they wouldn't kill me, would they? They hadn't so far.

"Could I at least get some water?" I said. "My throat's killing me."

I heard a grunt. "You asked for it, pal."

I heard the scrape of a chair and a rattle of keys. That was followed by a whack and a thump, then a series of thuds interspersed with a faint grunt or two, all while the keys continued to jingle.

I took a step back from the door, suddenly nervous. "You know, on second thought, I don't need—"

A latch clacked, and the door opened. Someone slipped into the darkness, closing the door behind them. Someone wearing a familiar pair of boots and tight leather pants.

"Kyra?"

She stepped into the wan moonlight, her body tense and her face drawn. "Good to see you're awake, and mobile. I wasn't sure you'd be after everything you've been through."

"*Everything I've been through?*"

"Come on, Jake. You're quicker on the uptake than this. How do you think I found you?"

"You were following me?" I said. "The whole time?"

"Not the *whole* time," she said. "I hid at the King's Theater. I mean, I'm the one who told you where the meeting would be, if you remember. Hell of a scene you made. I knew you were a badass, but you took down a *basilisk.*"

I pictured our second meeting. Kyra teasing me, coming onto me, spurning me. Had I missed something? "Why are you here?"

"I owe you my life. I'm paying back the debt."

"A point I made to you multiple times already. Didn't seem to sway you at the time."

"I changed my mind." She looked away. "As it turns out, maybe you *are* able to bring out the good in people. Even me."

I wasn't totally sure I bought it. "What happened after I got knocked out?"

"Bonesaw grabbed you, slung you over his shoulder, and followed Cobb out of the theater, them and a few of the remaining thugs. I followed the lot of you here. I was trying to figure out a good way to spring you when you distracted the guards."

"And where is here?"

"A mansion in Brentwood. Not sure whose."

"And my friends?" I asked. "Rodgers, Quinto. The Captain. The rest of the police strike teams?"

"Not sure," said Kyra. "I was focused on you, not them. I imagine they're still at the theater. Not sure if you noticed, but all hell broke loose after Cobb sicced that creature on the gang leaders. He timed it so several of his hidden teams of goons attacked the remaining gang troops right after it went down."

"I noticed."

"Then you know as much as I do. Could've been worse for your friends, I guess. I can't imagine there were many of the bad guys left once your pals went in." Kyra glanced toward the door. "Either way, it's time to go. I haven't scouted this place as well as I should've, certainly not as much as I would've if I were breaking in. There could be more guards here any minute."

"Aren't you forgetting something?" I said.

"What?"

"Shay. Where is she?"

"How would I know? I followed you, not her."

"*Kyra...*"

She sighed. "I overheard the guards mention another prisoner on the ground floor. I don't know if it's her. That's all I have."

"You're a life-saver."

"Technically true, but not if you keep up your current pace. Daggers, I was at the theater. I saw what you pulled off—or not, exactly. Those smoke bombs were a nice trick. But you can't keep it up. Look at you. You're a mess. I'm surprised you're still standing. You need to get out while you can."

"You know I can't do that," I said. "I have to save Shay. I have to stop Cobb."

"Oh, now you've upped your ambitions? You won't stop until the whole city is safe?"

"It's my job, Kyra. I know I may be in homicide, and most of the citizens I work with tend to be of the formerly living variety, but I do what I do to protect people. To save people. To make a difference."

Kyra snorted. "Gods, you really are a golden boy."

"Good thing you like golden boys. I mean...that *is* why you're here, isn't it?"

Kyra stepped closer to me. "You think I'd come between you and your partner? After you told me you loved her?"

"Maybe," I said. "Or maybe you came back for proof."

"Proof of what?"

"Proof that guys like me exist. Guys that would do anything for the people they love. Guys that would stand up for what's right, even if it means putting their own necks on the line. Maybe you came back for validation. For a glimmer of hope."

"You know, you're not *just* a golden boy," said Kyra, moving even closer. "You're a hopeless romantic. Don't worry. I like those, too."

She leaned in and kissed me. Not on the cheek, either. On the lips. Soft and tender, yet strong at the same time. It didn't last forever. Maybe a few seconds, but when Kyra pulled back, she was out of breath all the same.

"Sorry. Needed something else to remember you by. Go and get her, champ. And don't forget about me, okay?"

"How could I forget you?" I said.

Kyra smiled. "Oh, I don't mean in general. I meant when you send out the wedding invitations."

I snorted. "And where would I send them?"

"I'll be back—assuming you save the city from Cobb, that is." She opened the door. "Take care, Jake. And watch out for guards. I didn't clear them *all* out for you."

29

When I stepped into the hallway, Kyra had already disappeared. A couple of thugs lay on the floor, barely distinguishable in the darkness. I heard their slow breathing, though, so they weren't dead. A thread of smoke tickled my nose, which I traced to a lantern set atop a small table outside my room. Kyra must've extinguished it before coming in to save me.

I peered into the darkness around me, but other than the small table and chairs, the hallway seemed empty. Certainly, I didn't catch sign of my belt and other assorted personal effects, or a piece of furniture to contain them. No matter.

I knelt next to the first of the gently sleeping thugs and emptied his pockets. I didn't find much. Loose change, a package of chewing tobacco, and a pair of brass knuckles. I slipped the latter into my pocket, thanking Kyra once again for sparing me the beating I would've suffered at the wrong end of those, and moved on to the second thug. He didn't carry much more of significance, but he did have the set of keys I'd heard clinking before, not to mention a wicked looking blade, fourteen inches in length with an inwardly curved edge, all in an intricate sheath.

The keys I wasn't sure I'd need, but given there were a half dozen on the ring, I'd be stupid not to take them. Using the knife, I hacked a piece of the thug's shirt off, wrapped it around the keys, and tied it, shaking the bundle to make sure it wouldn't jingle. It didn't. Then I sheathed the knife and slipped it into my jacket's interior coat pocket. It didn't have the same weight or presence as Daisy, but I'd use it in a pinch.

I stood, ready to set off, but it occurred to me I shouldn't leave thugs lying around in the middle of hallways. Knocking folks unconscious was a permanent solution in penny dreadfuls, but in the real world, people woke up at inopportune times. Luckily for me, I had a perfect solution to the problem.

After dumping the thugs in my cell and locking the door with my newly commandeered keys, I set off down the hallway. I walked slowly, quietly, thankful I hadn't been stripped of the specialized boots I'd donned for trekking through the King's Theater. Not that feet wouldn't have been as quiet, but they weren't tailored for traversing gravel or the city's muck-filled streets or small stone paths set inside centuries old sewers.

I crossed a set of windows, these without heavy bars or shutters. Outside, trees swayed to and fro. Wind whistled, and rain rattled across the glass. Other than that? Silence. Where was I, exactly? Kyra had mentioned Brentwood, which explained the presence of vegetation instead of miles of brick and mortar as far as the eye could see, but *why* Brentwood? In whose manor? An abandoned one? The association of home-owners didn't look kindly upon those.

I wandered along, more or less sticking to the home's back wall, before I arrived at a staircase. A glimmer of light caught my eye from below, and I heard something. A voice. Maybe two. Laughter?

I took to the stairs, moving slower than before. I slipped my right hand inside my pocket, the brass knuckles sliding into place. Despite my newfound basilisk fighting experience, I still preferred beating on someone to going after them with a knife. Something about cutting into human flesh gave me the willies. I wasn't sure how Cairny did it, even on dead folks.

I paused at the bottom of the stairs and peered over the railing in the direction of the light. A glow flickered at the far end of the hall, but the voices I'd heard had quieted.

Even with only one fully functional hand, the element of surprise would give me the upper hand if anyone were to show up, or at least that was the lie I told myself to force my feet along the hall. More wind and rain battered the windows at my side, and in the far distance, I heard a peal of thunder. Shadows danced across the front of ostentatious decorative pieces: wrought iron chandeliers, the dozens of candles contained therein unlit, heavy drapes, tall bookcases crammed with tomes, a series of paintings, even a suit of armor for crying out loud. Apparently, whoever owned the manor had spent their efforts decorating the first floor and had run out of funds for the third.

Speaking of whoever owned the manor... The paintings which hung along the wall were portraits, depicting a series of young men dressed in fine clothes and standing in dramatic poses. The fashion in the first few were of the stuffy and dated variety, but they grew more modern as I walked down the hall. Each of them also had a brass plaque affixed underneath them. *Christopher Markeville. Anderson Markeville. William Markeville.*

I paused as I reached the last in line. It featured a lean young man, one with wavy brown hair and an aura of superiority. It was unmistakably a picture of Sebastian Cobb.

The plaque confirmed it—sort of. It read *Sebastian Markeville.* So...who the hell were the Markevilles? A long-lived crime family that had kept their efforts hidden over the years? Or had Cobb—Markeville, rather—split from family tradition, using his wealth to launch a career of a decidedly illegal persuasion?

I heard a cough and a loud hawk around the corner. I nearly jumped.

"Gods, I'm bored."

Another voice. "You signed up for this. What did you expect?"

"Not to play babysitter, that's for sure. Everyone else is out there, gettin' shit done. I mean, this is the night! And we're stuck here doing nothing."

"It's safer in here. Drier, too."

The first voice snorted. "The rain don't bother me. In fact, I think I'm gonna go have a smoke."

"Really?"

"Like I said. You okay on your own for a few?"

"Don't take long. You know how the boss feels about slacking off. Best not be lying about the rain, either. He'll smell the smoke on the upholstery."

"Yeah, yeah."

I heard a squeak of a chair, and I panicked, realizing I should've hid. As it was, my options were limited. I darted behind a set of drapes, hoping beyond hope the approaching guard wouldn't notice the awkward bulge and set of feet protruding from beneath them.

Footsteps came and went, and I breathed a sigh of relief—or I would've if I weren't worried about making noise. As it was, I counted to sixty before sneaking out from behind my cover.

I crept to the hallway's edge and peered around the corner, catching a glimpse of another nondescript tough sitting in a chair, idly rolling a heavy club between his fingers. Like the thugs who'd guarded my room, a lantern stood on a desk beside him, but Kyra hadn't come by to extinguish it.

I pulled back and considered my options. I could rush him. He looked alert, but I was pretty sure I could win, even with my left hand in the condition it was. I doubted I could silence him before he could yell for help, though, and unfortunately, I had no idea how many guys patrolled the manor's halls. I needed a quieter option. Something sneaky.

Years of reading mystery novels had taught me the best way to get someone's attention was with a whistle, ideally a birdlike one that sounded natural in occurrence. The only problem was I couldn't whistle to save my life. Shay had tried to teach me. Claimed it was simple, but I'd never managed it. The real question, though, was could I whistle to save *another's* life? With the fingers of my right hand curled around the brass knuckles, I put my lips together and blew.

I didn't whistle, but I did squeak out what sounded like an intermittent fart.

I heard the thugs's voice from around the corner. "That you, Chuck?"

On a whim, I tried again. This time, the sound was wetter if no less flatulent.

The goon's voice again. "What the *hell* is that?"

The chair squeaked, and I heard him approach. Gods, I couldn't believe it actually worked!

I waited patiently.

"Chuck, what are you—"

I blasted the thug in the side of the face as he turned the corner, hearing a crunch of bone as I made impact. He groaned and toppled, but I caught hold of him before he hit the floor, putting him in a headlock and squeezing tight. He only gurgled for a second or two before going quiet.

As silently as I could, I dragged him to the chair. I blew out the lantern's flame. Darkness had aided me thus far, and I planned on keeping it that way. Then I tested the handle of the door behind the thug's chair. Locked.

I checked my unconscious friend's pockets, where I found another key ring. My eyes were still readjusting to the darkness, but it looked the same as the ring I'd taken from my first jailer.

I started testing keys in the lock. Nothing on the first two. Upon trying the third, I heard a click.

My heart jumped into my throat. With trembling hands, I turned the handle and pushed in.

The darkness inside suffocated. If the room contained any windows, they were hidden behind heavy drapes. I heard the whistle of wind and the patter of rain, but nothing else.

A swish of air filled my ears. An explosion of pain erupted from the side of my head, and I tumbled to the floor.

30

R ed spots danced in the darkness in front of my eyes, and I grunted as a weight crushed me. Something sharp pressed against my neck, and I heard a voice.

"Don't move. Don't say a word of I'll cut you from ear to ear."

I blinked, the spots slowing their twirl. "Shay?"

Her outline began to take shape in the darkness. "*Jake?* Oh, gods..."

The sharp tool at my neck disappeared, clattering across the floor as Shay tossed it away. The knee against my chest lifted, and her arms enveloped me. "Gods, Jake, why didn't you say anything? I thought you were one of them."

I put my arms around her. Her breath warmed the crook of my neck. The tenderness and strength of her curves pressed against me. Her chest swelled as she breathed. Her scent filled my lungs. Not her lilac perfume—that was a faint memory—rather the purest scent of her, her natural smell, her aura of power and independence and femininity. I took a wracking breath and sighed, feeling a trickle on my cheek. My own, I think.

"Jake? Are you okay? Talk to me."

"Yes. I'm okay. I am now, anyway. Though physically, I've been better. Mentally, too. Gods, Shay, I was worried. I shouldn't have been. I mean, look at you. You can take care of yourself. I know you can, and the Captain made sure to tell me that. But I couldn't help it. I was petrified. I was a mess. But I'm okay now. You're here. *We're* here." I took another deep breath, trying to calm my frayed nerves.

"That's not true," she said. "About taking care of myself. I've been a wreck, too. The only things keeping me sane have been tearing this room apart in search of weapons and knowing you'd come for me sooner or later. I need you, Jake. I always have."

I felt her lips on mine, and we kissed. It wasn't what some might consider a passionate kiss. Our lips barely parted, and our tongues didn't meet. But it was a long kiss. Slow and tender. Our cheeks brushed against each other, both of them slippery. I wasn't the only one crying.

Shay finally pulled back. "Thank you for coming, Jake. And sorry for putting another dent in your skull."

"Water under the bridge," I said. "I wouldn't have expected anything less from you. Besides, the cumulative effects of brain injuries don't pile up until your later years. I'll be fine for now."

Shay rolled off and kneeled next to me, wiping her cheeks in the murky blackness. "Right. I suppose we should get moving. Where are Rodgers and Quinto?"

I sat up, my head still aching, along with most of my other body parts. "No idea. Kyra suggested they were still cleaning up the mess at the King's Theater."

"*Kyra?*" I couldn't make out her face, but I imagined Steele was giving me one of her raised eyebrow looks.

"Right," I said. "How much do you know?"

"Painfully little. But that ogre who the tattoo artist at Thicker Than Water described to us? You'll never guess who it is."

"Bonesaw," I said. "I'm way ahead of you. It's not your fault. A lot's happened since you were abducted."

"Fill me in, then."

"We're not out of the woods yet, but I can give you the quick and dirty version. Bonesaw's running with a new gang by the name of the Winds of Change, and they seem to be run by none other than Sebastian Cobb."

"The recruiter who you interfaced with during the Wyverns case?"

"The very same. Except his name isn't Cobb. It's Markeville. Apparently this is his estate—we're somewhere in Brentwood, by the way. I'm still putting together the pieces, but after he escaped following our bust of the Wyverns, it would seem he doubled down on his desire to head one of New Welwic's gangs. He rebranded his operation and set up a meeting with the heads of the city's most powerful organized crime operations. And he killed them all. Every last one. Sprung a trap on them in the heart of the abandoned King's Theater. It was a massacre, of sorts."

"Of sorts?"

"It was a bloodless affair. Markeville sicced his basilisk on them. Froze them in an instant."

"His *what?*"

"Basilisk," I said. "The mythical creature that can turn a person to stone with a glance? It doesn't petrify people, per se, but it does kill them, and cause rigor mortis to set in unnaturally quickly, as we found out following Cairny's analysis at my place."

"This isn't the time to be screwing with me, Daggers."

"I'm not. I should know. I fought the thing and won. Ripped its stomach open with a knife before dropping a body on it from four stories high. It was one tough son of a bitch. Messed my left hand up something good."

Shay took my hand in hers. I winced. "Careful."

"Daggers, you need medical attention."

"I know, but I haven't exactly had an opportunity to get any. I only woke up from a fist induced coma a half hour ago."

"They captured you, too?"

I nodded. "Kyra sprung me. Remember the elf thief who was trying to join the Wyverns alongside me and Bonesaw? I managed to recruit her help...somehow."

"*Somehow?*"

"Don't get jealous. She's into me, but the feeling's not mutual. She split as soon as she paid me back for saving her life."

"So we're on our own?" said Shay. "Still trapped in Cobb—I mean, Markeville's mansion?"

"Kyra and I have taken out three guards. One of them should be back momentarily. It's time to go."

Another peal of thunder sounded outside, distant but potent. Shay glanced toward her drapes. "Right. But Daggers? Before we go?"

"Yes?"

"I don't know what these Winds of Change goons are planning, but I don't think they're done. Bonesaw's the one who abducted me—I can fill you in later—but before dumping me here, he mentioned they'd capture you as well. Apparently the guys who came after you last night were only supposed to knock you around before kidnapping you. Regardless, Bonesaw said he'd wait to kill us until after they showed us something. Something big."

"Markeville insinuated the same when he captured me," I said. "Claimed I was too late. We'll figure it out later. Right now we need to get out of the frying pan. Need a weapon?"

Shay bent over and picked up a length of steel. "I'll stick with this one. Worked pretty well the first time."

"Only too well. Come on. Let's find a way out."

I moved to the door and checked for intruders. Hearing nothing, I motioned for Steele to follow and set back along my path toward the stairs. I imagined I could find an exterior door or accessible window from somewhere along the hallway.

I paused halfway along the stretch of Markeville portraits, holding an arm out to keep Steele from crashing into me.

I heard footsteps. Heavy ones, coming our way.

31

I pushed Steele back the way we'd come. "Back, *back!*" I said in a hushed voice.

I was too late.

"Well, well, well." Bonesaw's booming voice echoed down the hallway, crashing into us like an ocean swell. "Look what the cat dragged in—or let out of its cage, I should say."

I froze in my tracks. "You ought to steer clear of metaphors, Bonesaw. They're not your strong suit."

Lightning flashed. Long shadows splashed against the wall, including a massive black stain stretching from Bonesaw's shoulders. Darkness swallowed him back up, followed by a distant peal of thunder.

"You know, I've always liked you, Daggers," said Bonesaw. "That stunt you pulled in the King's Theater? Taking down eight of our guys and the boss's prized pet? I'll give it to you. It was impressive. Even when we were competing to get into the Wyverns, you had moxie. Flair. Creativity. That's rare in a cop. Maybe that's why I didn't see you for what you were until after the fact."

"Go," I whispered at Steele. *"Run."* Then louder, for Bonesaw's benefit. "Be honest, Bonesaw. You miss more than you catch. That's why guys like me have careers, relationships, and friends, and guys like you end up in prison."

Bonesaw held his hands to the sides. "And yet here I am. A prisoner no more."

"For how long?"

Shay whispered back. "I'm not running. I'm not leaving you."

Bonesaw moved a little closer. Fifteen feet. "I don't think the two of you've fully grasped what's going on yet. You think I don't understand metaphors? The Winds of Change? We aren't a gang. We're a coup, waiting to strike. And we're striking tonight."

"Shay," I hissed. Then louder again. "Speaking of which, we probably owe you some thanks. The gang unit will be happy to have five fewer crime operations within the city limits. Once we finish taking you down, we'll be up to six."

Bonesaw laughed, a powerful, malicious, booming sound that echoed off the walls. "Hah! You misunderstand me, Detective. I didn't say a takeover. I said a coup. The gangs were just the beginning."

"I'm staying, Daggers," whispered Steele behind me. "We're partners. I'm with you, for better or worse."

I couldn't fight her off. Not here. Not with Bonesaw bearing down on me. Besides, I didn't want to. I wanted to protect her, but I had to stop treating her like a liability. She might save my life. She had before, too many times to count.

I gave her a thumbs up behind my back. "The beginning of what, Bonesaw?"

"Everything," he said. "It'll be like the good old days. Remember when the Wyverns ran free, operating without restrictions? Maybe you're too young, but back then, the police took their cut and looked the other way. That's a decent system, but a costly one. We have a better one in mind. This time, your friends will be too afraid to say anything at all. They'll cower before us. The Winds of Change will own this city. It's a shame you won't be around to see it."

"We won't?" I said. "See, I got a different impression. That your boss, Markeville, wanted to keep us alive."

"He did. You hurt him, see. When you busted the Wyverns, he took it personal. Those dragons were the start of something special. An army that could bring the city to its knees. But the boss isn't like most men. He didn't pack it in at the first bump in the road. He hunkered down. Put his resources to work and found new soldiers for his army. The ones that would give him the edge he needed to effect meaningful change."

"I guess he chose wrong, then," I said. "Turns out his basilisks aren't too hard to kill once you know where to hit them."

"I wasn't only talking about the basilisk." Bonesaw crept toward the wall. Another flash of lightning lit the corridor. The chandelier above, the paintings at the wall, the suit of armor at Bonesaw's right. "Luckily for me, the boss is also the pragmatic sort. He won't be too bent out of shape upon hearing I had to kill you following your attempted escape."

I needed to put together a plan of attack with Shay, but I couldn't with Bonesaw bearing down on us and monologueing. I'd have to trust her, trust my own instincts, and hope for the best.

I gripped my brass knuckles in my right hand and shifted my weight to the balls of my feet. "You seem pretty confident about that, Bonesaw. You didn't fare so well the last time we went toe to toe."

"I've learned from my mistakes." Bonesaw pulled a poleaxe from the suit of armor's grip with a clang. "Besides, your half-troll friend isn't here to back you up, is he? All you've got this time is your skinny little elf bitch."

"I'm a half-elf," said Shay. "At least get it right, dumbass."

Bonesaw roared and lunged, swinging the poleaxe at chest level. I ducked and rolled, feeling a whoosh of air over me as Steele danced out of sight. Bonesaw tucked his poleaxe in and spun, whipping his foot at my head. I pulled it away just in time. His boot cracked the tile underneath with the force of his kick. I swore, scrambled to my knees, and dove. The blade of Bonesaw's axe sliced the void, cracking another tile with its impact.

I heard a heavy thwack. Bonesaw grunted, jabbing the butt of his axe in Steele's direction. The darkness turned her into an indistinct blur, but I heard her makeshift truncheon whistle through the air.

Bonesaw turned and lunged at me, jabbing with the pointed end of his polearm. I hopped back, slamming into the suit at the wall. A few pieces clattered to the floor around me. I ducked again as the blade flew through the air, crunching the suit's breastplate. I landed on a discarded shield, grabbed it, and rolled onto my back, catching Bonesaw's next swing square in its center. It rattled, shook, and split, the axehead protruding two inches through the metal.

Bonesaw roared and pulled back on the axe, ripping the shield from my grip like he might a sucker from a toddler. He swung the axe over his head, but Shay jumped on his back before he could bring it down, grabbing onto the axe pole for dear life.

I took the opportunity. I flipped onto my feet and launched myself into Bonesaw's midsection, brass knuckles first. A crunch of ribs met my fist.

Bonesaw didn't like that. He growled and slammed an arm into my side, sending me flying into the nearest wall. I groaned as the air left my lungs. My knuckles slipped from my grip, tinkling as they hit the floor.

Bonesaw reached over his back, latched onto Steele, and flipped her over him. She hit the ground with a crack.

"NO!" I stood and ran, pulling the knife from my jacket as I did so. Bonesaw aimed a boot at her head.

I hit him just in time. With his weight on one leg, my tackle sent us toppling to the ground. I used my momentum to drive the confiscated blade into the meat of his left arm.

This time, he roared in pain. He also lashed out, clubbing me in the head with his elbow. I tumbled across the floor. The blade ripped free from his arm. With my hands bloodied, I lost my grip. The knife clattered away, lost in the darkness.

His dark shadow descended on me. Huge hands wrapped around my neck, lifting me off the floor as if I were a rag doll. He whipped me though the air, slamming me into one of the nearby shelves. Books flew, and I had a brief sensation of *deja vu,* but at least when I'd collided with the bookshelf in my own apartment, I'd been in a position of greater power. Now I couldn't breath. Bonesaw's fingers were iron. My windpipe was being crushed into a diamond.

I sped a right hook at Bonesaw's face, but it bounced off harmlessly. I tried a jab with my left, only to have my fist scream in pain as the resulting jolt reverberated down my bite-ravaged hand.

Bonesaw grinned, his sneer a sickly yellow in the near darkness. "How does it feel, Daggers? How does it feel to *lose?*"

I saw movement. A dark blur. Then a brief flash caught in a stray moonbeam.

Shay screamed as she jumped on Bonesaw's back for a second time. I heard a wet slice. Blood splattered and hit me in the face. Bonesaw howled as my discarded blade sunk deep into his shoulder, right between his neck and clavicle.

His grip weakened to bronze, and I took advantage. I kicked out, landing a full-strength shin blow to his testicles. At the same time, Shay wrenched on the knife.

Bonesaw's hands vanished from my neck. I dropped to the floor, landing hard on my ass while he gurgled and tottered backwards, dropping to his knees. Books rained down around me, and I heard a slow creak.

"Crap!" I dove to the side as the bookshelf toppled and fell, striking Bonesaw square on the head as it crashed to the ground. Boards broke, something or *someone* groaned, and a cloud of dust sloughed off the top of the shelf.

I coughed and stood, massaging my neck. "Shay?"

The bookshelf creaked and shook. It rose off the ground, tipped, and toppled to the side. Bonesaw crawled out from under it, a dark sheen covering his face and neck. He reached up, gripped the knife that protruded from his shoulder, and yanked.

He cried out as it pulled free. "*Grahh!* Why I'm gonna—"

A rush of air swept past me, Shay at the helm. A weapon whistled through the air, catching Bonesaw in the middle of his cheek. Bone crunched, a wet, sickening sound, and he crashed to the floor like a four hundred pound sack of oranges.

Shay dropped the weapon and grabbed me by the arm. "What are you waiting for, Daggers? We need to get out of here!"

I spotted a flickering light in the distance. Now that I focused on it, I could hear shouts, too.

"What the hell was that?" I asked.

"The weapon? A mace."

"You found a *mace*?"

"On the suit of armor." Shay glanced up the hallway. "Daggers? *Come on!*"

"Right." Another lightning induced burst ripped through the corridor, searing an image of Bonesaw's mangled face into my memory, all red and black and bright white from the flash. I grabbed the mace and turned to the window. Glass shattered as I slammed the business end of the weapon through the pane. Another couple swings freed the remainder of the shards from the sill.

"After—"

Shay dove through the gap into the rainstorm outside.

"—you."

I jumped out after her and started running, angry shouts and flickering lamplight trailing us as we faded into the night.

32

A beat cop stepped forward as our rickshaw turned the corner toward the King's Theater's main entrance, waving and shouting at our driver.

"No way, pal! Active crime scene! Turn it around, now! Don't say a thing, just go."

A roaring brazier at his back cast him in shadows. A cap hid his blonde hair, protecting it from the incessant rain, but his voice and can-do attitude gave him away. "Phillips," I called as I hopped off the cart. "It's okay."

The young officer's eyes widened as he caught sight of me and the person who followed me off the rickshaw. "*Daggers*? Holy crap! *And Steele!*"

He took two quick steps toward us, arms outstretched as if he wanted to give us a hug, but stopped halfway. Likely he thought better of it—or he got his first good look at us.

He gaped. "Gods... You look like hell. I mean...sorry. No offense."

"None taken," said Steele. And there wasn't any. We'd taken good looks at each other. Soaked to the bone, bedraggled, with rips and tears in our clothing, splattered with blood, both ours and Bonesaw's. I still couldn't believe the rickshaw driver took a chance on us. Numerous others hadn't.

"Someone pay this man," I said, pointing to our driver as I headed toward the theater's entrance. "Double the asking rate. The Captain still here?"

"McCartney!" Phillips waved at another of the dozen cops patrolling the edge of the theater and pointed him toward our driver. "And yes, she is. The Captain. Here, I mean. Gods, Detectives. What happened?"

"And Quinto? Rodgers?" asked Steele.

"Still here, too," said Phillips.

"Take us to them."

I could tell Phillips wanted to know more, but he'd already asked once, and neither Steele's nor my tone invited further questions. The cops outside the theater noticed us as we approached. One of them nodded, eyes wide. Some of them murmured. And then the thoroughly unexpected happened.

They started cheering.

"Are you kidding me?"

"Hell yeah!"

"Daggers and Steele!"

"Give 'em hell, Detectives!"

I waved them down. "Alright, that's enough. Back to work. This night's far from over."

They simmered down, but only a little, their cheers following us as we passed through the King's front doors, into the lobby, and into the auditorium.

If I thought the front was well populated, the theater's interior put it to shame. Lanterns glowed all over, and people crawled along the aisles. Not just bluecoats; SWAT guys in black, CSU teams in white, even axe-carrying firefighters in khaki and crimson. White sheets dotted the landscape, some of them stained dark with red splotches, tens of them, but there weren't enough. A good dozen more toughs lay dead, beaten and bloody, free to the world to see. There must've been close to forty in the auditorium alone.

"Whoa," said Steele.

Phillips nodded as he led us down an aisle. "No kidding. Last I heard, the Captain and them had moved back to the orchestra pit. There's a, uh...well I don't even know how to describe it."

"A room full of dead gangsters, frozen stiff as boards?" I said. "Yeah, I know. What do you mean, moved back?"

"Well, there's..." Phillips spread his arms. "I mean, it's everywhere. Dead guys up front. In the pit. More in the back. Plus this crazy lizard thing—"

"A basilisk," said Steele.

"A what now?"

"I'll explain later," I said.

We reached the theater's front row, and Phillips led us down a ladder into the orchestra pit. Someone had hacked a hole in the makeshift barrier that had previously separated the pit from the auditorium, maybe one of the firemen or one of the thugs during the fighting that had taken place. Voices and flickering lights leaked out from within.

I stepped through the hole and found it much the same as I remembered it: cold, creepy, and full of dead gang leaders and their bodyguards. There were a few familiar, warm-blooded faces inside, as well.

Phillips cleared his throat. "Ah...Captain?"

Knox turned, her face drawn and her arms crossed. Her eyes turned into saucers as she looked past Phillips to us.

"Oh, thank heavens!" She ran to us, wrapping Shay and me in as wide a hug as she could muster. Her fierce grip belied her small stature, but it was still an awkward embrace, and not only because I'd never seen the Captain so outwardly emotional. Also because she only came up to my ribs.

Quinto, Rodgers, and Cairny knelt over a trio of bodies. It was Rodgers who first noticed us. "Daggers! Steele!"

Before I knew it, we'd been mobbed, our Captain-centric hug expanding to include everyone. Arms enveloped me. Hands grasped me on the shoulders and patted me on the back.

"Holy harvest, it's good to see you, Daggers!"

"Gods, Steele, are you okay?"

"You're a sight for sore eyes, the pair of you."

"Alright," I said. "Ease it up, will you? We're happy to see you too, but I've got bruises on top of bruises here."

The crew gave us space. The Captain adjusted her jacket and nodded. "Right. Sorry about that. You'll forgive us for our outbursts, Detectives. We were afraid you might be, well...you know."

"You assumed that without a body? Come on, Captain. You're selling us short. Steele especially, given how much confidence you expressed in her during her absence." I glanced at my partner. "You were right about her, by the way. She saved my life. *Again.*"

"I wouldn't have needed to if you'd been more focused during our fight with Bonesaw. I still don't know why you just stood there at the end."

"I'm not sure," I said. "Maybe I was out of it after he nearly choked me to death. Seeing him rise from underneath that bookcase and pull the knife from his shoulder was like seeing a zombie rise from the grave."

"So you were right," said Quinto. "Bonesaw was behind this. He's the one who abducted you?"

"Yes and no," I said. "He was involved, but he wasn't in charge. He was working for someone else."

"*Was?*" said Rodgers.

"I'm, ah...not sure he made it," I said. "Steele might've broken his skull. We didn't hang around to give him a physical."

Cairny blinked. "Dang, Shay. That's cold-blooded."

"It was him or us," Shay said. "I don't feel much remorse."

"So if Bonesaw wasn't in charge," said the Captain, "who is?"

"Sebastian Cobb," I said. "Or rather, Sebastian Markeville. You probably won't recognize the name, Captain, but he was my contact with the Wyverns during the case preceding your arrival at the Fifth. Obviously, he was never captured when we busted the Wyverns and their dragon hatching operation. At the time, I didn't have any reason to believe he was more than what he'd claimed to be, but I always had a sneaking suspicion he was more involved than advertised. And hoo-boy, was I ever right. He's the head guy, at least he is of this new gang. They call themselves the Winds of Change."

"I don't know Cobb," said Knox, "but Markeville rings a bell. A wealthy donor by the name of William Markeville. Gave a lot of money to the department over the years, but that was a long time ago. Twenty or more years back, if I recall."

"Right around when the Wyverns were active, I imagine," I said. "I wasn't sure if Sebastian was a first generation crook or not. Now I'm guessing not. Perhaps he's more audacious in the endeavor than his forebears, though."

Knox nodded. "Tell me everything."

"I'd be happy to," I said. "But could we get some towels? And a medic? I'm in a fair amount of pain."

Knox snapped at Phillips. "Officer?"

The young man's face dropped, but he scampered off, regardless of how fiercely he wanted to hear my tale of derring-do.

I took a seat and started with my descent into the sewers. It was an odd feeling. Sitting there, talking casually, surrounded by dead bodies, but all sense of normality had long since abandoned me. I'd killed a basilisk with a knife and a dead body dangling from a rope, for crying out loud.

As I talked, Cairny inspected me. She wasn't technically a medical doctor, but she knew enough about what could kill people to provide a diagnosis. I winced while describing the state I'd found the room we now sat in, and Cairny interrupted me during my description of the fight with the eight goons and the basilisk to inform me I'd probably broken a pair of metacarpals, something I already suspected.

I finished with the events at Markeville's manor, including Kyra's unexpected assist and springing Steele from her cage. "...and once we got out, that's when Bonesaw intercepted us again. As I already mentioned, it didn't end well for him."

The Captain, Rodgers, and Quinto had listened carefully throughout my report. The Captain in particular looked somber.

"We found the basilisk, as you already know," she said. "We weren't sure what it was, but Detective Quinto had his suspicions. You're certain Mr. Markeville was only in command of one?"

"No," I said. "But the way he reacted to her death implied it."

Knox nodded. "That's good. I can't imagine the destruction that beast could've caused if let loose. We're lucky as is that *this* is the worst that happened."

"With all respect, Captain, I don't think we're out of the woods yet."

She shot a furrowed brow in my direction. "No?"

"Markeville said I hadn't stopped him. Said I couldn't end what he'd already put in motion. That I was too late. I don't think it was an idle boast."

"Is this more than a hunch?"

"Bonesaw told me the same," said Steele. "That his boss was keeping me alive to show us something terrible down the line. Bonesaw repeated the same suggestion before we dealt with him."

"Ah...excuse me? Captain?"

I turned to see Phillips at the entrance, holding a stack of white cotton bath towels. They looked thin and scratchy, but they weren't covered in blood. Another officer stood at his back, one I didn't recognize.

Knox waved him forward. "Bring them here. And the medic?"

"About that..." said Phillips.

The officer stepped forward. "Sir? We need to talk."

"It can wait," said Knox. "What do you mean, you couldn't find a medic? Surely there's one here. Daggers needs attention. I'd like to have Detective Steele checked, too."

The officer persisted. "Sir, this can't wait."

"Spit it out, then," said Knox. "Make it quick."

"The district attorney, Captain," he said. "He's dead."

33

We sped past the city courthouse, its marble columns and shallow triangular topper still shining in the darkness of night, made bright white by the occasional flash of lightning. Phillips' towels had provided only a brief respite, as the rain continued to fall, whipping around on an unnaturally strong breeze. With a clatter, we pulled to a stop before a tall apartment building that stretched toward the angry sky overhead.

Shay and I hopped out of our cart, followed shortly by Quinto and Cairny in theirs, Rodgers and Captain Knox, and Phillips and the new guy, Officer Turtledove from the Grant Street Precinct. A couple of beat cops stood in the rain, a hearty bruiser and a heavyset one with a beard, none other than Poundstone and Gorman. They waited outside the apartment complex's front door, but they didn't brave the weather in an effort to flag us down or out a misguided sense of idealism. They were guarding the corpse.

I found it face down on the concrete, surrounded by a pool of blood that was slowly being washed into the street by rain. For some reason, I imagined I'd find the DA as I'd seen him before, clad in an impeccable suit, wearing imported leather shoes and with his hair carefully combed with mousse, but death hadn't spared him the indignity it did anyone else. He lay there in a white t-shirt and underpants, his hair plastered to his skull by the rain, his body broken and bent in impossible directions.

I cursed under my breath as the Captain pushed past me. She knelt next to the body, stretched out a hand, and touched the side of the man's face. "Oh, James..."

She'd known him better than any of the rest of us. Far better. As a general rule, the Captain didn't go out of her way to make friends. She didn't want to spread a sense of favoritism among her charges, no matter how benign the interaction might be. The fact that she came to Quinto's engagement party was surprising enough. He must've told her his intentions beforehand, despite whatever she'd said to the contrary. But District Attorney James Flint had been an exception. They'd had lunch on occasion, shared stories, and if the precinct's bi-monthly bulletin blasts were at all accurate, traded ideas on how to improve the quality of policing and the effectiveness of prosecution. I imagine she viewed him as more than a co-worker.

We stood there in silence, giving the Captain her moment to grieve. Lightning flashed again in the distance, and the peal of thunder crashed over us a few seconds later. The rain continued to fall, pattering relentlessly against the pavement. At least the summer warmth prevailed.

I thought I heard a sniff, and the Captain lifted a hand. "Coroner Moonshadow? If you would?"

Cairny stepped forth and kneeled next to the Captain, her hair turned into a midnight black waterfall by the rain. She pressed a couple fingers to the DA's neck, inspected his knee, tested his elbow, and rotated his head to get a look at the side facing the pavement.

"Injuries are consistent with a high velocity impact," she said. "What story did he live on?"

"The top one," said Captain Knox. "Sixth floor."

Cairny nodded. "It's hard to tell due to the rain, but based on the amount of blood and its radius from his body, he probably died on impact. I'm sorry, Captain."

Knox nodded, her face an emotionless mask. "Coroner Moonshadow? Stay here with the body. You too, Detective Quinto. Treat it as you would any other possible murder victim. Officer Turtledove? If you could arrange for transportation of the deceased? The rest of you, come with me."

The Captain pushed into the building's lobby, where a small crowd had gathered, staring at the scene in the rain-soaked darkness outside. One of them asked what happened, while another asked if he'd been pushed, but the Captain ignored them and headed to the stairwell, as did the rest of us.

I wasn't sure what I should say, or even *if* I should say anything. The Captain wasn't the outspoken sort. Far from it. She played everything close to the vest. Her hug at the King's Theater had been the greatest emotional outburst I'd ever seen out of her. But the way she strode up those stairs, quiet and purposeful—it worried me. Nobody was *that* good at keeping their feelings in check. Something brewed underneath her calm exterior. Something dangerous.

Apparently, no one else knew what to say to the Captain either. We arrived at the sixth floor breathing harder but otherwise in silence. We followed Knox to the end of the hallway, where we found the door to Flint's apartment thrown open.

We walked in cautiously. My hand itched, and I wished I'd gone into the back of the King's Theater to retrieve Daisy, though I knew I wouldn't need her. Not now, anyway.

Flint's apartment was of the modern, open variety. Doors on the left-hand side offered teasing glimpses into the bedrooms, but the kitchen, dining room, and sitting room had been combined into a long central space, adorned with mahogany, leather upholstery, and imported rugs. A pair of bookcases lined the walls, their shelves filled with thick legal texts, though I didn't see a desk anywhere. Perhaps one of the rooms to the side was an office rather than a bedroom.

All in all, the place appeared pristine—or at least the half closest to the entrance did. On the far side, wind whistled into the apartment through shattered floor-to-ceiling windows, the rugs at the edge of the floor damp and flattened.

We shuffled in. On second glance, I noticed a few things out of place. Pillows knocked from the sofa to the floor. A crack in the glass coffee table. A rug at a skewed angle. What I didn't notice was any damage to the floors.

"No claw marks on the wood," I said.

"*Claw marks?*" said Steele.

"From the basilisk. I noticed them at my place when I returned earlier today. It left them at the theater, too."

The Captain grunted. "Would've been hard to get one of those creatures up so many stairs without notice. But it's good news, I suppose."

Shay approached the broken windows. "Notice that?"

"Notice what?" I said.

"No crunching," she said, inching closer to the edge. "There are hardly any glass shards on the floor. I didn't notice any on the sidewalk either."

"Meaning what, exactly?" said Rodgers. "I can't imagine whoever threw DA Flint through his windows stopped to clean up after themselves."

Shay shook her head. "They wouldn't have needed to if the force of the throw carried them out. And it would've been quite the blow to carry the glass shards past the sidewalk to the road beyond. A concussive force. Yet the apartment seems fine."

"Daggers," said the Captain. "When you got knocked from your apartment last night, how was it you described the sensation?"

"Trust me, I'm seeing the parallels." I approached the windows, walking slowly. Heights didn't particularly bother me, but falling to my death did.

"We should probably knock on doors," said Rodgers. "See if anyone got a glimpse at whoever did this."

"I think we can safely skip that step," I said, peering over the edge. "If it wasn't Markeville, it was one of his lackeys. I don't see how this can't be related."

"Even if it isn't, it's in our best interest to assume it is," said Knox. "After what happened at the King's Theater, Markeville is wanted for the deaths of over fifty people. New Welwic hasn't seen a day this deadly since the St. Clementine's square massacre."

I gazed at the sky, an inky mass of angry clouds, shrouded by darkness and rain. "And it's not over yet..."

"So Markeville's at the top of our most wanted list," said Rodgers. "The question is, how do we track him? Daggers, you obviously lost him after Bonesaw knocked you unconscious. Steele, did you see him at the home he'd imprisoned you in?"

My partner shook her head. "I never saw him at all. Daggers clued me into his involvement. But we know where his residence is. We should send a team there immediately. Who knows what clues we can find as to his whereabouts."

"Clues, maybe," said Knox. "But not him. Not tonight. If his threats were sincere, then he has major plans. Call it a hunch, but I doubt Eric is the only one he's targeted."

"Then we need to figure out his motives," said Rodgers. "If we guess those, we can predict his next strikes. So is he out to cause chaos? Or is he focused on a more discrete goal?"

"Bonesaw said Markeville was going to make the city cower before them," said Shay. "Taking out the gangs must've been part of that, but this is a bigger piece. Targeting the police. Me and Daggers. District Attorney Flint. Maybe the rest of the justice system, too. The city government. The military, even, though I don't know how he'd have the strength."

Lightning flashed, showering the city in a bright white light, like that from one of Sherman Industries' electrical globes. My eyes widened.

"Maybe all of the above," I said. "But his next target might not be our biggest concern."

"What are you talking about?" said Knox. "Saving lives is always our greatest priority."

I waved everyone to the windows and pointed to the south. "Wait for another lightning strike."

It took a minute before the skies acquiesced to my request, but when they did it was with an eye-popping blast that sent shadows streaking to the horizon in three of the cardinal directions. The view to the south was obstructed, however, blocked by a giant, swirling cloud, gray and angry with muscular arms spiraling inward toward an opaque cone.

A cyclone. And it was headed toward the city.

34

Rain lashed us without mercy, the wind's powerful gusts pushing us to the side as we raced toward the city's shore. Our rickshaw drivers had abandoned us, all but one who'd helped Cairny take District Attorney Flint's body to the morgue, leaving Quinto, Shay, Rodgers, and the rest of us to our fate at the hands of the elements.

Lightning flashed and thunder rent the air as we reached Shoreline Avenue. Then again, and again, a series of blasts, all of them originating within the cyclone's churning maelstrom. Electricity crackled among the clouds, some of it arcing into the ocean below, other bursts sizzling and rippling through the dark clouds. Even at a distance, the cyclone glowed from within, an ominous purple hue. Despite the darkness, the sky had acquired a gangrenous tinge.

I stood staring at the storm, the trees at the edge of the road swaying and groaning, their leaves creating a white noise softer and more uniform than the relentless hammering of raindrops. Not a square inch of me was dry. My hair lay plastered against my face. Wind buffeted me, howling in anger.

The Captain shouted behind me. "How could we have missed this? These storms are slow developing. We see them coming. Sailors bring word. They give us time to prepare, to shelter."

"Doesn't matter, does it, Captain?" said Quinto. "It's headed toward land, whether we like it or not."

She must've agreed. "We need every officer we can muster. It's too late to evacuate the coast, but we'll needs hands to help in recovery. There'll be flooding. Wind damage. Buildings might come crashing down."

I glanced down the avenue. The streets were empty, cleared as much by the late hour as by the weather. Could people really be sleeping through the storm? If they hadn't known it was coming, perhaps. A cyclone hadn't struck New Welwic since I was a small child. Why would anyone suspect the wind was due to anything but a thunderstorm?

"But Captain," shouted Phillips into the wind. "We're stretched to the limit! The majority of the Fifth's still at the King's Theater. We're down to reserves."

"Then we'll bring what we can and ask for assistance with what we can't," said the Captain. "Officer Turtledove. Get back to Grant Street. Raise everyone you can. Tell them to wake everyone who's still asleep. Phillips. I want you to race as fast as you can to the New Welwic Main base. Make sure the army boys are on their way, if they're not already. Tell them to bring wagons, sand, shovels, the works. We're going to need it. If anyone asks, you tell them the mayor declared a state of emergency."

"But the mayor hasn't done any such thing, has he?" said Phillips.

"By the gods, he will have by the time the night is over," said Knox. "Now go!"

Phillips and Turtledove took off at a run.

"What about the rest of us Captain?" said Rodgers. "You know we're willing, but there's not a lot we can do against something of this magnitude."

Rodgers had it right. What could we do against so much rain, against hurricane force winds? Against *winds of change.*

Sometimes I could be so obtuse.

"Maybe there's nothing *we* can do," I said, turning away from the furious storm and back toward the others. "But there may be something *someone* can do."

"We're all ears, Detective," said the Captain.

"You're right," I said, shouting into the wind. "We shouldn't have missed a storm like this. We would've seen it coming. But this isn't a normal storm. I'm not an expert, but from what I understand, cyclones are big. Slow moving. This thing's anything but. We should've been drenched a day ago. Instead, this didn't hit until a few hours ago. It's unnatural."

"And yet here it is," said Knox. "It's improbability doesn't make it any less real."

"That's not what I mean," I said. "Markeville's gang. He named it the Winds of Change. When he confronted me following my fight at the theater, he said to me, 'The Winds of Change have arrived—and they are blowing.' I thought it was a corny one-liner, but..."

"Hold on," said Steele, pointing at the storm. "You're saying you think Markeville is *responsible* for that thing?"

"He had a basilisk as a pet. I'm not putting it past him."

"If it's magically driven," said Knox, "then we might be able to fight back."

"Exactly. We need to rally the city's witches and wizards. The Smarties." Technically, they were called the Strategic Magical Response Teams, or SMRTs, but Smarties sounded so much better.

"I can't authorize them," said the Captain. "We'll need the chief of police to give the order."

"We're already getting the mayor to declare a state of emergency, aren't we?"

The Captain set her jaw. "You're damned right we are. Shouldn't be too hard to get ahold of him. As a matter of fact..." The Captain paused, her eyes widening. "Oh, gods! How could I be so stupid!"

"What is it, Captain?" asked Steele.

"The chief," she said. "He lives on the coast, less than a mile from here. The storm's headed right for him."

It validated every piece of conjecture I'd already thought up—the importance of the storm, its magical nature, Markeville's plans—but I didn't have time to pat myself on the back. We took off at a run. Shay, Rodgers, Quinto, and I quickly outpaced the Captain, but she shouted the address at us and told us to keep going.

The wind pushed us into the street as we ran, rain whipping and swirling. The trees at the roadside gave way to a wall of vegetation, dense thickets of seagrape and holly trimmed into hedges. Then I spotted the first of the homes, modest two story structures made ludicrously expensive by virtue of their location. We passed a gate set between the bushes, then another. I wiped rainwater out of my eyes as I searched for the street numbers, my breath starting to come heavy.

As I looked, an orc with rain-slicked hair and a guy in a dark raincoat burst from one of the gates, running into the street perpendicular to our own. It couldn't be a coincidence.

My heart dropped as images of the DA flashed before my eyes, but I didn't let it slow me. "Rodgers! Quinto! Get those two! Shay and I'll check on the chief."

Quinto nodded, and the two of them sprinted after the pair with a renewed burst. I skidded around the open gate and kept going toward the home. The front door stood open, so I ran up the porch steps and hopped inside, Steele hot on my heels.

My heart pounded in my chest, and I took a deep, gulping breath. "Police! Anyone here?"

The house was dark as a cave. The wind howled, and rain lashed against the roof, battering it without mercy.

Shay yanked on my sleeve. "Upstairs. I heard a shout!"

I knew better than to question her elven senses. She pulled me onto a yawning black staircase, and up we went. I followed Steele, unaware of anything but the violent whine and roar of the storm, but she knew where she was headed. Her eyesight beat mine by a mile. It was how she'd found the weapons while we'd fought Bonesaw, no doubt.

We stumbled into a bedroom, its belly as dark as the rest of the house. In the center, a dark mass wriggled and moaned. Three dark masses. An adult woman, and two teens. Tied together, gagged and blindfolded.

I heard sobbing, but the woman must've heard us. She became hysterical, gurgling and moaning from behind her gag. Shay pulled her blindfold off as I knelt down to look at the ropes.

"They have him!" she shouted as Shay pulled the bundled rag from her mouth. "Oh, gods, they took him! You have to save him. Please!"

"They took your husband? The chief?" said Steele. "Who did? Where?"

I took the blindfolds and gags off the teens, who continued to shake and cry.

"I don't know," she said, her voice cracking. "We were asleep. They surprised us. Two of them, a man and an orc. I woke up to a yell. My husband's. They struck him in the head and came after me, blinding and gagging me before tying me here with our children."

"When was this?" asked Steele.

"What do you mean?" asked the woman. "Just now. Do something! They have him!"

"Daggers..." said Shay. "Those men. They didn't have him."

"I know," I said.

"What are you talking about? Please, get us out of here!"

I found the knots, but they were cinched tight. I wished I'd kept either of the blades from my earlier fights. "I can't get the ropes off. Got a knife?"

"My husband's and my room. Down the hall on the left. Under the right hand side of the bed, clipped into the frame."

I stood. "Be right back."

"Daggers." Shay stood and put her hand on my arm. "The screaming. It wasn't her. I still hear it."

"Maybe he's here," I said. "Keep your eyes and ears peeled. We might not be alone."

I stumbled into the hallway and hooked a left into another room. The bed loomed large in front of me. I knelt and felt underneath the edge, finding the hidden blade and pulling it free. The wind continued to howl, even louder now, and rain spattered against my face.

I looked up, blade in hand. On the far side of the bed, a glass door stood open. Wind and rain whistled their way through, but beyond the crash and howl of the storm, I could hear it, too. The shouts.

I stepped onto the balcony outside and scanned the yard. The churning cyclone continued to glow, closer now, still crackling with latent electricity, but I couldn't see anything in the yard. Nothing but trees and seagrass.

I heard it again, distinct this time. A shout for help. But from where?

Lightning flashed, illuminating the darkness. Still nothing, then the crash of thunder and another shout.

Gods, where was he? I looked around again, to the left, to the right, then up. Lightning flashed, and I finally saw him.

There at the top of the house, strapped to a massive iron cross, sagged the chief of police.

The lightning flashed again. Much closer this time.

35

"Gods, almighty..." I turned and raced to the bedroom with Shay and the chief's family. The chief's wife was sobbing when I returned.

"Find anything?" asked Steele.

I slipped the edge of the knife under the ropes and started sawing. "Listen to me, ma'am. It's going to be okay. Go downstairs. Take your children with you. Captain Beverley Knox of the Fifth Street Precinct will be there momentarily. Detective Steele and I are going to take care of your husband."

Hemp tore, and the ropes fell.

"You found him?" she asked.

"Downstairs, please. Shay, with me!"

I darted into the hallway and back out to the balcony. Shay followed me closely, but as soon as we stepped outside, she cocked her head. "There. I hear it."

I pointed as another flash and boom rent the sky. "Up there."

Shay's jaw dropped. "Oh, no..."

"Give me a boost," I said.

I tucked the knife into my pants, stepped onto the balcony railing, reached up, and grabbed the edge of the roof. Shay cupped her hands and brought them to chest level. "What can I do?"

"Stay here," I said. "Once I free him, I'll slide him your way. He looks in rough shape. Who knows if he can walk."

Another bolt of lightning crashed. A shower of sparks flew from a tree a few homes down the block. I heard wood splinter.

"Quickly, Daggers!"

"I know."

I planted a foot in Shay's hands, pushed off, and pulled with my good hand. Up I went, stepping off the drainpipe and onto the roofing tile. I lifted a leg, planted a boot, slipped, and fell.

I flopped onto the tiles, landing hard on my stomach. My hand cried out as the shock reverberated through my body, and I might've cried out in the more literal sense as well. My body began to slide, but I caught a boot on the drain and held firm.

Shay's voice carried on the wind. "*Daggers? You okay?*"

"Fine," I shouted.

"I'm coming up."

"Too late." I stumbled to my feet, digging my toes into the inclined surface as best I could. I took the ascent one step at a time, steadying myself with both hands, ignoring the pain in my left. The wind pushed hard at my back, but at least it mostly pushed me up the roof, not down.

The police chief watched me as I rose toward him, one eye half-closed and swollen, his face slicked from rain and blood. "Who are you?"

"Detective Jake Daggers, sir." I almost slipped again, but fell to a knee instead of to my belly. "I'm going to get you out of this."

"My family," he said. "Where are they?"

"Safe," I said as I made it to the top. "Unharmed, down below."

Lightning ripped through the darkness, almost blinding me with its ferocity. The thunderclap slammed into me simultaneously, and a nervous shiver rippled down my spine. I glanced at the skies. The swirling gray arm above us crackled with malice.

"Better hurry the hell up, Detective," said the Captain.

"Yes, sir." I pulled the knife from my belt and went to work on the ropes, the same kind the thugs had used on the man's family. "Can you walk?"

"I think so. Those animals who broke in went to work on me. Roughed me up pretty bad, but I don't think anything's broken. Won't know until I—"

A flash blinded me, and I dropped my knife. A series of explosions rang out around me, four in quick succession, filling my ears with cacophonous sound. Pressure waves blasted me in the chest. My world rumbled, rattled, and shook. Dark spots swam in the infinite pools of white before me, and I fell.

It didn't last long. I landed with a squeak and a bounce rather than a thud. Debris rained down upon me, and I blinked, trying to regain my sight.

Somewhere beyond the incessant ringing I heard Shay's voice. *"Daggers?* Jake, are you okay?"

I shook, or rather someone shook me. A familiar hand.

Shay swam into focus before me, her face gray and chalky. "What the...?"

Rain pattered against my face through the gaping hole in the roof above me, and I felt something gritty on my tongue. Plaster dust, quickly turning into mud by the driving rain. Exposed wooden beams sizzled and hissed, and I smelled smoke.

Shay left my field of vision. I blinked and turned, finding I'd landed on the police chief's bed.

He hadn't been so lucky. He lay on the floor, surrounded by smoldering wooden planks and shattered roof tiles. He wasn't moving.

Shay knelt next to him, shouting. "Chief? Can you hear me?"

She shook his shoulder before bending over and putting her ear to his mouth. She pulled back, a frustrated look on her face, before placing her hand under his nose.

"Is he alive?" I asked.

Shay looked up. *"What?"*

I could barely hear her over the ringing in my ears. "IS HE ALIVE?"

She nodded. "He's breathing."

I heard a groan. Looking up, I spotted another of the home's support beams sagging. I rolled as it cracked, falling off the bed as the three hundred pound beam smashed into the mattress. I hit the floor, my shoulders, back, and hand screaming in agony, while the bed collapsed in the middle. A shower of sparks flew off the beam, hissing and steaming.

I followed the beam to the hole, taking note of the red orange glow and flickering flames licking at the roof's underside. The battering rains might've soaked the home's exterior, but the attic spaces were still nice and dry. Perhaps the home might've survived a single lightning strike, but *four*?

"We need to get out of here," I shouted. "Fast."

Shay nodded again. "If you take him under the shoulders, I can grab his feet."

The wind screamed, tearing at the hole in the roof above us, the flames from the spreading fire swirling and licking at the dry wood like a hungry demon's forked tongue.

I swallowed hard. "Right." The home's windows rattled and shook as I stumbled to my feet. I ignored the throbbing pains in my back, legs, and hand as I hooked my elbows under the chief's armpits. Shay took his knees, and together we lifted.

I made it one step toward the hall before I heard a high-pitched whine. An angry, swirling gust rushed through the hole in the roof, turned in mid-air, and slammed me square in the chest.

I managed to hold onto the chief, keeping his head from bouncing off the floorboards as I fell hard onto my bottom. I grunted as I hit, the air billowing through my shirt and jacket and filling my ears with a resounding *whoosh*.

Shay had fallen to her knees. Her eyes widened. "Holy—"

The high pitched whine cut her off again. The house creaked, and windows cracked and shattered. The wind screamed through us, back the other way, crushing us against the floor with its force.

As it whipped by, I saw it, surrounded by a swirl of rain droplets, smoke, choking dust, and steam: two small spheres, devoid of particulates, set evenly in the center of the pressurized mass over a yawning void.

A face in the wind. A howling maw.

I staggered to my feet, leaving the chief at the floor. "Shay! It's not just a cyclone. It's a creature! Some being of the—"

Back through the hole dove the spirit, pressing Shay against the floor and slamming me into the wall on its way to the stairs. The flames rippled and spread. Timbers groaned. Another beam fell to the floor, raining down alongside a half-dozen two by fours, singed at one end and licked by flames at the other.

"A wind sprite, or elemental," said Steele, pushing herself off the debris at the floor. "How in the world did Markeville convince one to do his bidding?"

"*How* is the least of our worries right now," I said.

The chief coughed and groaned. His eyes fluttered. "What in the..."

Flames licked the walls in the hallway now. Despite the rain and the wind, I could feel heat rippling through the air. The howling intensified again.

"Get down!" I cried.

The wind rushed up the stairs, howling and shrieking. It whipped around the upstairs, circling toward the windows before doubling back. It swirled in the center, creating a tiny cyclone of smoke and splinters and debris. Its howl adopted a menacing tone.

"To the balcony," I said. "We'll jump!"

I grabbed the chief under his arms and dragged him to his feet as he mumbled and looked about, staring into the flames. Shay took him under the shoulder on the opposite side, and we bolted, but not fast enough. The wind tore through us again, sending us toppling into the remains of the bed as it whipped through the open balcony windows.

"It's no use!" cried Shay. "It's trying to keep us here! To cook us alive!"

I blinked, forcing myself to focus. Shay was right. We needed a way out, but the wind elemental seemed intent on preventing that from happening. Outside of a direct lightning strike, maybe it couldn't kill us itself, but the house fire would do that for it soon enough. Already the smoke hung thick in the air. My lungs ached, strained as they had during the fight back at the King's Theater.

There had to be a way to distract it. Something I could do to push it back, at least long enough for Shay to drag the chief to safety.

The elemental refused to give me time to think. It rocketed back inside, howling as it punched me to the far side of the room. My wet jacket sizzled at it bounced off the burning wall. The sound of rushing air filled my ears as the thing spun in a circle in the middle of the room. Sweat poured off me as the heat intensified. Steam hissed. Flames crackled. And still the spirit spun, pushing in every direction with tendrils of unseen air.

"Watch out!"

Shay pushed the chief to the side as another beam cracked and fell, showing sparks into the whirling dervish. As the fire motes hissed and steamed, the creature's mouth distorted as if in fear, and its eyes widened.

I wasn't much of a scientist. My willingness to comprehend the natural world extended only as far as it affected me personally, meaning I had a good grasp on the effects of alcohol on the human body and knew that gravity, from the standpoint of falling three stories with another individual on top of you to maximize the impact, was bad. But Shay, having grown up in a scientific household, had forced me to learn more about the sciences. Biology. Chemistry. Physics. The lot of them. And though I had no idea what might be able to harm a wind elemental, I did know that heat caused things to expand—air, included.

I grabbed one of the flaming planks strewn across the floor and whipped it at the miniature cyclone in the middle of the room, half expecting it to be thrown back at me with nose-crunching force. But the elemental didn't touch it. The smoky, swirling haze parted around the flaming plank as it flew, where it smacked into the far wall along its initial trajectory, untouched.

"Follow me!" I cried as I picked up another burning brand. "Get the chief to the balcony!"

I lunged at the swirling twister of smoke and mist, swinging the flaming end of the wood into its midst with outstretched arms. The wind howled and whipped around, threatening to extinguish my brand, but the flames stubbornly held. I pushed forward, cutting swaths through the air with my makeshift torch, and the spirit danced back, warping away from each stroke of my fiery onslaught.

Sweat dripped down my face, from the heat of the bedroom as well as exhaustion. I wasn't sure how long I could keep up the effort, not at gods-knew what hour of the morning, not after being worked over by a group of power mad thugs and lackeys, not after tangoing with a hundred and fifty pound demon lizard, freeing myself from capture, and beating back the baddest ogre ever to break out of prison. But I had to keep fighting. I had to get Shay and the chief out of danger. I just hoped the wind elemental wouldn't realize I wasn't the biggest threat.

My torch was but a match compared to the raging campfire of the home around us, and yet the spirit seemed to fear *me*. Perhaps it didn't posses the ability for critical thought, but for whatever reason, fear me it did, and that gave me some measure of control.

"Daggers!"

Out of the corner of my eye, I saw Shay and the chief stumble onto the balcony. Tossing the brand at the gaping maw, I turned and ran.

Steele and the chief disappeared over the lip of the balcony and as I reached the doorway, but unfortunately for me, the wind elemental wasn't permanently cowed. A powerful blast of wind slammed into my back with a shriek, lifting me off my feet and sending me soaring. I rebounded off the top of the balcony railing, spun, and tumbled into the darkness of night.

I couldn't help but think about that whole gravity being bad bit as I tumbled through the air, and how Shay was supposed to be the prescient one...

36

I tucked my injured hand in close to my body before I slammed into the dirt. A bone-rattling, teeth-shaking jolt shivered through my body, and my head whipped and slammed against the earth.

Believe it or not, the earth gave. I stumbled to my hands and knees, spitting wet grit from between my teeth. Sand. Of course. Apparently, living at the coast contained a few ancillary advantages besides the view and nice breezes.

I heard an angry shriek and looked up. A whoosh of air streaked from the burning home, trailing smoke and ash and sparks as it rose into the sky like a phoenix. As it fled, the howling winds seemed to die, slowing from hurricane force to merely strong. Rain continued to beat down, though, and I welcomed it. The droplets felt deliciously cool on my fire-baked face.

The house groaned and shuddered. The roof over the upstairs bedroom sagged and collapsed, taking most of the left-hand side of the home with it. Sparks flew, steam hissed, and flames danced in the wreckage.

"Carol! My kids!"

I followed the cry to the chief's shadowed face, still slick from blood as he stumbled around the edge of the house.

Shay followed him. "Sir!"

I rose to my feet, feeling every bone, muscle, ligament, and tendon within me groan and complain, but I forced myself after the pair of them. At a walk, mind you.

When I arrived at the foot of the home, I found the chief with his arms wrapped around his wife, his kids latched onto the pair of them in a massive hug. The flames from the home danced, sending shadows flickering over the four of them. If not for their incessant crackle and the still potent roar of the winds, I'm sure I would've heard a sob or two.

Captain Knox stood nearby, at a respectful distance, with Shay in her arms. She saw me approach, disengaged, and came to me.

The hug she gave me was quick. Economical. "Are you okay, Detective?"

"I'm still alive."

She glanced at the chief and his family. "The city owes you a debt."

"I know."

Shay joined us, taking position at my elbow. She touched me on the arm. "I didn't see what happened. You drove it away before jumping down?"

"Let's go with that," I said. "It sounds more heroic that way."

Shay smiled, despite it all.

The fates refused to let us have a quiet moment. Quinto's booming voice cut through the night. "Captain!"

We turned to find him and Rodgers trudging our way from the direction of the street, pushing a pair of battered, handcuffed thugs in front of them. The long-haired orc and the guy in the raincoat from earlier.

The chief noticed them, too. He disengaged from his family, motioned for them to stay put, and walked toward us.

He blasted the orc in the jaw with a right hook when he arrived, and then slammed another fist in the raincoat-clad guy's stomach as he started to say something.

He surveyed the lot of us, looking like hell. I probably didn't look much better. Hell, I probably looked worse. "Captain Knox. Damn it's good to see you."

"Likewise, Chief," she said.

The chief looked at me. "What did you say your name was, Detective?"

"Daggers, sir."

"And this is your partner?"

"Yes, sir," said Shay. "Steele, sir."

He nodded. "I owe you my life. Mine may not be worth much, but you saved my family, too. I owe you an undying debt of gratitude. I do not say that lightly. Thank you."

Steele and I echoed each other. "You're welcome, sir."

He shifted attention to the newcomers. "You're detectives as well?"

"Yes, sir. Rodgers and Quinto, at your service."

"I also owe the two of you for catching these foul murderers. Thank you, as well." He stared into the sky, eyeing the swirling clouds with their intermittent crackles of lightning. "Gods, what the hell is going on? First, I get abducted in my own home. Then this cyclone shows up, and that *thing* attacks us. What was that, Detective?"

I think he meant me. "Not sure, sir. A wind elemental or sprite is our best guess."

"It's a long story," said Captain Knox. "A bloody one, and one whose ending isn't written yet."

"What do you mean by that, Captain?" said the chief.

"Fifty men are dead at the King's Theater," said Knox. "Goons, mobsters, and criminals, mostly. But it's not just the city's dregs meeting their maker. Good ones have been lost in the fight, too. District Attorney Flint, for one."

"*Gods...*" The chief eyed the captives with murder in his eyes. "You mobilize the army yet? What about the rest of our boys? How many precincts?"

"Working on it," said Knox. "All of the above."

"Good. All of you, come with me. I want to know everything, but let's get out of this damn rain first."

The man gathered his family and funneled us out his property's front gates. I thought he might take us to a neighbor's, but instead he crossed the street to a three story building, the split commercial and residential sort. He stopped under a sign depicting a rat with bubbles around its head and with a mug in hand. The words read "The Rat's Nest."

"Felipe usually keeps this place open at all hours," muttered the chief. "Probably better this way."

He reared back, kicked the door open, and walked in.

We followed him into a bar, replete with booths, chairs, and tables. The only thing it was missing were patrons and barkeeps. Despite the name, the place actually looked pretty nice. We followed the chief around the large circular bar in the middle. Once at the back, the chief dug around behind the counter, struck a match, and lit one of the lanterns on the bar.

"Have those two take a seat," he told Rodgers and Quinto. They obliged by planting the captives into a pair of chairs.

"Fasten them," he said.

Rodgers and Quinto did that, too, unlocking and re-locking the pair's handcuffs around the chair back's bars. For whatever it was worth, the two thugs had apparently decided to invoke their right to remain silent.

"Good," said the chief. "Detectives Rodgers and Quinto? If you two managed to chase down and apprehend this pair, then I trust you to handle yourselves out there. You're familiar with the Old Town Precinct? It's about five blocks from here. Please escort my family there. I sincerely doubt Captain Markow will be in at this hour, but if he is, appraise him of the situation. If not, tell whoever's there to find him. This is an all-hands-on-deck situation. Captain Knox. You've said you've already rallied the Fifth?"

"Yes, sir," she said. "Grant Street is on high alert, too. They'll be spreading the word. And I sent one of our best to check on the armed forces."

"Excellent," said the chief. "Detectives Rodgers and Quinto? I'm commandeering this post for the time being. I know the owner. He won't mind. When you're done rallying the troops, rouse the runners. They'll be hard to find at this time of night, but spread word that we're doubling pay until further notice. They'll come out of the woodwork like termites, then. Order them to take direct routes between precincts, and to station themselves at key intersections for faster transit. Also be sure to tell them to take care of themselves. Who knows how bad this storm is going to be. After that, you're to return here. Dismissed."

Rodgers and Quinto didn't even look disappointed as they left, which was more than I would've been able to muster. Then again, they were better cops than I was, and they hadn't been through the same hell I'd been over the past six hours.

The chief waited for the sounds of Rodgers, Quinto, and his family to die amidst the howling winds and beating rains before addressing the Captain. "How bad is it? What are we dealing with?"

"With all due respect, sir," said Knox. "Detective Daggers is the one to tell you. He and Detective Steele have been at the epicenter of this since last night."

"Since *last night?*" The old badger glared at me. "Why wasn't I appraised?"

"There wasn't anything to be appraised of until to-day, sir," I said. "Last night, I was attacked in my home by a pair of goons not unlike these two. Suffice it to say, I came out on top. Literally, in one case. Don't ask. We were pretty sure it was a gang case, but we didn't have any motives until today. That's when Detective Steele was abducted. Long story short, we managed to locate a known associate who we thought might've been in-volved. An ogre by the name of Bonesaw. He's dead now, but his boss is very much alive. A former Wyverns operator by the name of Sebastian Markeville. Goes by the last name Cobb, or used to. Started a new gang by the name Winds of Change. He's behind everything. The slaughter at the old King's Theater. A basilisk attack. Your own assault and attempted murder, along with the elemental-driven cyclone."

"What's his current location?"

"That's what we're trying to find out, sir. We were working on that when we found out about District Attorney Flint's murder. That in turn got derailed by the cyclone's arrival and trying to save you, sir."

"Succeeding in saving me, Detective." He eyed the Captain. "We may need to enlist the aid of the SMRTs."

"That's why we're here, in part, sir," said Knox.

He nodded, turning his gaze to the captives. "You're with the Winds of Change, is it? I don't suppose anyone wants to tell me about their boss, Markeville? His location? His plans?"

The chief circled them slowly, his stance coiled and menacing despite his injuries, like a jaguar sizing up his prey. "No? No one wants to be the snitch? Can't say I'm surprised. What's in it for you, right? You're both going to jail for the rest of your lives. But you do realize I get the final say in *where*, right?"

The orc spat at him, though the spittle barely cleared his own shoes. "Go to hell, pig. You don't scare us. The winds of change are blowing."

"I was rather hoping you'd say something like that."

The chief crossed to the bar, lifting up a hinged portion before heading behind it. He leaned down and popped back up with a worn wooden bat in hand. He hefted it, a grim smile spreading across his face.

"Told you I knew the owner," he said. "This place doesn't get rough often, but he likes to err on the side of caution. You're all free to excuse yourselves for this portion of the interrogation. Might make forgetting it ever happened a little easier."

"Hey, now," said the guy in the raincoat. "You can't do this. You're the po—"

The chief's bat took him square across the jaw. Blood sprayed, and a couple teeth flew into the darkness. That blow alone got him to moaning. His tougher-than-nails orc friend held out a little longer, but he was sobbing within minutes, too.

I'm not some doe-eyed idealist. I know what happens behind the scenes at times. Hell, I'd toed the line myself on more than one occasion. Gotten rough with more than one suspect. I'd even done it early on in Shay's and my tenure. I didn't think any less of the chief for doing what he did. The thugs in front of him had beaten him. Tried to kill him. And even worse, at least in his eyes, tied and gagged his family and left them to die in a home that, if all things went according to plan, would've burned to the ground after being struck by lightning.

No, there was no mercy to be had at the hands of the chief, and no pity to be had on my part. But that didn't mean I had the stomach for it. And the chief was right. Better to see as little of it as possible in the event that someone, *anyone,* ever bothered to ask how those two gang members happened to end up as bloody, mouth-breathing piles of pulp in the back of a bar across the street from the chief's house.

Shay joined me, walking to the other side of the bar as the chief's bat bit into the goons with wet thuds and stomach turning crunches. For was it was worth, the Captain stood by his side, her face carved from stone.

Shay crossed to a chair and sat down, but I headed behind the bar. I started rummaging through the bottles, looking for something to fit my needs.

"You want to grab me something while you're back there?"

I looked up, surprised. "You never go for hard liquor."

She shrugged. "It's been that kind of night."

"It has," I said. "But as nice as a shot of Glendale might be, that's not what I'm after."

I couldn't see Shay's face well in the darkness, but I could feel the force of her raised eyebrow. "Then what are you doing?"

"Pocketing some insurance."

I found a trio of flask-sized bottles, each of them filled with a caramel-colored liquid. The labels said they were brandy, but I wasn't familiar with the brand. Either way, I slipped them into my interior jacket pockets, then kept rummaging, eventually finding a box of matches under the counter near another unlit lantern. Hopefully the box would stay dry in my jacket, but under these condition, who knew? I'd still need cloth, though. I snagged some dish towels and started ripping them into strips.

"Seriously, what are you up to?" asked Shay.

"You don't think this is over, do you?" I asked. "Markeville's still out there. Whatever he has planned, we need to stop him. He may be weakened, but don't doubt for a second that he'll go down without a fight. I'm just trying to even the odds."

The sounds of the chief's wetwork faded, and I heard low voices among the sobbing. Rapid footsteps preceded the Captain around the edge of the bar.

"Well?" I said.

She headed for the door at a jog. "It's the mayor. He's the next target, and Markeville might be heading this task up himself. Come on! We don't have a moment to lose."

37

I didn't cherish the idea of abandoning the chief, and not because I was afraid for his well-being. Rodgers and Quinto would be back momentarily, and anyone who could survive being heavily beaten, lashed to a rooftop during a cyclone, and struck by lightning could handle himself with two barely conscious thugs. Rather it was the chief's emotional state I doubted. Left to his own devices, I wasn't sure the goons would live to see another sunrise, and as much as I cherished justice, I preferred the official kind, not the street variety. But we had bigger concerns at the moment than the chief's emotional anguish and the safety of his prisoners.

Shay and I dove after the Captain, plunging once again into the pounding rains and heavy winds. The cyclone's center continued to bear toward the city, but it appeared to have weakened despite its closer proximity. Maybe it was my imagination—the storm's winds couldn't match those the elemental had unleashed on us in the chief's house—or maybe my fight with the elemental had weakened it, in turn lessening what the storm could muster.

My body groaned as I ran. My hand throbbed, my head ached, pins and needles stabbed at the undersides of my feet and into my shins with every step I took. I'd need an accountant's help to tally the bruises I'd acquired over the past day. On top of that, my stomach rumbled. The burger I'd consumed was a fleeting memory, a mirage of meaty goodness on a heat-rippled horizon, and all I wanted to do was lie down and sleep for twelve days. Yet still I ran.

I'd never considered myself a hero. One of the good guys, sure, despite my rough edges. Shay'd helped me sand those down. I rarely went on the sorts of fist-to-face tantrums the chief had embarked on tonight. I'd broken up with my alcoholic mistress, no matter how much the clinking bottles in my jacket cried out to me. I spent time with my son, paid my alimony, and generally treated people with kindness and respect, if not without the occasional bit of snark. But I was serious about my job. I cared about justice, public safety, and the rule of law. Being a homicide detective had grown to be more than a job for me. It was a career. My life's work.

That still didn't make me a hero. Heroes were folks who put their lives on the line for the public good, those who knowingly ran into harm's way for the mere chance to save others, whether guaranteed or not, like firefighters and the hardasses on the SWAT team and the occasional leotard and cape-clad lunatic who roamed the streets at night. Yet here I was, darting into danger with my body on the verge of collapse, chased by a whirlwind formed of unnatural forces in the wee hours of the morning, and why? Not for the woman I loved. She'd been freed. Not for my career, either. Everything I'd done since heading into the sewers outside the King's Theater had gone beyond the line of duty. Yet still I ran. Still I persevered. Why? Because I cared about the city. Because I cared about people other than myself. Because I wouldn't knowingly let others face the same risks, same dangers, and same fears I had, damn the risks! And because it was the right thing to do.

It occurred to me then that even those people the rest of us recognize as heroes don't see themselves that way. They're just out there, doing the right thing, too.

Unlike with the chief of police's residence, I didn't have to ask the Captain for directions as we traveled. We all knew where the mayor lived. The penthouse suite of One Freemont Plaza.

The newspapers had covered the story with unwavering interest. Throughout his tenure in office, Mayor Greenburg's most vocal campaign had been in the modernization of New Welwic. He'd proposed new public works, taller buildings, bigger universities, and better quality housing for all, so it was no surprise that when Bock Industries came along with their revolutionary generator, followed immediately by Tanner Sherman and his electrical globes, that Mayor Greenburg moved heaven and earth to outfit the city with said lights. Not that they'd spread to every corner yet—the darkened streets that greeted us on our sprint to his condo were proof enough of that. But they continued to spread, and One Freemont Plaza was their epicenter.

The brand new Freemont Building, only a month past its official opening, was the toast of the town. At an absurd fifteen stories tall, it was by far the tallest structure in the city, double its closest competitor. I'd yet to see it in person, but word was Sherman's inventions had been integrated into the core of the building. Not just his electrical lights, but electrical pumps to carry water to the highest floors, an electrically driven lift to carry passengers and cargo to the same levels, and even a contraption to convert electricity into sound. A sounder, they imaginatively called it, though word was the thing had only been installed on the ground level.

We saw the building stretch toward the clouds as we approached, many of its windows lit even now with that all too white electrical glow. We kept running, crossing the rain-soaked street and dashing into the lobby.

It spread out before us, every bit the epitome of modern luxury. White marble floors, twenty foot high ceilings of gilded tin tile, exterior glass as far as the eye could see, all lit by hundreds of Sherman's electrical globes. A wide welcome desk, also topped with marble, curved into a wide 'U' at the center of the lobby. Stairwells stood past it, as well a steel grating with a fat black button to the side and a gauge over the top. The lift, perhaps?

I glanced to my right, then my left, water dripping from my coat to the polished floor underneath. For all of the Freemont Building's amenities, it seemed to be suffering from a major shortage.

"Where are the doormen?" I said. "The guards? Shouldn't there be some?"

Captain Knox nodded, her breath labored. "There were when I visited a few weeks ago. Even at this hour of the morning, there should be several. This isn't a good sign."

"So we're too late?" said Shay.

"Only one way to find out," I said, moving toward the stairs.

Shay grabbed me by the sleeve. "Daggers, don't be stupid! If the guards are gone, that either means the Winds of Change have come and gone, or worse, they're still here. We have no idea how many men they have, how well they're armed, or what their plans are. We don't know anything. No offense, but as much as I appreciate you freeing me from Markeville's prison, you got lucky. You're exhausted. I can see it in your eyes, in the way you walk. We all are. We need to wait for backup, and of more than one kind."

"You mean the mages and witches," I said.

"You saw the elemental same as I did," Shay said. "It rocketed into the night when we escaped from the chief's house. It may have played a role in the attack you suffered last night, and it almost certainly took part in the murder of District Attorney Flint. And we have no idea how to deal with it."

"Not entirely." I tapped my jacket, causing the brandy bottles to clink. "The fire scared it. That's how I was able to beat it back while you pulled the chief to safety."

"Scared it, yes," said Shay. "Killed it, no. And if an entire two-story building on fire didn't kill it, what good will a bottle bomb do?"

"It'll be enough to scare it again," I said. "Which may not be much, I admit. But if it gets me close enough to Markeville to deal with him, maybe that'll be enough. Think about it. Elementals and spirits don't take orders from people. They don't care about money or power or fame. And yet Markeville has managed to get one under his control. I don't know how. Maybe dark magic or another form of coercion. But it *is* under his control, I have no doubts about that. We need to break that link."

"How exactly would you propose doing that, Detective?" said Knox. "Last I checked, you had neither the knowledge nor the ability to sever supernatural links."

"I'm willing to bet a swift boot to Markeville's head would do the trick."

"Careful, Detective," said Knox. "It sounds like you're advocating for precisely the sort of thing your department fights."

"Never, Captain," I said. "Just a bit of well-timed unconsciousness, that's all."

"There is precedent for it, though," said Steele.

We both turned and looked at her.

"What do you mean, Detective?" said Knox.

"The use of lethal force is permitted in some instances, notably where the loss of human life is an imminent risk."

"This isn't a hostage situation," said Knox. "At least we're not aware of it being so."

"That's not exactly what I meant, sir," said Steele. "If Markeville is in command of the wind spirit, and we have to assume he is, then he's putting the entire city at risk. There will be loss of life from this storm, beyond what he's already caused. You know that. That's why you advocated to activate the army, not to mention SMRT."

Captain Knox took a deep breath. "You may be right, but it's a moot point, mostly because you were also right in your previous assessment. We can't do this ourselves. I know where my limit is, and I'm far past it. I'm also lucid enough to know that both of you are in rough shape. We'll wait for backup."

"But sir," I said. "The mayor... What if we'd arrived at the chief's house fifteen minutes later than we did?"

That hadn't been the right thing to say. The Captain's face turned gray, and her eyes shadowed toward the floor. "Then it'll be my burden to bear, Detective Daggers. We'll wait ten minutes. Detectives Rodgers and Quinto, at least, should be on their way shortly."

We settled in behind the welcome desk, our gazes split between the lift entrance behind us and the front doors. My mind raced with nightmare scenarios, so I forced my idle hands to work, using the opportunity to convert the brandy bottles and towels I'd taken from The Rat's Nest into bombs.

As it turned out, the Captain gave our fellow detectives too little credit. The cavalry showed up in five.

38

My heart skipped a beat when the front door opened, letting in a powerful gust of wind and a momentary roar of the storm, but instead of a herd of bloodthirsty Winds of Change gangsters coming to clean up the messes laid bare by those before them, it was Rodgers and Quinto who waltzed through the door, followed by a half-dozen beat cops in sodden blue uniforms, truncheons at their sides.

They weren't the SWAT officers from the King's Theater, or the magic-slinging badasses in the SMRT program. The assembled cops instead looked like late night dregs, but beggars couldn't be choosers. They'd have to do.

Captain Knox waved them over. "You're a sight for sore eyes, Detectives."

"Got here as soon as we could, Captain," said Quinto between gulps of air. "The chief barely let us catch our breath before sending us out. Said the mayor could be in danger."

"We suspect he is." She eyed the assembled officers: three men, a woman, a male elf, and a hulking, grayish-green skinned mutt of indeterminate sex. "You're from the Old Town Precinct?"

"Yes, ma'am," said the one in front. "I'm Officer Watley. These are Officers Dunbar, Chelios, Navarre, Falynn, and Djorkert. At your service."

"What about the mages, Detective Quinto?"

"We sent word, Captain," he replied. "The runners are in full force. Communications are still a nightmare, but I got notice the army's on its way. I imagine the witches and wizards won't be too far behind."

"But you don't know for sure." Captain Knox ground her teeth. "*Damn...*"

"Sorry, Captain," said Quinto.

"No need to apologize, Detective," she said. "You're doing all you can. You all are. But we can't wait any longer to assess the situation. If there's even a small chance to save the mayor, we have to take it. Follow me."

"Excuse me, Captain," I said. "*Follow you?*"

"Yes. It's a simple instruction."

I hesitated. "But...who'll interface with the Smarties when they arrive? Or the SWAT teams?"

Captain Knox didn't quite smile. Her show of teeth had a more animalistic quality to it. "I appreciate your concern, Daggers, but you've lost your mind if you think I'm sending the rest of you in without putting my own neck on the chopping block as well. Let's move!"

The Captain led the way to the grating next to the stairwell and yanked it to the side, revealing the lift's interior. It wasn't as luxurious as I'd expected. Rather, it

resembled a jail cell the size of a closet. A single electrical globe glowed at the top, casting rays that died
amid a jumble of pulleys and chains that stretched into
the darkness above.

"I don't know how many people this thing can take,"
said Knox. "Maybe six. Daggers and Steele, you're with
me. Some of you from Old Town, as well. Rodgers and
Quinto, bring up the rear, either on the stairs or after
the lift returns, your call."

Rodgers nodded. "Might wait. I think we could use
the rest."

The rest of us piled into the cage, standing shoulder
to shoulder in the tight space. The Captain pulled the
grating back into place.

"You sure this thing is safe?" I asked as she cranked
on a lever at the side of the cage.

"I haven't heard of anyone dying yet."

I nodded, thinking to myself the lift had only been
operational a month. It had time. Then we waited. And
waited. And waited some more. The thing took forever,
the dial for the stories creeping clockwise as we trun-
dled up the darkened chute, wheels whirring and spinning in the shadows around us. It probably would've
been faster to take the stairs, though we might not've
been in any condition to fight when we'd arrived at the
top. And perhaps we wouldn't need to fight, but the
implications of that possibility weren't rosy.

Finally, the clock hand reached the rightmost portion of the dial, and a bell chimed.

Knox pulled open the grating and the door beyond
it. "Stay alert."

We filed after her into a hallway as brightly lit and poshly decorated as the ground floor, but we didn't have to guess where to go. Other than the stairwell to the side of the lift, there was but one door in front of us. It stood open, the doorjamb gashed and the lock's strike plate hanging loosely at the side.

The Captain swore and hopped through. I darted after her, wishing I'd keep hold of *any* of the weapons I'd wielded during the long night.

Perhaps I shouldn't have worried. No one jumped out to slash at me with a rusty dagger, or club me over the head with a leaded pipe. Rather the apartment appeared empty, much like the DA's place but without the shattered windows.

The main difference was the level of opulence between the places. Compared to Flint, the mayor might as well have been a king. Crystal chandeliers hung from vaulted ceilings, thick cherry bookshelves lined the walls, couches dotted the cavernous living room, dressed in leather and draped with deftly woven throws. Apparently, green-lighting luxury construction projects came with its perks.

"Mayor Greenburg?" called Captain Knox. "Are you here? Spread out, all of you! Search for signs of him."

A knot formed in the middle of my stomach, the sort that usually did when I knew a conclusion was foregone. With the door in the state we'd found it and the mayor not responding to the Captain's calls, that suggested two likely scenarios, neither of them good. I wondered if I'd find a bloody corpse or nothing at all in the man's bedroom.

It was the latter, thankfully, though the red silk sheets covering the bed gave me a scare. I skirted around to the master bathroom, ignoring the unfair levels of luxury the mayor lived in as I searched for blood or signs of struggle. I found neither.

I stepped back into the bedchamber and called out. "Bedroom's clear!"

I heard another shout. "No one in the office!"

Shay. "Kitchen's empty!"

The wind gusted and roared outside, and I wondered if perhaps the top of a massive, cloud-scraping monument wasn't the smartest of places to wait for an oncoming cyclone to strike. Then another thought crossed my mind, or rather my gut. The windows were closed. The doors to the balcony were, too. And yet...I'd been fooled once. I should at least check.

I cracked open the balcony door and immediately regretted my decision. Wind buffeted me, much stronger than what gusted at ground level. Rain lashed me in the face, ripping away whatever small measure of dryness I'd acquired since arriving. The dark clouds swirled overhead, close now and still crackling with lightning. I didn't want to stare at them, but I reasoned that looking down was an even worse idea.

With one hand holding the doorjamb for support, I took one step onto the balcony and looked up.

I wasn't sure exactly what I saw hanging from the edge of the building above me. It looked like a construction crane, except far smaller than what I imagined might be needed to erect a building such as this one. I also imagined it would've been dismantled at the conclusion of the work on One Freemont Plaza, yet something dangled from the end of it.

Something that moved. Something human-shaped.

"*Oh, gods...*" I stepped back into the bedroom and called out. "Captain! I see the mayor!"

I'm sure she heard me, but whatever response she'd crafted was cut off by screams of terror, crashes, thumps, and shrieks of pain reverberating through the apartment from the direction of the front door.

An oily voice followed them. "*What do we have here?*"

39

I darted to the bedroom door, poked my head around the edge, and surveyed the landscape. Two of the officers who'd joined us in the lift lay on the floor, one of them motionless and with a growing pool of blood seeping onto the tiles around them, the other writhing in agony, clutching his abdomen as blood stained his jacket black. A group of five goons crowded the penthouse's entrance. Water dripped from their clothes and their hair, forming puddles at their feet. All of them wore heavy leather vests and combat boots, held crossbows, and had long dirks strapped at their belts. Two of them were busy reloading, while the others held their weapons at the ready.

Markeville stood in their center, an evil sneer stretching his lips. He, too, held a crossbow, which he aimed down the middle of the room. The bolt shot free with a twang, thudding as it embedded itself in the topmost cushion of the couch nearest the windows.

"Come out, Captain," said Markeville, handing his empty crossbow to a crony in exchange for a fresh one.

"You, too, Detectives Daggers and Steele. No point in delaying the inevitable."

The Captain's voice called out from behind the couch, and I noticed a hint of her faded auburn hair poking over the top. "Who's delaying the inevitable, Markeville? You think you'll walk out of here a free man? We've mobilized the city against you. Police. Fire. Military. The Strategic Magical Response Teams. They're on their way as we speak."

"But they're not here yet, are they?" he said. "Which makes your boast all the more ironic."

"No it doesn't," I called. "It makes her boast anemic, or flaccid, or any other of numerous adjectives that could apply both to a poor bargaining position and your own manhood."

Markeville's gaze shifted toward my doorframe. "Really, Detective? Now, of all times, you're going to resort to childish insults?"

I glanced at the far side of the room. Shay had called out that she'd cleared the kitchen. Which door led there? The goons hadn't spread out yet, had they? And the other officer who'd come with us—where was she?

"If now's not the time, then I don't know when is," I said. "Might as well get them in before I die. A nice whiskey sour would hit the spot, too."

"I'm not planning on killing you yet, Detective, though we are getting tantalizingly close to that moment. I want you to see the futility of your actions before you die. See the world you've worked so hard to craft rot and crumble before you."

I considered my options. I had to assume Shay was alive. The Captain was too, but we wouldn't be for long.

My fear of being caught weaponless in a combat situation had been realized far too quickly, and as much confidence as I had in my ability to take Markeville one on one in a fair fight, his troop of goons armed with blades and crossbows tilted the scales in his direction. There wasn't much of anything I could do against that many bows. Not with the mayor's home so open, so cavernous. I might get lucky and avoid a shot if I dove behind a couch like the Captain had, but I'd never close on them before sprouting several bolts from my chest and neck.

Of course, I *did* have the brandy bombs. I'd hoped to save those in the event I had to dance with the wind elemental again, but they were missiles, after all. I could pitch them across the room and create carnage. They might provide enough of a distraction for me to close on the goons—at which point they'd cut me to pieces with their blades, while the rest of my friends and colleagues burned to death in a fiery inferno after failing to evacuate a burning building fifteen stories above ground.

There had to be a better strategy, but what? I needed to do *something.* Sitting around twiddling my thumbs wouldn't get me anywhere...*or would it?* Markeville and his buddies must've come down from the roof, after all. Their sodden clothing gave it away, even if the mayor's presence above didn't.

"I can't wait to see it," I called back.

"Excuse me?" said Markeville.

"The death and destruction and ruin. Can't wait."

"Are you being sarcastic, Detective?"

"A little. More ironic, though. I figured you could use a few pointers on how to use that rhetorical device properly."

Markeville laughed, a bone-chilling, hollow guffaw that echoed around the mayor's home with all the warmth of a banshee's shriek. "It's a shame I have to kill you, Detective. I'm going to miss your banter. So many of the antagonists I've faced over the years have possessed the mental capacity of a gnat. You're on the level of an ant, at least."

"And yet you're the one who doesn't understand irony," I said. "You know what? Screw it. While we're both alive, let me give you a broader lesson, because irony isn't as cut and dry as most people think. You see, you've got your verbal irony, which is what most people classify as regular irony, but it's also the most commonly misconstrued. That's when you say one thing but mean another. You get a lot of ironic similes of that sort. Clear as mud. Sharp as a bowling ball. That kind of thing."

The Captain hissed at me. "Daggers, what the *hell* are you doing?"

I waved her back from the confines of my doorframe. "Then you've got your situational irony. That occurs when an action results in the opposite desired effect. Like, say, if you tried to kill me and ended up dead yourself. Oh, how sweetly ironic *that* would be."

"I tire of this, Detective," said Markeville. "Maybe I was wrong. Gnat seems more appropriate after all."

"Wait," I said. "I haven't even gotten to tragic and dramatic irony, yet. You're going to *love* those. Well, you will if you assume we're all pawns in some omnipotent being's grasp, our fates already sealed, signed, and delivered."

A crossbow twanged, and a bolt sprouted from the doorjamb opposite me.

"Men," said Markeville. "Advance. Cripple him if you must, but don't kill the Detective. Same for Steele, wherever she's hiding. Murder the rest."

Crap… I reached into my jacket for the bombs and matches, hoping I'd be able to light one before being gutted, when time finally caught up with Markeville.

I'd expected our backup to burst into the mayor's office with a collective roar. Instead, I heard a swish and a crack of bone, followed by a howl of pain before everything exploded into a cacophony of yells and crashes.

I turned the corner and darted into the action, unprepared for the full extent of the melee into which I'd be diving. Crossbow bolts flew as readily as curses. Blades and truncheons cut through the air as Rodgers, Quinto, and the rest of the officers pushed Markeville and his goons into the room, but the thugs fought back with unbridled ferocity. Already the elven officer lay on the ground, clutching a wide gash in his side. Quinto slammed a fist into one of the thug's faces even as a crossbow bolt slammed into his shoulder, causing him to cry out in pain.

I narrowed in on the closest gangbanger. *Take them one at a time, and try not to die.* That was what any brawl or battle boiled down to, but it was hard not to worry about the forest when facing a single tree.

Shay darted out from a doorway as I bore down on the thug from behind, a honing steel in hand. Her eyes flickered toward me, taking stock of me, the thug, and the rest of the situation in a fraction of a second, same as I had.

The goon noticed us a moment too late. He turned toward me, slicing the air with his long knife in an effort to cut the arm of my oncoming fist.

Lucky for me, I'd decided to kick him. My boot landed on the side of his knee. He wobbled and grunted as Shay's honing steel took him on the back of his neck, between the shoulder blades. He spun on his good foot, tying to use his momentum to cut Steele open from ear to ear, but I used my momentum too. I kept going, catching his forearm and slamming the rest of my weight into his shoulder joint. Something popped, and he screamed. Shay's second honing steel blast caught him across the nose. It shut him up.

Shay and I simultaneously turned toward the fighting, but somehow it had already ended. Two more officers lay on the floor, bloodied but conscious. Two of the goons joined them, one with a crossbow bolt sticking through his chest, another with his neck twisted to the side at an unnatural angle. Rodgers and the orc hybrid, Officer Djorkert, I think, were tag teaming one of the others, beating him into submission with truncheons. Quinto had the last in a one-armed headlock, slowly choking the life out of him. Blood streaked his coat underneath the bolt that sprouted from his shoulder, the arm hanging limp at his side.

The Captain shouted at us as she popped from behind the couch. "Get Markeville! Go! I'll help Quinto!"

Officer Djorkert ran to the door as Rodgers blasted the goon underneath him with one last boot to the face. Shay and I ran to the hallway, too.

We paused there for a second. The lift stood at the ready, meaning Markeville had taken to the stairs. The question was up or down.

It wasn't much of a question, really. Winds howled and rain echoed down the stairwell from above.

"Follow me," I said as I hopped up the stairs. Bare electrical globes illuminated the concrete steps, four sets of ten as I raced toward the heavens. The last set were slick from rain.

I paused a couple steps shy of the open door. Wind howled past it, carrying with it driving rain. The cyclone's angry dark clouds churned and spun. I couldn't believe how close they appeared, looming over the tall spire of a building like an apocalyptic prophecy. Had the height of the building brought us so close to the storm, or had the storm travelled to us? By the gods, was the cyclone specifically targeting the Freemont Plaza Building?

"I see him!" said Officer Djorkert.

I did, too. Markeville stood there, near the edge of the roof, the winds and rain howling and whipping around him. Despite their ferocity, he seemed at ease. His body didn't tilt when the winds blew past. His hair, damp though it was, didn't flutter, nor did his shirt and jacket. He simply stood there, uncaring, as if the storm didn't exist, as if none of the violent carnage from the mayor's apartment had come to pass.

"Come on," shouted Officer Djorkert over the roar. "Let's get him!"

"Wait!" I said, but Djorkert had already rushed into the rain. She stumbled across the roof, bearing down on Markeville, truncheon in hand.

And then the wind intensified. Djorkert hunched and dug her heels into the concrete, but it wasn't enough. With an ear-splitting shriek, the wind pushed Djorkert to the side. She toppled and fell, skidding across the roof. I thought I caught a hint of a scream as she flew over the side, disappearing into the empty night.

Shay swore behind me. "*Gods...*"

The wind shrieked and swirled, whipping rain into the stairwell, and once again I saw the face. The beady eyes and wide open mouth. The same one I'd seen at the chief's house, now free of smoke and debris but otherwise the same. It rushed toward the open door, howling with rage, but at the last moment, it pulled away, the eyes wide and the mouth puckered.

I think it recognized me.

I turned my back to the door and pulled one of the fire bombs and matches from my jacket. "I'm going out there."

"*Are you crazy?*" said Steele. "You saw what happened to our officer, right?"

Rodgers knelt behind Shay, a look of fear pitting his face. "You don't need to be a hero, Daggers..."

I struck a match against the side of the box. Nothing. "I'm not trying to be a hero. I'm out here doing my job, same as everyone else."

"Nobody else has a death wish!" said Steele.

I struck another match. Still nothing. "I don't have a death wish. But we have a duty to defend the city. To serve and protect against all forces that would seek to do harm to the citizens of New Welwic. All *forces*. Right now, Markeville is the least of my worries. It's that elemental we need to stop. It'll tear the city apart if we don't stop it, and call me crazy, but I think that's exactly what Markeville wants. But the quickest way to it is through him."

"You want to kill him?" said Rodgers. "Knock him out? Whatever. Doesn't matter. Fine. Let's grab a cross-bow from downstairs. I'm a decent enough shot. I can pick him off from here."

The wind roared behind me. I struck another match. It caught.

I lit the cocktail's wick, which took quickly thanks to the brandy that soaked it. "You saw what the wind did to Djorkert. It can push a crossbow bolt out of Markeville's path if it wants to. But the spirit is scared of me. I can see it in its face, which means I can take him."

"Daggers, please..." Shay's face was wet, but only partly because of the driving rain.

"Do you trust me?" I said.

"Of course."

I leaned in and kissed her, a quick peck on the lips. "This won't take long. Promise."

I plucked a second cocktail from my coat and lit it with the first, then turned toward the door. The wind roared by, swirling before coming to a stop ten paces beyond the exit.

I stepped into the squall with more confidence than I'd thought I could muster. The wind bellowed and blew, but it didn't push me off my feet.

I took aim at a spot immediately underneath the wind spirit's hovering face, threw my bomb, and prayed.

It flew true, enveloping the face in a gout of flame that licked hungrily up into the sky.

The wind whipped around the fire, the elemental's face flying with it. The thing's mouth widened, and the wind slowed.

I pulled the last bottle from my coat, lit it, and tossed the second. The flames engulfed the spirit's face again. It shrieked, a more high-pitched sound than I'd heard earlier, and it shifted toward the building's lip. I followed it with my third and final cocktail. The flames licked the edge of the building, and the face shot into the darkness with a panicked whine.

The bright lights of the explosions only now seemed to register with Markeville. He turned as I started to run toward him, calling out through the whipping winds.

"You don't know when to quit, do you Daggers? Don't you know when you're outclassed? Outmatched? Out—"

I hit him at full speed, planting both of my hands square in his chest and pushing with all my might. He flew backward, his arms flailing as he toppled over the edge of the building. His scream cut through the shrieking winds, fading as he plummeted toward the ground.

"Gods, that asshole doesn't know when to shut up." I brushed my hands on my pants, hearing another shout somewhere on the wings of the wind.

I turned, wondering what I'd forgotten. That's when I spotted the makeshift crane and remembered that the mayor was dangling sixteen stories in the air.

40

The wind picked up behind me, and I stopped in my tracks. I turned, wondering why I hadn't ever considered what might happen once Markeville died. I'd assumed the elemental would flit away, that the winds would die, the clouds would break, and the stars of the night sky would shine down on me like the smiles of ten thousand thankful gods. But what if I was wrong? What if I'd set free a power only one man had figured out a way to control, a power that could blow the entire city to its foundation in a fit of rage, all before the magical Smarties could come to contain it?

Those thoughts and more raced through my mind as the winds whipped and swirled and cried out. With a surge, the air pushed against me like a wall. It forced me onto my bottom with a thud. But it wasn't the elemental that flowed over the edge of the roof, ready to pick me up and cast me into the eternal abyss.

It was Markeville, born through the air on invisible wings. He landed lightly a few paces in front of me.

I blinked and stared. "How... *How did you...?*"

Markeville took a step toward me, his hands clenched tightly in fists. "You know, Detective Daggers, I'm finding it irksome that for all the expense they've cost me and for all of their power, neither of my pets have been either able or willing to kill you."

I stumbled to my feet, forcing down my fear. "Incapacitate me."

"Excuse me?"

"You said you didn't want to kill me. Not yet, anyway. Stands to reason you wouldn't demand it of your pets. That doesn't explain why you sent your basilisk after me, but in retrospect, you didn't know the ghost in the smoke at the theater was me, did you? And I can only assume you wanted to scare me back at my apartment, not petrify me. What happened? Your pet elemental get too feisty? It blew me out my window before you got a chance to confront me and gloat?"

He leveled a finger at me, the same way a serial killer might threaten a man with a knife. "You angered me at the theater, you know, but I can appreciate it now. Your ability to suppress fear with my pet bearing down on you. You're a lot like me in that regard."

"What are you spouting on about, Markeville? I'm nothing like you. You're a twisted, power-hungry freak."

"Twisted, perhaps," he said. "But power hungry? Only in the same way as you. We both respect the power of fear. We're able to harness it. Use it. That's how you tricked my elemental. I can see that now, as you can surely see I didn't kill anyone—the gang leaders, the district attorney, your police chief—out of spite. I don't dangle the mayor from a harness over a hundred and fifty foot drop out of malice, or push a cyclone into the streets for the sheer joy of it. I do it for the *power*. The power that fear provides."

"Sorry to break it to you, but the chief's alive," I said. "And you're wrong. Fear doesn't grant you power. It only takes it away from others. I don't use fear as a weapon. I *extinguish it*."

I imagine Markeville had quite a speech planned for me, probably to tell me about the love lost between him and his father, his days as a youth being tormented by classmates, the sick pleasures he got out of retaliation, how he'd grown to realize the irrational impact of terror, how Shay's and my actions with the Wyverns had irked him but only provided a minor roadblock in his power-mad quest to bring the city to its knees.

I surprised him by not giving a shit.

I lunged at Markeville while he was still focused on the remains of his evil monologue. I sailed a punch at his face, but the man ducked and wove out of the way. I followed it with a kick and another punch, both of which he avoided. Apparently, that was enough to piss him off. He stepped into me as I jabbed, landing a hard blow to my ribs.

I grunted but managed to trap his arm under my own. We spun about, each of us throwing punches with our free hands, him using his attacks to free himself while I hung on for dear life, landing short, choppy punches and elbows to his shoulders and chest. The wind swirled around us, whipping rain and debris in a tight circle inches outside our radius, but whether because of fear of me or of hurting Markeville, it refused to interfere.

With a wrench, Markeville pulled free, but I dove on him, wrapping him up by the legs. He kicked at me, hitting me on the forehead and then on the mouth. A sting rocked my lips as my teeth cut into them, and I tasted hot blood.

The blows loosened my grip. Markeville pulled away, though I ripped a shoe from his foot in the process. He stumbled to his feet a few paces away, his chest heaving from exertion and his eyes wild with anger.

I spat, my saliva tinged red, and stood, facing off again. Somewhere past Markeville I caught a glimpse of Rodgers in the stairwell. Was he waving at me? "What's wrong, Markeville? Don't like your chances against me? Don't tell me you're *afraid*."

Markeville laughed again. "Scared of *you?* Why would I be?"

"I'm stronger, faster, and smarter than you. Without your henchmen and your beasts and the wind at your back, you're nothing."

The man cocked his head. "Not faster, surely. And perhaps you've noticed, but it's not as if I have to take the stairs to get away."

I coiled my legs underneath me, ready to dart after him. "Try me."

Markeville smiled. "I'd rather not. Besides, you're going to be too busy to catch me."

"Why's that?"

"Because you're predictable, Detective."

Markeville's eyes narrowed in focus, and another lightning bolt rent the sky. It hit somewhere behind me, overwhelming me with bright white light and ear-splitting sound. I didn't want to glance over my shoulder to see what destruction it had wrought. I didn't want to take my eyes of Markeville, but he was right. I couldn't help myself. I was predictable.

And then I realized that wasn't what he'd meant. The makeshift crane dangling the mayor over the edge of the building creaked and groaned, a smoldering black mark spread across its base. A wooden gear at the bottom shuddered and slipped, the spring-loaded finger holding it back crumpled and bent.

I took off toward the crane at a dead sprint. The finger cracked and snapped. The gear flew into a spin, taking with it the length of rope coiled at its side.

I dove and latched onto the rope with barely ten feet of it left in the coil, but the mayor's momentum refused to cooperate. The rope slipped in my grip, burning my palms and sending knives of pain lancing through my injured hand. I held on anyway.

It wasn't enough. My feet slipped on the wet concrete. I went down as the rope slipped free of the mangled ratchet system. I skidded across the roof, holding on with everything I was worth as the mayor's weight yanked me toward the edge.

The homunculus inside me who manned my panic button mashed it frantically, but I refused to give in. Twisting my body, I swiveled my feet in front of me with a foot and a half to spare. I dug in my heels and braced for impact as the soles of my boots hit the roof's lip. My muscles cried out and cursed my impudence as we made landing. The rope slipped another foot in my hands before I stopped its forward motion. I heard a crack and a twang, and somewhere over the roar of the winds, another panicked scream.

"See, Detective?"

I glanced at Markeville. He stood where I'd last seen him, a smug grin spread across his face. "Told you. Too predictable. See you around, Detective—assuming the storm doesn't kill you. My pet isn't fully in control of it, you understand."

I grunted, my legs straining against the edge under the combined weight of the mayor and whatever contraption they'd strapped him into. It was then I realized Markeville had won. There wasn't anything I could fasten the rope to. I was lucky to have sunk my feet into the roof's lip for support, and though I could probably drag the mayor up to safety—slowly, given the excruciating state of my left hand—I wouldn't be able to stop him. Not from here. Not by myself. None of us would if he could float away on an invisible cushion of compacted wind.

I'd failed. Markeville knew it. That's why he laughed, that same haunting killer clown laugh he'd burst forth with in the mayor's penthouse. He laughed as the wind swirled at the edges of the roof, his evil eyes belying the forced humor in his voice.

And than I saw her. Shay, racing toward him from the open door.

I chill ran down my spine, and I cried out. "Shay, NO!" But the wind tore the words from my mouth, casting them into the darkness and rain. Just as they'd cast *her* over the edge.

I guessed *I'd* be safe because I'd driven the wind elemental back, because I'd scared it with fire and because I'd do it again with gouts of flame from my hand-crafted bombs. But Shay hadn't done any of that, and I hadn't made myself clear. I'd simply told her to trust me.

Maybe the elemental had been distracted by my plight, or Markeville's preoccupation with me bought her some time. She almost made it—but almost only counts in darts and drunken love making.

The wind picked up as she closed on him. He turned and whipped an arm at her, as if directing the elemental's fury in her direction. The wind lifted her off her feet. She reached out, grasping at Markeville's arm for purchase, but her hands slipped off his wrist, and the wind carried her up.

And Markeville with her. He cried out as the wind lifted him, too. The pair hovered for a moment, suspended in the air, lashed by winds and rain, and then I saw it. A glint of metal, stretched between Steele's and Markeville's outstretched arms. Handcuffs. Shay'd cuffed herself to him, tying her fate to his own.

Or at least to an extent. A rope trailed her from the waist into the stairwell, stretched taut by the wind's efforts to take her.

Markeville shrieked. The wind set them back down. The madman dove at my partner, but she was ready. Another metallic flash gleamed in her free hand. One of the knives from the brutes downstairs.

Markeville howled as it bit into his side. Steele pulled back for another stab, but Markeville used her cuffing trick against her. He pulled her in using their tethered wrists, catching her free hand in his fist. He swept his legs underneath hers, and the pair crashed to the concrete, Markeville on top.

Cold dread poured through me, nothing at all like the panic I'd faced with the decision to save the mayor or capture Markeville. This was far worse. Now a new choice bared its yellowed, rotten teeth. A choice between lives. The mayor's or Steele's.

I grunted and strained, straightening my legs. The rope moved with me, but it wasn't enough. I couldn't drag the mayor to safety. Not in time to save them both.

Markeville slammed Shay's blade hand against the concrete roof. The blade clattered to the side, and his hands shot to her throat. His eyes widened into saucers of hate, his teeth a snarling vice as he squeezed.

The mayor's screams drifted over the edge of the roof, high-pitched and frantic. I tried to let go of the rope, tried to force my aching hands apart, but they wouldn't budge. His death would be on my hands. I'd have made the choice. Me, and no one else.

Then Markeville stiffened. His face froze, and blood seeped from between his teeth. Steele wasted no time, slamming her palms into his chest. He toppled, falling face first to the concrete at Shay's side. A feathered bolt protruded from his back, over his left side a few inches down from his shoulder blades. A perfect shot to the heart.

Behind him, crouched in the stairwell, Rodgers tossed his crossbow to the ground and darted toward Shay. He made it halfway before the wind started to weep.

41

I t began as a soulful dirge, a reedy song filled with sorrow. It whistled through the wind, coming from before me and behind me, over the edges of the roof and down in the black ink below, from everywhere all at the same time. The elemental face I'd seen raced through the rain and darkness, its features wide, stretched either by pain, sadness, or ecstasy.

The face blurred as it circled me three times in quick succession. I felt the winds strengthen with each of its passes. The reedy whistle grew in intensity, focusing into a dangerous whine.

I cried out to the others. "Rodgers! Steele! Get down!"

They'd felt it, too, the swirling winds growing stronger and pushing in. Rodgers dove to the ground, latching onto Steele's tether.

I didn't have any such luxury. With the rope still clutched between my aching hands, I flattened my back against the concrete, willed as much strength into my legs as I could, and said a prayer.

I'd never been the religious sort, but this time I meant it.

The wind swirled, pushing harder and harder, whipping faster and faster. The whine turned into a shriek and the shriek into an apocalyptic roar. The winds tore at my clothes. My jacket's hem slapped back and forth, battering me with blows. The wind pulled at the rope, forced itself into the crevices at my back. Beside me, the remains of the crane groaned, creaked, and pulled free, disintegrating into pieces as the winds blew them off the edge of the roof and into the night.

I closed my eyes and pressed harder into the concrete underneath me, picturing myself as a pancake or a slug or a puddle of molasses. The rope strained in my hands. My muscles screamed. Maybe I did, too. I didn't want to die. Not with so much of my life ahead of me. Not at the hands of a degenerate like Markeville. And I certainly didn't want to die knowing Shay awaited the same fate as me.

I'd do anything for her. *Anything.*

My body lifted off the concrete. Air fluttered the clothes at my back, and I knew it was over. But as suddenly as I'd been lifted, I fell.

I smacked back into the roof, my head spinning as it bounced. With a deafening roar, the winds abandoned me. I cracked my eyes. In the distance, I saw the face, stretching and fading as it careened toward the heavens, taking the anger of the winds with it.

I twisted my neck toward Rodgers and Steele. They were still there, hobbling to their knees. Somehow they'd made it, too. I'd been too scared to look. The rope had held tight, I guess.

As I gawked, my own rope slipped. I clenched with all my remaining strength. My forearms burned with exertion, and I heard the mayor scream. "Guys? A little help?"

Rodgers stumbled to his feet and ran over. I think Shay would've too if she hadn't still been tied at the waist and shackled to Markeville's corpse.

Rodgers grabbed the bit of rope that protruded behind me. "Got you, Daggers."

"Pull!" I said.

I pushed with my legs and yanked with my arms. With Rodgers' muscles working in tandem with my own, we drew the rope up, two to three feet at a time. The cries for help neared, and within twenty seconds of work, the top of the mayor's head appeared.

"I've got the rope," I told Rodgers. "Pull him over the edge."

Rodgers obliged. He grabbed him by the shoulders and tugged. With a grunt, the mayor flopped over the side, tied and bound to a heavy chair, his clothes bloodied, his face bruised, but still very much alive.

His skin was gray and his entire body shook. He mumbled the same thing over and over. *Gods. Oh gods. Oh gods.*

Suddenly Shay was at my side, long knife in hand. How she'd managed to secure it in the wake of the wind elemental's death throes I'd never know, but she went to work on the knots keeping the mayor in place.

"It's alright now, sir," she said. "It's going to be okay. We're police."

The knife sliced through the ropes, and the mayor fell to the concrete, barely putting his hands out in time to soften the fall. His eyes were full moons. "Oh gods, I... Thank you. *Thank you...*" He started to sob.

I didn't think any less of him for it. I might've cried myself if not for the adrenaline coursing through my body, creating a greater buzz than any espresso ever could've.

Shay tossed the knife to the side and wrapped me in a hug. I felt her warm breath on my neck, and her voice sounded soft in my ear. "Jake. I was so worried. Are you okay?"

"I'm okay. Are you?"

Her chin dug into my clavicle as she nodded. "I'm okay. I love you, Jake."

"I love you, too, Shay."

We sat there for a long moment, clutching each other, enjoying the sound of each other's breath and the slow patter of the dying rain around us. I counted the beats of Shay's heart, focused on them, felt them slow over time. Rodgers collapsed to the ground beside us, but he didn't say anything. I imagine if his wife, Allison, were here, he would've reacted in the same way.

"Nice work, by the way," I said to Steele. "Where'd you find the rope?"

"A maintenance closet, by the top of the lift," she said. "I think Markeville might've left it there. There were more supplies than I would've expected."

"I hope he *did* leave it there," I said. "You know, given how I lectured him about situational irony down below."

Shay smiled. "You never quit, do you?"

"I don't plan on it." I smiled back. "Thank you for saving my life. *Again.*"

"You would've done the same for me," she said. "You have, in fact. It's kind of what we do now, I guess."

"Still pretty ballsy, though. How'd you know you'd be able to get close enough to Markeville to cuff him?"

"I didn't. But I had to try...despite objections to the contrary."

Rodgers looked over. "Come on, now. You have to admit, that was totally crazy. I still can't believe the rope held."

I reached over and clapped him on the shoulder. "Hey, at least she *had* a plan."

He sneered. "Don't give me any of your lip, either. I had a plan. To shoot Markeville with a crossbow. Turned out pretty well, didn't it?"

"Eventually," said Steele.

I cocked an eyebrow. *"Eventually?"*

"I *may* have fired half a dozen bolts into the wind before Shay decided to try the rope," said Rodgers. "I guess the wind elemental finally got distracted enough at the end for me to get a clean shot. Good thing I didn't give up, eh?"

"More than a good thing," I said, squeezing his shoulder. "A great thing."

"Daggers! Steele! Rodgers!"

The Captain's voice cut across the lingering sounds of the storm. She walked from the rooftop door, helping Quinto beside her. A makeshift tourniquet fashioned out of a bed sheet had been wrapped around his shoulder, and another around his leg. He limped as he walked. Apparently he'd taken a slice to the leg, too.

Rodgers and I got to our feet and took the big guy off the Captain's hands. "Quinto? How you doing? You going to make it?"

He winced and nodded. "I won't be taking part in intramural scrummage games anytime soon, but I'll live."

Rodgers shot his partner a smile. "Hell of an engagement present, huh?"

"The present will be having Cairny there to take care of me," he said. "I can't think anything better."

"You mean other than not getting shot and stabbed in the first place, right?" I said.

He snorted. "Yeah. That."

The Captain helped the mayor to his feet, trying to reassure him with a soothing tone. "It's alright, Mayor Greenburg. We've got everything under control."

I glanced toward the skies, wondering if that were true. The winds and rain had slowed, and the clouds seemed to be thinning, but the elemental hadn't been defeated, only chased off. I hoped it would be enough.

As if on cue, the universe answered me. The clouds at the horizon parted. Not much. Just a smidgen. But enough for a trickle of purplish-pinkish light to creep over the horizon.

As I've said before, I'm not a religious man. More spiritual than anything else. But I took the vista as one that was heaven sent, and beyond that, as a sign.

Namely, as a sign that I could finally get some sleep.

"Come on, Detectives," said the Captain as she led the mayor toward the door. "We're not done yet. Help me get the wounded back to the main floor, and then we'll need to make sure everyone in this building is still okay."

I sighed. *The story of my life...*

42

I stood at the top of the steps in front of city hall, dressed in the official blue policeman's uniform that I never, *ever* wore. Until this morning, I hadn't touched it since I'd been promoted to detective. It was a miracle I still fit into it given how much weight I'd gained since then. Luckily for me, I'd lost it all under Shay's supervision.

She stood beside me, dressed in her own official blue duds. A crowd milled before us at the base of the steps, a collection of service members, first responders, journalists, city officials, their families, and a nice group of bystanders as well. To our right stood a podium, centered on the stairs a few steps below us. It remained empty for now.

The sun shone down upon us. A bead of sweat formed at my temple. I lifted a hand to wipe it away before I realized I'd picked the wrong hand.

I grumbled. "I hate this cast. I can't wait to get it off. It itches so much."

"Get used to it," said Shay. "You've got another two weeks. And you should be counting your lucky stars it was a clean break. Could've been much worse."

"That bite was anything but clean," I said. "You never got to see the basilisk. It smelled like a dead weasel."

"I said the *break* was clean," said Shay. "You're being obtuse."

"Not to mention a baby," Quinto huffed from behind.

I turned to look at him. He stood there next to Rodgers, his arm in a sling and a crutch under one armpit. Both he and Rodgers were also outfitted in their barely used official uniforms.

"Couldn't you have loomed over someone else?" I said. "Having you right behind me is cutting back on the empathy I'm getting over my hand."

"What a shame." Rodgers nodded to the side. The other injured officers who'd aided us during the raid of the Freemont Plaza building stood beside us. One of them had Quinto doubled up on number of crutches.

"Point taken," I said.

I glanced at the podium again. It was still empty. I sucked on my lips and shifted my weight between the balls of my feet.

"Why are you nervous?" asked Shay.

I tucked my good hand into my pocket reflexively. "Why aren't *you,* is the better question. You actually *like* ceremonies?"

"Relax, will you?" She squeezed my arm. "We're all in the same boat. It'll be over before you know it."

Just as I was about to make a joke about prostate exams, I heard a rumble among the crowd. I looked to the side and saw the Chief of Police descending the steps, the commendations on his blue uniform sparkling in the mid-afternoon sun. A purple bruise marred the right side of his face, but otherwise he looked as tough and grizzled as ever.

He stepped to the podium to generous applause. He lifted a hand, beckoning for silence, but it took a good twenty seconds for the crowds to acquiesce. "Thank you. Thank you very much. Ladies and gentlemen; officers and detectives; lieutenants and captains of the New Welwic Police Department; members of our city's fire and emergency medical response teams; our armed forces; members of the city council; Mayor Greenburg, and all of your friends and families and colleagues, thank you for presence.

"One week ago today, our city faced off against evils both unnatural and also quite human in their essence. All of you are aware of at least one manifestation of these evils. The cyclone which struck our city on the night of the twenty-seventh was swift, potent, and deadly, and made all the more so by its unexpected arrival. Only thanks to the timely efforts of our police officers, firefighters, medical first responders, and members of our national guard were we, as a city, collectively able to minimize the loss of life that would otherwise have materialized from such a deadly storm.

"Sadly, however, the storm was not without its victims, nor were the forces responsible for its sudden manifestation. Today, we join one another here to honor the memory and mourn the loss of those individuals who made the ultimate sacrifice in defense of our great city.

"For Officers Mason Wayne and Celina Rodithas, their day began like any other. A warm meal, well wishes to their families, and off to work. Little did they know a cyclone would hit the city that night, bringing with it powerful lightning strikes that would raze over a dozen homes and businesses to the ground. But Wayne and Rodithas were officers of the law. They knew that from the moment they put their uniforms on until the moment they removed them, their duty was to the city. To protect others from harm. Wayne and Rodithas did just that, saving eight citizens from a burning three-story dwelling before paying the ultimate price when said building collapsed. Today, we mourn and honor their sacrifice.

"Officers Wallace Dunbar, Mario Chelios, and Lucretia Djorkert also answered the call of duty. When their fellow servicemen and women called upon them for aid, they came without question. They braved the fierce winds and driving rains, joining their fellow officers and detectives in the pursuit of the villains who attacked the city through both conventional and magical means, fully aware of the danger involved. When their fellow officers were trapped, cut off by terrorists with murderous intent, they fought back, sacrificing themselves to save their fellow man. Without their efforts, even more of our friends and colleagues would be dead, and our city less safe. We mourn their sacrifice as well. If you would please honor their memory with a moment of silence."

I bowed my head in respect, as did those around me. Silence reigned over the hall's steps, broken only by the steady hum of the city.

"Thank you," continued the chief. "But we do not assemble here today merely to mourn those we have lost. We also join here in celebration, to honor those still living among us whose quick thinking, sacrifice, determination, and bravery saved countless lives and helped protect our city from future threats.

"First among them: Of the Old Town Precinct, Officers Dedrick Watley, Julia Navarre, and Filverel Falynn. Along with their fallen compatriots, these brave officers stepped forth when faced with the call of duty. Risking danger to life and limb, they helped quash a violent insurrection, and their actions at One Freemont Plaza aided in the elimination of a savage terrorist. For this, they will be awarded medals of exceptional merit. Officers? Please step forth."

The three officers stepped or hobbled to the podium. The crowd cheered and clapped as the captain of the Old Town Precinct stepped forward to bestow each of them with their decorations. As the cheers subsided, they returned to their posts.

"Next," said the chief. "From the Fifth Street Precinct. For their tenacious pursuit of their fellow officers in the gang-infested war zone that was the King's Theater, for their enduring bravery in the face of armed opponents at One Freemont Plaza, and for their pivotal role in the elimination of the terrorist who sought to place our fine city under his thumb, it is my great pleasure to present Detectives Gordon Rodgers and

Folton Quinto the prestigious Police Combat Cross. Please come forth, Detectives."

Rodgers and Quinto shuffled past us to even greater applause. I caught Cairny's beaming face in the crowd as Captain Knox stepped to the podium. The Captain shook each of the detective's hands before draping a medal over their necks, a brilliant silver eight-pointed cross with golden trim.

Rodgers and Quinto took their positions behind us as the Captain continued his speech. "Also from the Fifth Street Precinct, a detective who has distinguished herself spectacularly in her first year of service, Shay Steele. For tenacity in the face of her kidnappers, for quick thinking and courage in the subduing of a dangerous escaped convict, and for exceptional bravery in the face of enemies both mortal and supernatural, it is my distinct honor to present her with the Department's Medal of Valor. Detective?"

The chief looked back, and Shay stepped forth to thunderous applause. She dipped her head, and Captain Knox placed a six-pointed golden star over her neck. The Captain shook her hand, and the chief did the same, leaning over to whisper something into her ear. She nodded her head before returning to stand next to me.

My arm trembled even before the Captain continued. "And finally, another member of the Fifth Street Precinct's finest. A twelve year member of the homicide division. A true champion of justice, Detective Jake Daggers. During the thirty-six hour window that encompassed the arrival of last week's life-threatening cyclone and the terrorist and criminal acts that preceded it, this brave officer survived multiple attacks on his life. He doggedly pursued his partner's kidnappers, defeating countless numbers of their ranks with his intellect, creativity, and physical skill. He single-handedly eliminated a creature most of us would've cowered before, helpless and afraid. Atop a fifteen story building, he braved supernatural winds and rains to help subdue the terrorist behind that night's attacks. Because of his quick reflexes, he saved Mayor Green-burg from certain death. And along with his partner, Detective Steele, he personally saved the lives of me and my entire family. It is with the utmost gratitude and respect which I present to him the department's high-est accolade, the Medal of Honor. I can think of no one more deserving of it. Detective?"

With wobbly legs, I stepped forward. The crowd erupted in applause, clapping and cheering with even more force than they had for Steele, if that was possi-ble. I dipped my head as Captain Knox placed the golden, twelve-pointed star over my neck, leaning into my ear as she shook my hand. "Congratulations, Detec-tive. I couldn't be prouder."

"Thank you, Captain." My legs felt a little stronger, and my heart beat a little steadier.

The chief shook my hand, too, leaning in as well. "My sincerest gratitude, Detective. I wouldn't be here if not for the actions of you and your partner. This city owes you an immeasurable debt, as do I."

"Thank you, sir."

The cheers followed me as I returned to my post. The chief beckoned for silence once again with a raised hand. "Thank you. Finally, I'd like to take this opportunity to once again thank all of the officers and detectives behind me, all of our fallen brothers in arms, and every member of the fine New Welwic Police Department. Because of your actions, your bravery, and your relentless pursuit of what is right and true, this city remains a paragon of liberty, prosperity, and creation. Thank you, each and every one, for your service, and may the gods bless us all."

Once again, the crowd erupted in applause, and this time I joined them in cheer.

43

The crowd slowly started to disperse, but only the non-police contingent. Rather than leave, those officers, detectives, and police spouses who'd milled at the foot of city hall surged onto the steps with the rest of us. I'd assumed they mostly wanted to glad-hand the chief, and although there was a fair amount of that, Rodgers, Quinto, Steele, and I weren't exempted from the action. Dozens upon dozens of officers and detectives, most of whom I'd never met, came up to give one or all of us their appreciation and thanks. Even the captains of the Old Town and Grant Street precincts came by, congratulating us and telling us that if we ever needed anything to stop by and ask. I lost track of how many hands patted me on the back and how many times I repeated the words "Thank you."

At some point among the jubilation, Cairny snuck through the crowd and wrapped her beau in a huge hug. She beamed as she looked into Quinto's eyes, and the big lug gave her as warm a look back. They kissed, their faces framed against a backdrop of blue.

I felt a touch on my arm. "They sure are cute, aren't they?"

I smiled at Shay. "They are. Which is no small feat given how awkward they are."

Shay snorted. "You're just jealous."

"Of their happiness?" I said. "A little. Not as much as I would've been, once upon a time. I'm pretty happy with where I am now."

"Only *pretty happy?*"

I was saved from answering that by the appearance of a set of jowls surrounded by wrinkles and granite. "Detective Daggers. Detective Steele."

"Captain Armstrong," I said, shaking his hand. "I didn't know you'd be here."

"Wouldn't miss it for the world," he said. "Though it would've been nice if someone had sent official word. I swear, once you retire it's like you fall off the face of the earth."

"Budget cuts, probably," I said. "Can't pay for the postage."

"You blame everything on budget cuts," he said. "Steele? Congratulations. I always knew you'd be a boon to our department. Glad to see I was right."

"Much appreciated, sir," she said. "Thanks for taking a chance on me. And not kicking me out once you realized I wasn't psychic."

"Please," he said. "Performance was all I ever cared about. I just wish I could've seen past your resume to your real potential. Daggers? Take good care of her, will you?"

"I've been doing my best, sir. But among the two of us, she's the better caretaker by far."

"Glad to hear it. I'm happy for you two. Keep up the good work." The Captain spotted Rodgers and went to shake his hand. At the same time, Quinto descended on us. He clapped me on the shoulder, too hard as was his usual.

"So, Daggers. I guess it's time for you to retire. I mean, you're never going to top this."

"I'd be fine with that if it means I never suffer through another assassination attempt, basilisk attack, or fight with a wind elemental atop a fifteen story sky-scraper," I said. "But you and I both know that's not going to happen. It's cute you think I have enough cash on hand to retire though."

"Don't you believe him," said Steele. "He's making a killing on his Sherman Industries stocks. He'll be a cutting-edge technologies magnate in no time."

"That's me," I said. "Part time homicide detective, part time venture capitalist. Although after today, I'm thinking my newest business venture should be en-dorsements. I don't think I've ever had so many people clamoring for my attention."

"And all of it's well deserved, old friend," said Quinto. "Anyway, Cairny and I are headed to the police gala. We'll see you there?"

"You bet," I said. "It's probably time we get moving, too."

Shay peered toward the street, which was still clogged with pedestrians. "The hardest part is going to be finding transportation."

"Oh, ye of little faith," I said. "Quinto? See you there. Follow me, Steele."

I led my partner down the steps, weaving through a maze of congratulations and handshakes. When we reached street level, I turned left and headed a good hundred paces down the street. There, past a group of people trying to hail carts off the street, stood a lone rickshaw, its driver impervious to calls from those on the sidewalk.

He looked up as we approached. "Afternoon, Detective. Everything go as planned?"

"So far," I said as I hopped into the back. "Thanks for waiting for us, Toby. You know where to go."

As Shay and I settled into our seats, Toby took off at a run, leaving the mass of officers in the dust at the foot of the hall's steps.

"Thinking ahead, were we?" said Steele with a smile.

"It's the hallmark of our species," I said. "I knew this would be a zoo, and it's still hot enough that I wanted to get out of the sun as quickly as possible. Aren't you glad you brought me along?"

"Kind of hard to leave you at the precinct, seeing as this was a ceremony to honor *all* of us, but yes, I am. I'm always glad to have you along."

Our driver took a turn, our cart's wheels clattering over the cobblestones. "You know... I wanted to talk to you. About Markeville, the kidnapping, the Winds of Change. All of it."

"It seems unreal in retrospect, doesn't it?" said Shay. "If not for the broken bones and scars, it almost could've passed for a bad dream. I'm glad it's over. I just wish so many people, good and bad, hadn't had to die. Sorry, I'm babbling. You wanted to discuss an aspect of the case? Don't tell me you think we missed something."

"No, nothing like that," I said. "This isn't like the Wyverns case. Markeville's dead. The Winds of Change are done."

"So what do you want to talk about?"

"You. Us," I said. "In all the post-case discussions about Markeville's psychological profile, his family background, the involvement of his lackeys, his connections to outside groups, smugglers and elemental shamans, I realized I never told you probably the most important thing I realized in this case. And that's how incredibly proud I am of you. How you dealt with adversity, both before and after being kidnapped. How you fought alongside me, never wavering, never tiring. How you stood by me, no matter the risks. I've always known what loyalty was supposed to entail, but I don't think I've ever experienced it in such a way. What I'm saying is, I'm incredibly honored to serve by your side, Shay. To be your partner, in more ways than one."

Shay smiled and looked at me, her eyes soft and inviting. She leaned in and kissed me, a quick peck. "I couldn't have expressed my own feelings any more eloquently, Jake. Everything you've told me, I feel the same for you. Even when it scared me, I understood your actions. Your motivations. And I'm so proud to have gotten through it with you. I hope to the gods we're never faced with anything of that magnitude again, but if we are, I know I'll be fine as long as you're at my side."

She looked down, her eyes suddenly concerned. "Are you okay? You're trembling."

"I am?" My left arm was shaking a little. I tried to make it stop. "Guess so. Sorry. It's an emotional day. I never thought I'd be honored by the department in such a way. Then again, I never thought I would've done anything deserving of the honor in the first place."

"You're too hard on yourself, sometimes."

Our cart slowed to a stop. Shay looked at the surrounding buildings, her body tensing. "Wait...this isn't the gala. Daggers, careful."

She made as if to jump out of the cart, but I caught her by the arm. "Shay, wait! It's not a trap. I told Toby to bring us here."

Shay put a hand to her heart. "Goodness, Daggers. You gave me a fright. With the kidnapping last week—"

I felt like an idiot. "I know. I'm sorry. I should've thought this through better."

"Thought what through better?" She took another look around. "Branzino's Restaurant? Why are we here? They'll have food at the gala, you know? Besides, they look closed. The shades are all drawn."

"They *are* closed," I said. "At least to most people. Come on."

I hopped down and extended a hand. Shay took it and followed me, but she eyed me with suspicion. "You're kind of weirding me out right now, Jake."

"Sorry about that. Just follow me, okay?"

I opened the door and ushered her in, closing the door behind us. We had to wait a moment as our eyes adjusted.

"Um..." said Shay.

With the restaurant's shades drawn and blackout curtains hung over them, not a single ray of afternoon sunlight crept in, but the space wasn't completely dark. Far from it. Dozens upon dozens of candles flickered and danced, set upon tables, shelves, and booth backs, filling the room with a mellow golden glow, like a forest full of fireflies. Rose petals littered the floor, creating a path between the tables.

"Daggers... This is beautiful."

I took her hand and led her along the path. We walked deeper into the room to a clearing of sorts, where one of the tables had been removed, replaced instead with a ring of rose petals that gleamed a dark purple in the candlelight.

"Shay," I said, taking both of her hands in mine, feeling clumsy because of my cast but doing it anyway. "There's more I wanted to talk to you about today beyond last week's case. I *am* proud of you. So incredibly proud of how you dealt with every obstacle that came your way. You show a level of rationality and a calm, collected cool that belies your experience. It's amazing to watch, and it makes me wonder how I ever managed to solve crimes before you came along. You're a pleasure to work with, and my only regret is that I didn't treat you with the respect and appreciation you deserved from the get-go. But we can't change the past. All we can do is learn from it and grow. And I have grown, in large part because of you. I don't know if you realize the influence you've had on me. It's hard for me to think back to the days before you joined the force, and not only because of all the blows I've taken to the head."

I smiled, and Shay snickered.

"No, it's hard for me to look back to those days because I can hardly recognize who I was at the time. You probably remember it clearly. I was overweight, out of shape, slovenly dressed. My apartment was a pig sty. But it wasn't the physical attributes I find hard to reconcile. It's who I was on the inside. I've always maintained that I have a heart of gold, but for so long it was covered up, hidden behind layers of hurt and despair, years of emotional neglect, drowned in a bath of alcohol, and shielded with juvenile humor. But somehow you saw past that, and moreover you were able to pull back the rotten layers, to toss them aside like the rose petals around us.

"Shay, you were the one to help me through that transformation, and it wasn't always easy, was it? For me, or for you. I didn't always want to change. Even though my heart was in favor of it, the mind sometimes disagreed, or vice versa. But little by little, you chipped away at the hardest parts of me, sculpting me into something worthwhile. The best version of me that had always been inside."

Shay gazed within me, her eyes deep and soulful and incredibly blue. My arm had started to shake, and my legs felt like they might give out at any moment, but I couldn't stop now. I had to fight through it.

"Shay, you're the most incredible person I've ever met, and I don't say that lightly. I've already told you how much you impress me with your intellect, your tenacity, your bravery, your deductive wit. You're a born leader even though you may not always see yourself as one. But that's just the tip of the iceberg. You're funny—hell, even funnier than me! Not a day goes by that you don't make me laugh and smile. You challenge me mentally and physically, though I don't hold those forced workout classes against you. You always seem to know best. You're the most beautiful woman I've ever met, and you manage to exude that beauty despite being the feistiest, most badass female detective the Fifth has ever seen!"

Shay lifted one of her hands to her heart, and she looked like she might be on the verge of tears. "Oh, Jake..."

My heart had started to beat out of my chest. I was sure Shay could hear it. "It's true. Every last word. And when I think ahead to the future, I can't bear the thought of you not being there, of you not being a part of it in some way. I love having you as my partner, but that's not enough. Not for me. Because I don't just love you some of the time. I love you every minute of every day. And I can't imagine wanting to spend a moment of my life with anyone else."

With shaking legs, I dropped to one knee. Shay gasped as I reached into my coat pocket and produced a small black box. I popped it open, revealing the ring inside.

"Shay Simone Steele...will you marry me?"

Tears streamed from Shay's face, and she fanned herself with her free hand. "Oh gods, Jake. Yes! Absolutely, a hundred percent yes!"

I pulled the ring from its case and slipped it onto her finger. Shay pulled me to my feet and wrapped her arms around me, sobbing tears of joy.

I held her back as tight as I could. Time lost all meaning. I could've stood in her arms for a minute or an hour and I wouldn't have known the difference. But I didn't have to know any more, because forever more, until the ends of time, Shay would be with me.

And that made me the happiest man in the world.

A WORD FROM THE AUTHOR

Thank you, my readers, for tagging along with me on this amazing journey through the lives of Daggers and Steele. It's hard for me to believe how far they've come, Daggers especially. I always knew where I wanted them to end up, but I didn't always know how they'd get there. I'm as glad as you are that they made it to the finish line safe, sound, and happy.

This isn't necessarily the end for Daggers and Steele, but it is *an* end. I might come back one day to tell more of their story if I feel I can do it justice, but in the meantime, it's off to other, new writing endeavors. I hope you'll join me on those as well, when the time comes.

Thank you again for your support.

Sincerely,
Alex P. Berg

ABOUT THE AUTHOR

Alex P. Berg is a mystery, fantasy, and science fiction author, a scientist, and a heavy metal aficionado. Connect with him at www.alexpberg.com. If you'd like to be notified when new books are released, please sign up for his mailing list on his website. You will only be contacted when new books come out, your address will never be shared, and you can unsubscribe at any time.

Word of mouth is critical to author success. If you enjoyed this novel, please consider leaving a positive review on Amazon. Even if it's only a line or two, it would be a *huge* help. Thanks!